TARNISHED PROPHECY, SOUL DANCE BOOK THREE

SHIFTER PARANORMAL ROMANCE

ANN GIMPEL

Edited by

ANGELA KELLY

Edited by

DIANE EAGLE KATAOKA

CONTENTS

TARNISHED PROPHECY

SOUL DANCE, BOOK THREE

Shifter Paranormal Romance
By Ann Gimpel

COPYRIGHT PAGE

Edited by: Angela Kelly and Diane Eagle Kataoka

ISBN: 978-1-959551-06-5

BOOK DESCRIPTION

Germany, 1940

Magic runs strong in Ilona, a gypsy seer. Powerful ability isn't valued in Romani women, so she focuses her fortunetelling on inconsequential details. Nothing that could come back to haunt her caravan if a prediction went bad. Rounded up and dumped in Dachau prison camp, she has plenty of time to rue her decision to downplay her ability. If she'd taken the time to scry her own future, she'd still be free.

A wolf shifter, Jamal made the mistake of wedding a Romani woman centuries ago. His arrogance caused both death and heartache, and he's been alone ever since. The recent threat of vampires joining the Third Reich has provided ample reason for shifters and Rom to lay their ancient enmity aside and work together, but their détente is fragile.

Jamal and a group of shifters come across Ilona after her escape from Dachau. Vulnerable, terrified, she's fully prepared to fight. Her courage and mettle touch places in him he'd thought were dead, but she's Romani. His last relationship ended so badly, the last thing he needs is to fall for another gypsy woman. He wrestles his tumbling emotions into submission, but when she trains her enigmatic, gray gaze on him, his resolve first weakens and then vanishes entirely.

CHAPTER 1

Ilona Lovas pressed into the shadowed place where her bunk attached to the wall, wishing night would last forever. At least at night, she could lie down and no one bothered her. Stacked in three layers on both sides of a drafty barrack building, the beds consisted of wooden slats. Nothing to cushion them and no blankets unless you were one of the lucky ones who hadn't been stripped of every single possession on your way into Dachau. She'd been told she was on her way to a work camp, but it was really a prison.

The fine, old medieval village of Dachau sprawled around the camp. There had to be gypsies left who hadn't been imprisoned, but efforts at telepathic communication failed to raise anyone at all. Ilona thinned her lips into a harsh line. Everyone was running scared. If any Romani remained, they were keeping a very low profile. Help wouldn't come from any quarter beyond her own efforts. Tears threatened—hot and bitter—but she blinked them back. No energy to do anything that wasn't essential, and crying was an indulgence.

Barely three weeks had passed since she'd been plucked from the streets of Augsburg for the high crime of being a gypsy. All she'd been doing was shopping in the open-air market. For once, she hadn't even stolen so much as a sweetmeat. Three weeks, but it may as well have been three years. Life in Valentin's caravan had been difficult, but it was paradise compared with where she was now. At first, she'd nurtured the hope Valentin would show up to claim her. It would be easy enough to figure out where she was, but for all his bluff and bravado, he was a coward underneath. Besides, even if he'd risked himself, like as not he'd have ended up an inmate.

No one who wasn't Aryan had any rights in Hitler's Germany. Maybe someday the war would be over and…

Who am I kidding? At this rate, I'll be dead before

three months have passed. Waiting out a multi-year war isn't even a remote possibility.

Her stomach cramped from hunger and she wrapped her arms around her middle, trying to think about something other than food. She'd attempted to wrangle an assignment in the kitchen where she could steal more to eat, but so far the Nazi officers marched her—and every other woman in this building—through the streets of Dachau each morning to a garment factory where they sewed Nazi uniforms twelve to fourteen hours a day.

No food. No water. Not even a bathroom break. Some of the women soiled themselves and were forced to sit in their own filth as tears of humiliation mingled with the thread and fabric.

Fury washed through her, and she curled her hands into fists. No one should be treated this way. None of them were guilty of anything—except being gypsies or Jews or immigrants or malformed or mentally deficient.

Her little brother, Aron, had been with her the day she'd been taken prisoner. They'd been separated at Dachau's gates where she'd been forced to stand with other women, and he'd been prodded into a group of teenaged boys. He'd slipped away from them, though, and made a run for it with three guards hot on his heels. Heedless of punishment, she'd sent magic zinging after him to add speed to his feet, but something dark and malevolent stepped between them, halting the flow of her power.

A strikingly beautiful man robed in scarlet with waist-length dark hair and eyes the shade of a turbulent ocean stared at her as he probed her mind. A predatory smile revealed elongated fangs.

Breath whooshed from her, and her throat thickened in horror.

A vampire. It had to be a vampire. Nothing else could feel so profane.

Who would've thought they even still existed? She'd read about them, but from all accounts, they'd never moved out of Egypt where they'd been a true scourge in ancient times.

The vampire was still focused intently on her. Waves of sexual heat poured from him, snaring her in their net. The lust felt perverse, wrong, but she was rooted in place. She didn't have enough magic at her disposal to both keep him out of her mind and move away from his leering gaze. Even placing herself behind the other women wasn't possible. She tugged at a foot, but it refused to budge.

Damn but he was strong. Far stronger than any Romani. Stronger than the occasional shifter she'd run across as well.

The Nazis who'd taken off after Aron trotted to the vampire, pointing in the direction they'd just come from. Her brother—always wily and a fast runner—had clearly given them the slip, but his chances against a vampire wouldn't be good. At least the SS officers had refocused the creature's attention away from her. She felt dirty, like she'd taken a bath in smut, but her body was hers to command again.

She had to warn Aron, so she risked telepathy, doing her damnedest to shield it from the vampire still deep in conversation with the Nazis.

"Aron! They just sicced a vampire on you. Go to ground. Wind power around you. Remain there until tonight."

Her brother didn't answer, which probably meant his full magical ability was focused on flight. The vampire didn't even look up. Ilona inhaled raggedly. Good. Maybe the fell creature hadn't noticed.

A club landed on the backs of her legs, and she yelped.

"Gypsy bitch!" a guard snarled. "Get moving. Next time, the club lands on your head."

She'd staggered into the camp, her calves on fire, and her stint in Hell had officially begun. At least she hadn't been forced to entertain the German officers, but it was only a matter of time. They grabbed women at random each night. When the women returned at dawn, their faces held a resigned, drawn look and they shook their heads sadly, refusing to talk about how they'd been used.

Soon, her half-starved state would erode her magic. When that happened, her ability to make herself invisible to the Nazis trolling through the women's barracks each night wouldn't be there anymore. It was probably the only reason she'd escaped their net so far.

Yeah. When that happens, I'll be fair game for any bastard with a hard on.

Risking death was better than being raped, and an idea took form. Later this morning when her group was on its way to the garment factory, she'd summon power—while she still had some—create an invisibility illusion, and run. Better not to go far. She'd go to ground the first opportunity she found and wait out the day. When night fell, she'd make her way out of Dachau.

Saliva flooded her mouth, and her gut clenched from nausea. She might have vomited from nerves if she'd had anything in her stomach. Could she pull this off? Why hadn't she done something before? When the answer came, she felt ashamed. She'd been waiting for Valentin—or someone—to rescue her. Or for the Nazis to announce they'd made a mistake. She was innocent, and they were releasing her.

Except that hadn't happened to anyone during her brief tenure in Dachau. The only way out of this place would be in a box if she didn't take matters into her own hands. Soon, she'd be too weak to leverage the amount of power required to vanish from prying eyes. It wasn't just cloaking herself. She also had to plant a suggestion in the guards' minds that they'd never seen her.

Hard to raise an alarm for someone no longer on your mental roster of prisoners. They might have a paper list, but she'd never seen them use one.

Ilona scrunched her eyes shut. They felt hot and gritty, and a headache pounded behind one temple. Where would she go—assuming she pulled off her escape? Not back to the caravan. Associating with gypsies wasn't safe. The guards had stolen her rings and bracelets and hoop earrings, so nothing marked her as Romani. Her hair was dark and curly, but she had gray eyes, and lacked the sharp facial features common to her people. She couldn't pass as Aryan, but at least she might not be pegged as Rom absent her jewelry and colorful, flowing skirts.

Thinking about skirts reminded her that her prison clothes would have to go…

Stop! One thing at a time. My first focus has to be escape. Once I'm hidden somewhere, I can work out the rest of it.

She relaxed her muscles, which had tightened into rocks, but sleep was out of the question. Dawn couldn't be far off. She had a plan. One she'd put into action because it was better than fading away and dying in Dachau. The guards dragged dead bodies out of her barracks each morning. If she waited too long, she'd meet the same fate, but not before she'd been raped. She'd been young and strong when the Nazis captured her, but those resources were dwindling.

Fear—the same terror that turned all the prisoners into mewling ninnies dancing to a malevolent Pied Piper—lodged behind her breastbone and accentuated every beat of her heart. She pushed it back. She'd need its energy for her flight, and only a fool frittered away resources.

~

ILONA WALKED at the tail end of the line of women plodding to the garment factory. Dawn was just breaking, and the gunmetal sky spit sleet. She knew better than to talk, and she kept her hands clasped in front of her. With downcast eyes, the human queue moved like an undulating snake through deserted streets. Dachau might always have been quiet at this hour, but she bet it had never been this quiet. Everyone avoided the Nazis for the best of reasons. They no longer needed a reason to imprison you in a world that had turned upside down. A world where no one asked questions anymore.

Sleep continued to elude her for what was left of the night, but she'd traded her ambivalence about escaping for acceptance. She'd try her best. If it worked, she'd be on her way to freedom. If it failed, death would end her misery.

The woman in front of her stumbled but recovered and kept moving before a guard could swat her with a baton—or shoot her outright. Prisoners were a commodity. Nothing more, nothing less. Easier to kill the weak and move on. New prisoners arrived daily. So many, some of the barracks stuffed them two to a narrow bunk. At least it was warmer that way.

Ilona girded herself and tapped into her magic. One more block and she'd have to do this. If she waited much longer, they'd be at the factory, and escape would be much harder.

Impossible after the women were herded inside.

Once she began, she'd have to be quick. If any of the guards felt her magic—and they might if they were gypsies hiding what they were—the jig would be up. Of course, it would be all over for them too because she'd finger them for being just like her.

Takes one to know one.

A grim smile parted her lips, but her head was down so no one saw it. Her hands shook where they were clutched in front of her, so she gripped them hard enough to hurt. Casting spells was easier if she had the use of her hands, but that part would have to wait until no one could see her.

She inhaled deep, blew it out, and did it again aiming for a calm, clear center. Her power had always been strong for a Romani. Her fortunes smacking of clairvoyance rather than pretense. Ilona let her power build. She wouldn't get to do this again if it turned to shit.

Means I have to get it right the first time.

Magic spilled through her. So much, she feared luminescence dancing around her might give her away. Working fast, she reached into the minds of the half dozen guards flanking them and the dozen women nearest her.

"You have never seen me. You will not miss me."

Ilona repeated the suggestion twice more. Three was a power number, and she wasn't leaving anything to chance. No sooner had the third iteration left her mind than she drew invisibility from the crown of her head to the soles of her feet and stepped out of the line.

She'd planned to wait long enough to see if any of the guards raised an alarm, but the specter of freedom was heady, and she couldn't force herself to turn as she'd planned to watch the line move away without her.

Heart pounding and throat clotted nearly shut with anxiety, she ran as fast as she could down a side street, and then another one, angling toward the road out of town. After the first few minutes where she'd expected bullets to rip through her spine, her breathing eased a little.

She'd pulled it off—at least for now. Maybe

going to ground wasn't such a good idea. She had no idea if she'd eradicated herself permanently from the guards' memories, or if her magical intervention would fade. She'd employed subliminal suggestion before, but always when her caravan was within hours of leaving a town. By the time a gadjo discovered she'd hoodwinked him, it was too late to do anything about it.

Not that no one ever drove after caravans demanding the head of the gypsy who'd cheated them, but Valentin always dealt with them. She didn't know if anyone had ever come after her, claiming she'd played them false.

She took stock of her magic. It was weakening, but she had enough left to clear the ancient town's walls. Once she was outside Dachau, she could take to back ways, and she wouldn't need to be invisible.

Clothes.

She'd need something other than her prison garb. The only other option was holding onto her invisibility spell permanently—and she didn't have enough magic to do that.

Ilona scanned the street. Nothing here. She'd been to Dachau with the caravan numerous times, and she tried to remember where shops that sold clothing were located. And then she rolled her eyes. She had no money, and all the shops were still closed. Besides, no one in their right mind would sell anything to someone dressed in prison garb.

Not insurmountable. I can break in.

She winced. Stealing a few Reichsmarks from the gadjo paled in comparison with what she had in mind, but she had no choice. Her striped prison suit had to go, and it was too cold to be naked. Never mind the type of attention that would garner.

A quarter mile to the east brought her to a lane of shuttered women's dress shops. Most were multi-story, which no doubt meant the proprietors slept upstairs. Toward the end of the street, a door opened, and a buxom, blonde woman swathed in gingham and a white apron bustled out, leaving the door ajar behind her.

If it wasn't an opportunity, Ilona had never seen one. She hurried up the steps and inside a cozy room lined with samples. Except they were one of a kind. The sharp-eyed woman who'd just left—maybe to go to market—would notice if anything hanging from the hooks adorning the room were missing.

A curtained alcove was inset on the rear wall. She hustled through it, hoping to find more clothing. After all, this place had to have stock to sell beyond the display samples. Her heart pounded so hard, she expected to hear footsteps clattering down the stairs demanding to know what was going on, but silence reigned from the house's upper levels. Piles of clothing scattered through the back room. Exactly what she needed.

Without stopping to check sizes, she scooped a woolen skirt, wool tunic, cotton shirt, and thick jacket beneath one arm. A stack of sturdy socks beckoned, so she took a pair of them too and extended her invisibility illusion to cover everything.

She'd just moved beyond the curtain, intent on the door, when the woman returned carting a bucket that smelled heavenly. Fresh milk. Meant a cow was nearby. Her mouth watered, but she froze in place willing the woman to move back upstairs with her pail. She'd obviously procured the milk for breakfast.

So far, the goddess had shielded Ilona from harm, but she wasn't under any illusions. The Nazis offered generous bounties for the return of escaped prisoners. This shop didn't look prosperous enough for its owner to turn down a hundred Reichsmarks.

The woman crossed the shop, moving

carefully to keep milk from sloshing onto her shiny, wooden floor. Ilona would have employed a small spell to speed her on her way, but she needed to conserve her magic. It wouldn't last forever.

The woman stopped near the curtain, her nostrils flaring. She made a face, as if she'd smelled something putrid. Ilona clamped her teeth together to keep them from clanking against each other and giving her away. She could shield her visual presence, but not her stench. She hadn't had a bath since the Nazis captured her. Her nose had adapted, but she must be ripe as rotten cheese.

"Piotr," the woman yelled.

"Yes, Momma." A child's voice floated down the stairs.

"Get the mop, bucket, and lye soap. It stinks in here. Must be that smelly customer we had yesterday, although she didn't seem to be quite that rank while she was in here."

"Before breakfast?" the child inquired.

"Yes, before breakfast." The woman sounded annoyed. "It will take me time to cook something and time for the floor to dry. No reason they can't happen together."

Ilona edged toward the door, taking care to be

silent and praying a squeaky floorboard wouldn't give her away. The woman had closed the door, but if she'd just start up the stairs, her heavy tread would hide the snick of the latch when Ilona let herself out.

Sighing and muttering in German, the woman disappeared behind the curtain, pail still in hand. Before her son could appear with the mop and bucket, Ilona let herself out deploying still more magic to dampen the noise of the latch. Milk would have been wonderful, but she didn't have time to hunt down the cow.

She felt lightheaded from all the power sluicing through her, but ran anyway, picking a direct route that would lead out of town. A quarter hour later, staggering and panting, she cleared Dachau and hunted for something, anything, that would hide her from prying eyes for long enough to change clothes.

A small stream cascaded down a muddy hillside before vanishing into a thicket of bushes and trees. With the last of her fading energy, she staggered up the hill choked with a blanket of leaves and crisscrossing tree limbs. Her feet ached in their ill-fitting prison shoes, and her arm clutching the stolen clothing cramped.

Once she moved beyond sight of the road, she

loosed her magic. Not having to maintain invisibility shored up her flagging strength, but not by much. Ilona worked her way through a slight opening in the vegetation and stopped in a grove of oak trees. The stream cut through them, which meant she could bathe. Maybe next time she stole something, her reek wouldn't almost be her undoing.

If she hadn't been so exhausted, she'd have whooped aloud. She was free. She'd pulled it off against daunting odds. Locating a dry spot, she piled her new clothing atop it and stripped off her stinking prison suit. It would be better if she could find a place to hide it, but that wasn't likely. When she was ready to leave, she'd wad it up and bury it beneath the thick carpet of leaves and debris.

Unbuckling her shoes, she waded into the creek. Her teeth chattered from the cold, but she squatted in the water and washed weeks of grit and grime from her body. Even though she was beyond cold, she tilted her head until her hair was immersed and scrubbed her scalp with sand from the creek bottom, rinsing it well. Once she was as clean as she could get absent soap and shampoo, she moved upstream and drank her fill. Food would have to wait until her power wasn't as depleted. She could lure small game—mice and suchlike—but not until she'd rested.

She should have escaped right after they'd captured her. Today proved she could have, but fear had held her back. No more. She couldn't eradicate her fears, but she was done giving in to them.

Ilona made her way to where she'd left her clothes, gratified no one had come anywhere close while she bathed. She hadn't seen any human tracks on her way up the hill, but it paid to be cautious.

She aimed to remain free. Not an easy task, but one she was prepared to die for. As she wrapped herself in the clothing, she savored the finely woven fabrics next to her skin. The socks had been an indulgence, but they padded her feet, making the prison shoes less painful. It would be lovely to replace them, but she wasn't about to return to Dachau. Maybe she'd risk a cobbler's shop in another town, but not this one.

Ilona eyed her discarded prison attire and stopped worrying about it. Surely, she wasn't the first to escape Dachau. No one would associate the shapeless mass of sackcloth with her, and she'd left the prison before they'd gotten around to stenciling a number into her forearm. By the time anyone found her prison clothing, she'd be long gone.

Sleep beckoned, but she had to put some miles between her and her current location. As many as possible. She'd taken the southern route out of town—the opposite way from Augsburg. Munich was ten miles away. It might be a good place to lose herself. Maybe even a good place to find work. She couldn't walk that far without rest, but she could maybe make half that.

There were probably Rom caravans in Munich, but if she'd wanted a caravan, she'd have headed back to Augsburg. She wasn't exactly done with being a gypsy, but she was done associating with them. Guilt nagged. The Rom were her people, but she couldn't do much to save them from Nazi persecution. Hell, she was having the devil's own time saving herself.

Ilona made her way along the steep hillside until she came to a dirt track leading roughly where she wanted to go. She pulled the hood of her jacket over her head to hide her dark hair and made as good a time as she could.

Where was Aron? Had he made it out of Dachau too?

She started to raise her mind voice, and then remembered the vampire. If they were in league with the Nazis—and it certainly appeared that way—the one she'd seen that day could scarcely be the only one. Magic to hide herself was one thing. Projected power quite another. The last thing she needed was undue attention—or any attention at all.

She'd been worse than a fool to deploy power standing in the yard outside Dachau's gates. If she wanted to remain alive, she'd have to do a better job checking for who might be sensitive to magic before she summoned it.

Ilona murmured a quick prayer thanking Isis for her escape and asking her to watch over Aron. Today had gone surprisingly smoothly. Maybe it boded well for both their futures.

Do not grow complacent, her inner voice cautioned.

All it takes is one vampire—or a car full of Nazis—for my carefully balanced world to shatter.

CHAPTER 2

Jamal Jabari slowed the Mercedes to a crawl, crimping the wheel to avoid a pothole that might well be the death of his front axle. Maybe trying to coax the heavy vehicle many miles to the end of this road was a mistake, but he couldn't turn back now. The ruts were deep enough it would be impossible to get the car headed back the other way.

I'll drive until I can't. Then I'll figure things out from there.

A whuffling growl reminded him that his wolf, bonded to him for hundreds of years, disapproved of most modern inventions. Cars were at the top of the heap. For some reason, the wolf hated being trapped in a car. It had never minded wagons, but they weren't noisy. Nor did they stink of oil and gasoline. Jamal's senses were far more acute than a normal human's were, and he wasn't overly fond of the hot metal reek of an engine. He did appreciate getting from point A to point B in a hurry, though.

Color flashed in his rearview mirror, and he chuckled. Hadn't taken the gypsy wagon following him long to catch up. Horses were definitely a better bet in these conditions. Tairin was in that wagon, along with Elliott Brend, a gypsy mage.

Mirth faded, replaced by guilt. Tairin was his long-since-grown-up daughter, but her mother had been Romani. He'd known full well the penalties for mating outside his blood—and his wolf had given him untold grief for falling in love with Aneksi—but none of that stopped him from following his heart. He'd passed himself off as Romani and joined Aneksi's caravan. Tairin had been their love child.

Thank the goddess no one had looked at him too closely during the thirteen years he'd spent with the caravan. Rom had varying degrees of magic—nothing as strong as shifter power—but if they'd wanted to, they could have determined he wasn't one of them. He'd known he was living on borrowed time, but he couldn't convince Aneksi to leave her caravan.

In truth, he hadn't tried very hard, and destiny snared them. Tairin hit womanhood—a time when she had to either shift or die. He and Aneksi quarreled. His temper won out over judgment, and he'd left them both.

Jamal winced. He'd failed in his duty to both his daughter and his shifter heritage. No excuses for not preparing Tairin for her first shift. Never mind that shifters didn't look any more favorably on mixed blood pairings than the Rom. His people had censured him and made it abundantly clear if he left his pack to care for his daughter, they'd banish him forever. He'd stayed with his shifter clan, but he'd never felt the same about them—or himself.

Two hundred years passed before his daughter hunted him down. An angry, alienated Tairin, but he didn't blame her.

A snort blew past his lips. He wouldn't have been surprised if she'd wanted to meet him in open combat. They'd gotten past that, though, and he was grateful for the opportunity he'd let slip through his fingers so long ago: a chance to protect and support his daughter. He vowed never to give her cause to regret letting him back into her life.

A large, black bird flapped toward him, its beak clacking open and shut. He recognized Meara in her vulture form. She'd overflown the route and was clearly on her way back.

"Stop," her mind voice commanded.

Meara was one of the first shifters. Their kind dated back to the making of the world, and Meara had flown out of heat and light when Earth spun out of the sun.

Jamal drew the car to a halt. Tairin and Elliott's wagon rolled close to his back bumper before stopping too. No question about moving off the track. He couldn't. The ruts on both sides of his tires were too deep. Guessing what was coming, he shielded his eyes from the flash of blue-white light that presaged Meara's shift. Sure enough, the passenger door clicked open, and she climbed inside. Long, gray hair cloaked her nakedness, and she regarded him with a pair of shrewd, amber eyes.

"Are there problems?" he asked, concerned about the two gypsy caravans ahead of them. Meara had declared this spot safe from both Nazis and vampires, but maybe something changed between yesterday and now.

"No problems. Not yet, anyway." She settled against the seat cushions, her nostrils flaring. Maybe she didn't like the smells of a gasoline engine any better than he did.

Jamal put the car in gear and moved forward at the same snail's pace he'd adopted before. Meara wanted something, but peppering her with questions wouldn't hurry things up.

"There's a blanket in the backseat," he told her. "In case you're cold."

Meara made a squawking sound, not unlike her vulture might have. "Why does everyone always assume I need clothing?"

He considered correcting her, but remained silent. He'd suggested the blanket for her comfort, not in lieu of the garments she never wore.

Meara rolled her shoulder blades and shook long hair out of her face. "I'm the one who suggested the Rom hole up back here—and I still believe it will be safe for a while—but we need a better plan."

The car hit a bump and sloughed sideways. Jamal corrected the steering. "What kind of plan?"

"I had something more aggressive in mind. Going to ground and waiting for the vampires to find us—and they will—isn't wise."

He narrowed his eyes to thoughtful slits. Working in concert with the Romani, they'd wiped out a dozen vampires, including the master vamp who'd created the nest. But they'd missed at least four who worked directly for Hitler…

"What are you thinking?" Meara demanded.

"Several things." Jamal organized his thoughts. "If it hadn't been for Tairin and Elliott stumbling onto that nest, we'd never have known about the vampires' link to the Reich—"

"That surprised me." She spoke over him. "And very little does. It also explains a lot."

"Like how the Reich rose to power so quickly?" Jamal cut in. "That seemed odd to me too as I watched it unfold. With vampires fueling the Nazi war machine, though, it makes perfect sense how people ceded power to them and sat back while atrocities mounted up."

"Convenient for them humans can't sense magic, eh?" Meara arched a brow and sank deeper into the plush leather seat.

"Plays right into Hitler's *rule the world* plan," Jamal agreed.

"Which is a good lead-in to why I'm in your car and not flying around outside. Elliott and Tairin snuck into Dachau and poisoned about fifty SS officers. It was a start, but we need to organize and do a whole lot more to undermine the work camps."

"I'm guessing you have something in mind." Jamal cast a sidelong glance at her tall, thin form. Hair swathed her from head to foot in waves of silvery gray. No wonder she'd dismissed his offer of a blanket.

"I do. Once we get to an area where the caravans can stop for a few days, I will raise as many shifters as I can. Most Rom aren't as strong as Elliott—"

"He's a shifter now," Jamal reminded her.

Meara rolled her amber eyes. "As if I could forget. I was there when Tairin's wolf bit him to stymie the master vampire's attempt to steal his body. Regardless, he'll be far stronger now than he was as a Romani mage. It doesn't change the fact that most Rom can barely light a candle."

"Where are you going with this?"

"When we work with the Rom, it potentiates both our magics and makes the Rom strong enough to withstand vampire mind control tactics. We'll need every magic-wielder we can locate to launch a coordinated attack."

"The Rom aren't warriors," he argued. "What if they'd rather hide than fight?"

"Not an option. The vampires caught our scents when we scavenged their nest. They won't rest until they locate all of us. Vamps are arrogant. They assume that if they find us, killing us—or turning us—will be easy. We could sit back and wait for them to attack, but I far prefer to do everything in our power to subvert the Nazis—and their vampire sidekicks. To the extent we can keep them off balance, never knowing when the next stealth attack will happen, we might have a chance of doing enough damage to erode their power base."

"Might work." Jamal thought back to things he'd overheard the Romani discussing. "Michael and Stewart will fight. So will the others who went with us to wipe out the vampires—assuming we can find them. The other caravans are either heading out of Germany or going into hiding, just like the two ahead of us."

"Might have been better to keep the Romani together, but there were too many to have any hope of sequestering them in the same place."

An image of brightly painted wagons and horses adorned with bell-studded harnesses flashed through Jamal's mind. "Even if they'd transitioned to cars—rather than their wagons and horses—gypsy caravans would be impossible to hide. I'm worried about the ones ahead of us, but we seem to have moved far enough off any beaten track to avoid notice, at least for a while."

A corner of Meara's mouth twisted downward. "It's a whole new world out there. I never thought I'd live to see a day when we fought side by side with Romani. Or expended energy protecting them."

Something about her words caught his attention, and he angled a glance her way. "Even though you helped plan our offensive against the vampires, you didn't believe it would come together?"

"Something like that, but I recognized the necessity of what we were doing. My doubts would only have gotten in the way, so I buried them deep." She showed him a mouthful of teeth. "Good thing too. Once we got there, we were in the thick of it immediately."

Breath hissed through Jamal's teeth. He hadn't expected the battle to last long, but it was over far faster than he'd reckoned. Vampires weren't used to being confronted. That had worked in his group's favor and helped secure their victory, but the remaining vampires wouldn't make the same mistake.

"How many of those hell-spawned bastards do

you suppose are running loose out there?" he asked.

"More than the four who raced back to where we killed their master and kin." Meara's tone held grim underpinnings, and she screwed her face into a frown. "My guess, and it's just that, is Hitler promised the vampires unlimited blood and sex. That kind of inducement would have drawn many nests, not just the one we destroyed."

Jamal swallowed back distaste. He hated vampires with their bloodlust and dead-but-not status. Why the hell hadn't the fuckers died out a few centuries back?

"Because they need very little to survive. And yes, I was in your mind, but that's the least of our worries..." Meara swung her head around and stared intently out the side window.

"What?" Jamal focused his magic where Meara was looking. Something pricked the edges of his power. Gypsy. Whatever it was had Romani stamped all over it.

"Do you suppose the caravans stopped before they reached the spot I directed them to?" Meara thinned her lips over her teeth.

"Don't know, but they don't obey you like our people do."

She hissed out a snarl, much like a pissed off

vulture might have. "Stop the car. If they ran into trouble, we'd do well not to drive right into it."

"If we're sensing the same thing, it's the wrong way. The road continues north, and what I scented is east of us, but not by much."

"Whatever it is, we need to check it out."

Jamal looked for a place to pull the Mercedes off the rutted track, but didn't find anything. In the end, he simply drew the car to a stop. By the time he got out, Meara stood in front of the car.

Elliott and Tairin's wagon halted right behind them, the horses blowing and stamping.

"What's happening?" Tairin called from the wagon's box. Tawny hair cascaded down her back, and her liquid dark eyes crinkled at their corners with concern.

Elliott pulled the wagon's brake to keep the wheels from rolling. His dark hair was braided to keep it out of the way. He jumped down and held out his arms to help Tairin. Not that she required assistance, but he was taking care of her, and it made Jamal's heart glad his daughter had found someone who loved her.

Meara stalked to Elliott. "Tell me what you sense."

He furled both brows and inquired, "What am I supposed to be sensing?"

"Uh-uh." Meara shook her head. "I don't want to influence you."

Elliott shut his eyes. Power flowed from him as he extended his hands and turned in a full circle.

"Well?" Meara prodded.

Elliott opened his blue eyes. "I sense gypsy power, but it's coming from two directions. Did the caravans split up?"

"Same conclusion I came to," Tairin said and focused her gaze on Meara. "Do you know why they split forces?"

"Not sure they did," Meara replied. "They're not the only Romani in the universe. Besides, there's no road leading to one of the places I sense Rom power. I'm going to shift and see what I can find out."

"We could all shift," Jamal suggested.

"Yes, shift," his wolf concurred, anxious as always for freedom.

"If we do"—Tairin looked askance at her father—"we need to be stealthy. Nothing like three wolves to totally spook a group of gypsies. Even the ones who know what we are haven't spent any time with us in shifted form."

"My wolf likes the idea." Elliott grinned. "But

then he's been nattering about running free for hours."

Tairin trotted back toward the wagon, removing clothing as she went. Elliott followed her, and Jamal began shucking clothes and tossing them into the back of his car. Light flashed around Meara, and she took to the air before the phosphorescence around her had faded.

Jamal finished undressing and summoned shift magic. His torso shortened and his limbs moved beneath him. By the time he was stretching out his paws one at a time, Tairin and Elliott had joined him. His daughter's wolf looked a lot like his, black and gray with tawny markings. Elliott's wolf was pure black.

Pride swelled in Jamal as the trio took off, running as a pack. This was what shifters were meant to do. Form family groups and protect one another. Even though he'd chosen his pack over his daughter, his joy in running free hadn't returned until now.

"You suffered long enough," his wolf observed.

"I deserved to suffer. My hubris and arrogance were my undoing. I decided the rules didn't apply to me. The one who truly suffered from my lapse in judgment was Tairin, though."

"Would you make a different choice if it were offered?"

The wolf's question caught him by surprise. It was something Jamal had asked himself many a time, but he'd always quashed that line of thought because he couldn't go back.

"Well?" the wolf prodded.

"Yes. I'd choose my daughter. I let the pack railroad me into doing what they thought was right. The time for that would have been before I joined my life with Aneksi's. Once that happened, the dye was cast, and I should have stuck with the path unfolding before me. To abandon my daughter, particularly after the Rom burned Aneksi alive, was unconscionable."

"We didn't know about Aneksi's unfortunate end for quite some time," the wolf reminded him.

"Not for certain, but if I'd let myself look closer, I'd have realized Tairin wouldn't have sought me out unless she had no other options. She was raised Romani, and she'd never have left the caravan unless she had no other choice."

"Still, it was many moon cycles after Tairin came to our settlement before our kin told you of her visit."

Jamal sent his thoughts tumbling backward. The wolf had a better memory than his—or perhaps less tendency to bury what it didn't wish to dwell on. Months had passed since Tairin's visit by the time he'd been summoned to appear before the shifter council. When he'd asked why they hadn't let him know sooner, one of the council elders told him it was to ensure he made the right choice—on the heels of a series of wrong ones.

He could have left. Tracking his daughter would have been simple enough since he could always find her through their wolves.

So why didn't I?

Squawks from Meara's vulture broke into his thoughts. He glanced upward and saw her circling to land. Jamal ran lightly to her, along with Tairin and Elliott.

"I found one gypsy only a few hundred yards from here," Meara announced.

"By himself?" Elliott asked, sounding surprised.

"Herself," Meara corrected. *"And nervous as a cornered hare. Her magic is strong enough, she senses you moving toward her, but she's half-starved and weary to her bones. She'll stand and fight, but I sense desperation in her."*

"Wonder why she's out here by herself?" Tairin mused.

"Probably the same reason we are," Elliott countered. *"Hiding from the Reich."*

"Yes, but we have each other. It's not natural for a gypsy to be by herself. Particularly not our women."

"You were." Jamal eyed his daughter.

"Sure, but I'm half shifter. Makes a difference. And I wouldn't have been alone if my caravan hadn't burned Mother. Maybe this woman's caravan banished her too."

"Possible," Jamal agreed.

"Meanwhile," Tairin went on, *"I'm thinking we'd be better served to approach her in our human bodies."*

Jamal's wolf groaned. *"I've barely had a chance to stretch my legs. And I haven't caught so much as a mouse."*

"I heard that." Tairin nudged her father with her snout. *"Glad my wolf's not the only unruly one."*

Jamal tossed his head and asked Meara. *"How much farther to the place you directed the caravans to?"*

She canted her head to the side, regarding him through intense, avian eyes. *"We have covered perhaps three quarters of the distance. Maybe another mile, certainly less than two."*

"I suggest we return to where we left the car and wagon. We can reclaim our human bodies and our clothes. Once we're in a more palatable form, we'll approach the gypsy and offer assistance." Jamal gazed from one to the other, seeking agreement.

"She may not want our help," Meara cautioned.

"We can't just walk away and pretend we never came across her," Tairin argued. *"I chose my wolf form for a hundred years because the people I stumbled across were all monsters. Meara said the woman is desperate. No matter what the rest of you do, I will at least offer aid."*

"I shall await your return here," Meara said. *"I don't require clothing, but I'm less human than the rest of you, and if I approach the gypsy by myself, I might frighten her so badly she flees. We can't afford the time to hunt her down. Nor do we want to chase her into the Reich's arms."*

"Or another vampire nest," Elliott added sourly.

"Have you sensed one?" Tairin twisted her head so she met Elliott's gaze head on.

"No, but I'm fairly certain there have to be more than the four vampires we saw tearing down the roadway with Hitler's motorcade. If I'm right, it argues for another nest."

"Same conclusion Meara and I came to," Jamal said.

"Move, people." Meara punctuated her words with a squawk.

"Thank you," Tairin said.

"For what?" Meara angled her head to the other side.

"Being compassionate. It's rare enough these days, but when we quit caring, we may as well sign on with the Nazi party."

Jamal licked her snout. *"I'm pleased by who you've become. Honored you share my blood."* He wanted to say more, but emotion choked off the words so he spun and took off, racing for the Mercedes and his clothes.

The other wolves paced him, pack energy strong and vibrant.

"Happy," his wolf said as it covered the short distance back to the car. *"We survived two centuries of misery. I'm grateful our time of penance is over."*

Jamal winced inwardly. *"I never meant to make you mourn along with me."*

"I didn't say that to give you yet one more thing to feel guilty about. We're bondmates. I knew what I signed up for. We share everything. Bad times and good. Even though danger surrounds us, my heart is light."

"I love you for sticking by me. You could have left any time."

"What kind of wolf would that have made me? Open your heart, bondmate. Let joy in. You've been pushing it away with both hands ever since the council told you about Tairin."

It was good advice—if he could put it into practice. His wolf was both wise and loyal.

"Indeed." Whuffling laughter rippled past the wolf's jaws. *"I am all that and more. Hurry now. Let's find out who that gypsy is. Probably some old fortuneteller who got tossed out of her caravan for one too many shenanigans."*

Jamal reached the car and called the magic to bring his human form back into ascendancy. He pulled on slacks, socks, shoes, shirt, and jacket. By the time he was ready to retrace his steps, Tairin and Elliott had joined him.

"Ready?" he asked.

"Never readier." Tairin favored him with a smile and loped toward where they'd left Meara.

CHAPTER 3

Ilona sensed power converging on her. The air was electric with it, charged with magical potential. Three days had elapsed since she'd escaped Dachau. She'd remained on back roads and hadn't made much progress, although she felt certain Munich was fairly close.

Hunting to eat meant she was still hungry, but not as starved as she'd been in the prison camp. She hadn't felt safe enough to risk building fires, so she'd eaten everything she caught raw. At first, it disgusted her, but she'd gotten past that quickly. At least she'd had plenty of fresh, clean water. She'd even taken another bath earlier today.

Skirting the small farms in the area proved

easy enough, and she'd managed to avoid the few people she'd seen by hiding behind trees and large bushes. Things had gone smoothly.

Until now.

What the hell was heading toward her? Not vampires. Certainly not Romani. What was left in the magical realm? Druids. Fae. Shifters. In truth, the only magical creatures she'd come across in her twenty-seven years were other Romani, a handful of shifters, but only from a distance—and the vampire outside Dachau's walls.

Valentin had barely been literate. He'd employed several men—mostly blood kin of his—to read and interpret the Romani lore books that had been handed down from generation to generation in his caravan. Aside from whispered tales around their fires at night, she had no true knowledge about other people who carried magical ability.

Ilona gathered power and rose to her feet, facing the direction the threat came from. Many moved toward her. More than she could possibly dispatch, but she'd go down fighting. She hadn't snuck out of Dachau to lie down and give up now.

Did they know she was here? Or was their path toward her chosen at random?

Ha! Not very likely.

Magic jumped to her summons and spilled through her. She narrowed her eyes to slits and waited for whatever approached to show itself. Didn't matter much what it was, so she stopped wasting mental energy on conjecture. She'd find out soon enough.

They were coming closer. Closer still, but then something happened and the wall of power stopped for long, heartrending moments before moving in the opposite direction.

Jubilation flowed from her firmly planted feet over the top of her head in a wave of heat. They didn't know about her. Couldn't, or they'd have kept on coming. She blew out a tight breath, followed by another. Beyond any reasonable expectation, her luck was holding. Goddess knew why, but it wasn't wise to question these things.

She sank back into a crouch to give her trembling legs a break. The clearing where she squatted had several plusses. Clean water and a rocky cave to shelter her from rain. Game had been plentiful so far, and a nearby farm had two cows. So far, she'd been too frightened of discovery to sneak over to the cows to steal some milk, but one of these nights, she would. Whoever owned them didn't milk them often enough, their lowing testament to uncomfortably distended udders.

She might be close to Munich, but she wasn't in a rush to subject herself to any city with Nazis driving through its streets. Churches offered sanctuary, but not to those like her. The Catholics were almost as anti-gypsy as the Nazis. While rumor had it they were helping the Jews, that aid hadn't yet extended itself to those like her.

She'd had time to think about where Aron might have gone. If he'd escaped, he'd probably headed for Valentin's caravan. They'd been in Augsburg, but it was anyone's guess where they were now. For all she knew, Valentin might be trying to escape Germany. It wasn't the brightest plan since it would involve crossing a border where the caravan would be stopped, searched, and like as not sent straight to a work camp.

But then, Valentin wasn't a mental giant. Most of his energy went into hiding his homosexual dalliances. The ones he was certain no one knew about.

Ilona curled her lips into a sneer. Of all the caravans to be born into, his was the worst. She'd met most of the other caravan leaders in the region, and they'd seemed like reasonable men…

She raked her hands through her unbound

hair and tied it into a sloppy queue low on her neck. Her mind was wandering because she was so relieved not to have to deal with the confrontation that had seemed inevitable a little bit ago. Her instincts told her to avoid Munich. They hadn't steered her wrong yet, and she'd do well to listen to them. She'd been in this clearing since yesterday and had yet to run into anyone. Maybe she could remain here. Winter would be hard, but it would end eventually. Her stolen clothing was warm and well made. New boots could wait.

The specter of being alone—maybe for years —dragged at her, but being by herself beat being dead by a good, big bunch. The war had to end someday. If it ended with Nazis running the show, she'd deal with it then. Meanwhile, her life had devolved to its simplest terms.

Shelter.

Warmth.

Food.

She was a decent thief. She could make the occasional run into Munich to add to her supplies, so long as they didn't close off the city and post guards. She might even spend an occasional night with the cows in their cozy barn.

From what she could tell, the farmer never visited them once the sun went down.

Ilona pushed upright and stretched, rotating her arms above her head. She'd take things as they came, and now was time to hunt so she'd have something for supper. Greens grew thick and plentiful by the creek, along with anise and wild onions. If she got lucky and snared a rabbit, she could approximate a stew, albeit a cold, uncooked one.

She made a mental note that she needed a cookpot if she ever got brave enough to enter Munich. Those were easy to steal, easy to find discarded in rubbish bins too. She'd just paid out magical threads to draw game her way when the sense of power heading toward her returned.

Ilona froze. Was it the same people as before? Had they sensed her and gone back for reinforcements?

"Don't be ridiculous," she hissed. "If they're as strong as I think, they know I'm by myself."

She redirected her power, seeking, probing. Four people were coming toward her, their magic subtlety different than it had been last time. Was this a different group? What were the odds of that?

I have no idea. I haven't been here long enough to know who passes this way.

Ilona balanced power between her hands, watching it arc blue-white in the afternoon air. Whoever approached now didn't feel as threatening as they had before, which argued they were something different. Unlike the first batch of power, this one kept coming on a trajectory aimed right at her.

They knew where she was. Had sensed her with their brand of magic. She swallowed around a dry throat, determined not to show them how frightened she was. She angled her gaze at the small cave. Even if she attempted to hide, their magic was strong enough to ferret her out.

"Who's coming this way?" she called, pleased her voice hadn't trembled.

A tall, thin woman with silver hair that cascaded to the ground walked around a thick tree bole and entered the clearing. Her amber eyes gleamed with intelligence, and she held herself ramrod straight.

"My name is Meara. We mean you no harm."

Three others melted out of the forest and flanked Meara. Two were men, one with long black hair, and the other with shorter tawny locks. The woman's hair fell to her waist and was the same shade as one of the men's, a rich, tawny chestnut. The men wore simple, dark trousers and dark jackets. The woman was dressed in a colorful skirt and tunic with a jacket tossed over her shoulders, very much like a Rom might have attired herself.

Ilona scanned them with power, and her eyes widened. "Why two of you are Romani. Partway at least."

The woman with tawny hair stepped forward. Her deep brown eyes with amber irises crinkled at the corners when she smiled, and she extended a hand. "Right you are. I'm half Romani, and my name is Tairin."

Ilona clasped her extended hand and didn't want to let go. For all her inner reassurances about being fine by herself, she'd missed the presence of others. A lot.

"And I'm Elliott." The man with black hair stepped forward, draping an arm around Tairin. "I'm not sure what I am now, but I was a Romani seer for most of my life." His eyes, which were a clear, pure blue, twinkled merrily.

"I'm Jamal." The other man joined them. "Tairin's father."

Ilona let go of Tairin and tried to see into him. Magic boiled through Jamal, strong magic, but she couldn't figure out what he was. He was a beautiful man, though, with the same liquid, dark eyes as his daughter. Tall and slabbed with muscle, he radiated an understated menace, but it wasn't directed at her.

"What exactly are you?" Ilona blurted. Perhaps she'd made a mistake being so bold, but this man couldn't be the source of Tairin's Romani blood.

The woman, who was cloaked in her silver-gray hair and nothing else, closed from one side. "He's a shifter like me, and you have nothing to fear from any of us."

"Shifters?" Ilona's breathing quickened. Romani hated shifters, and vice versa. So much so, any contact at all was forbidden, which was why she'd only glimpsed them from afar. Her eyes darted from side to side, but flight was impossible. These people could morph into animals and run her down. Once they did, they'd have teeth, claws, and could tear her limb from limb. Her stomach clenched, and it took all her willpower not to wind her arms around herself and wail.

Tairin reached for her again. "Take my hand. It's all right. We sensed you here by yourself—actually, Meara did—and we wished to offer assistance if you need or want any. If not, we'll be on our way."

Ilona stared at Tairin's hand. The hand had given her comfort before, but she didn't clasp it. Would the other woman snare her with magic? Force her to do something she didn't want to?

Tairin shook her head. "No. I'd never do anything like that. And yes, I helped myself to your thoughts." She dropped her hand to her side and squared her shoulders. "You probably don't know much about shifters. Most Rom don't, but we're long lived. Two hundred years ago, I was run out of my caravan after my first shift. Life on the road was hard. So hard I spent a very long time as a wolf. It was my idea to see if we could help you."

She leveled her dark gaze on Ilona. "Can we? Why are you out here all by yourself?"

The kindness flowing from Tairin undid Ilona and tears welled. She blinked them back. "I—" She choked on the words, cleared her throat, and tried again. "I was with Valentin's caravan. The Nazis took me from the market in Augsburg and put me in Dachau."

Elliott's eyes widened, and a look of naked admiration washed over his face. "You escaped."

Ilona nodded. "It was either that or die." She

shrugged, suddenly uncomfortable. "Not much of a choice when you got down to it."

"We're headed toward two caravans setting up not far from here," Meara broke in. "If you'd like to come with us, at least there will be blankets and fires and food."

"But you're shifters," Ilona sputtered. "Rom won't accept you."

"That's the kind of thinking that got Mother burned alive and cut me off from the shifter half of my kinfolk. That hatred meant I was cast adrift with nothing but my wolf." Tairin's pleasant expression vanished, replaced by something much harder.

Ilona thought she should keep quiet, but macabre curiosity drove her, and she asked, "How old were you when that happened?"

"Thirteen. I know all about choices where death is the alternative." Tairin tipped her chin upward. "Are you coming with us? If not, we'll leave you to your evening."

"Don't waste a moment worrying we'll tell anyone about finding you," Elliott said reassuringly. "We're trying to stay one step of the Nazis and vampires too."

Ilona inhaled raggedly, and her heart skipped

several beats. "Then I'm not the only one who's seen them."

"If by *them*, you mean vampires," Meara said dryly, "you are not. We killed a dozen quite recently, but there are many more where they came from."

"We? You and the Romani? Working together?" Ilona's voice came out as a squeak.

"Yes. That *we*," Jamal replied, dry humor lining his words. "What's your name? We gave you ours."

"Ilona. Ilona Lovas."

"Well, Ilona Lovas," he went on, his gaze never leaving her, "I don't want to hurry you, but you have to decide. We're late meeting the caravans as it is. If vampires are lurking, the gypsies will need our help."

Ilona turned away. It wasn't easy. She could have spent forever staring at Jamal, but that was stupid and beside the point. He might be beautiful and alluring, but he was a shifter. She was Rom. No future in that.

I'm being ridiculous. I could be dead tomorrow.

Ilona refocused. What should she do? She'd sworn off caravans, but these were in hiding so maybe they'd be safe for a little while. She turned back to face everyone. "Which caravans are they? Who are the leaders?"

"Michael and Stewart," Elliott replied. "I was seer for all the caravans, and I know Valentin."

"You wouldn't make me go back to him? Not that he was cruel to me," she hurried on, "but it's not safe being a gypsy in a city anymore. If they could abduct me from the marketplace, they could take anyone. I—"

"No, I'd never force you to do anything you didn't want to. Besides, I'd be surprised if any of us saw any of the other caravans again." Elliott cut into her flow of words. "The ten others each had plans. Some were remaining in Germany. Others were going to try to leave."

"If I go with you and it doesn't feel right…"

"You'd be free to leave," Tairin reassured her. "You're a gypsy, not a prisoner."

A tightly wound place inside Ilona loosened a little. "Okay. Thank you for your offer. I deeply appreciate it. Lead out, and I'll try not to hold you back."

Meara nodded. "Good choice. You're scared, but you're not letting it stand in your way. Plus, your magic is strong. You'll be an asset." She focused on the others. "I'm flying back to reassure the others nothing happened to us. See you soon."

"Guard your eyes," Jamal cautioned.

Ilona shut her eyes, but a flash of light seared her corneas anyway. When she pried her lids open, a large, black vulture winged away from them, flapping hard.

"That's her?" Ilona pointed with an unsteady hand.

"Yes. Meara was one of the first of us, and her magic is abundant and powerful," Jamal replied.

"Are all of you birds?" Ilona asked, fascinated in spite of herself.

"No. We're wolves," Tairin replied. "Let's get moving. We'll lose the light soon."

Ilona fell into step next to her. Elliott was on her other side and Jamal behind them. "What other forms can shifters take?" she asked.

"Bears, coyotes, mountain lions, hawks," Tairin rattled off. "Lots of possibilities, and I'm sure I missed a few."

"You were raised Romani?" Ilona looked sidelong at Tairin and saw her nod.

"Not just raised Rom. Once I stopped being a wolf, I retreated to Rom caravans. Had to switch them out every twenty years or so—"

"Otherwise the women would notice you weren't aging," Ilona broke in.

"Exactly. You know how it is. Everyone wants

to be youngest, prettiest, but there's not much tolerance for anyone who remains that way." Tairin laughed, and the sound warmed Ilona's heart.

"Never thought I'd hear laughter again. Or laugh myself."

"How'd you escape Dachau?"

"Invisibility spell plus suggestion. Eventually, the guards and my fellow prisoners will remember me and wonder what the hell happened."

"But you've moved beyond their reach. Who taught you magic?" Tairin narrowed her eyes. "Valentin never struck me as particularly competent in that regard."

Ilona thinned her lips into a tight line. "He's not, but there are several older women in his caravan who command potent magic. One was my mother."

"Was? What happened to her?"

"She caught pneumonia. We were between cities. By the time we got to Berlin and I took her to a hospital, she was too far gone for them to save her." A familiar, dull ache settled behind Ilona's breastbone. Her mother had died last winter, almost a year ago, but she still missed her.

"And your father?" Tairin probed.

"Never knew who he was. Mother never would tell me, and after a while I stopped asking."

When she looked up, Ilona saw a wagon and team parked behind a sleek dark car. "These are yours?"

"Yes. We were on our way to talk with you earlier in our shifted forms, but Meara overflew where you were and called us back. Said you were skittish and four shifters would scare the daylights out of you."

Ilona snorted. "Three wolves and a vulture would have been a little hard to wrap my mind around, yeah." She shook her head. "I'm still having trouble assimilating Rom working side-by-side with shifters. It seems wrong."

"But it isn't. Not really. The lore books were what kept the old rules in play. Apparently, years back, a mixed blood shifter mated with a mixed blood Rom and produced a hell-spawned child. No one had any idea about genetics hundreds of years ago, so they created a blanket rule that Rom and shifters couldn't even talk with one another."

Tairin paused to take a breath. "Turns out our magic actually strengthens when we work together. Shifter magic grows more powerful, but so does Romani. It's how we defeated a nest of a dozen vampires."

Jamal pulled around them, heading for the automobile. "You can ride with me, Ilona," he called over one shoulder.

Her heart did a funny little dance in her chest, but she told it to stand down. He'd offered her a ride to the caravans. He had space in his car. If she didn't go with him, she'd be stuck riding in the back of the wagon.

Tairin squeezed her hand. "See you very soon. The caravans are only about a mile from here. I want to hear about the vampires you saw. The men will want to know too."

"Yes," Elliott seconded. "We certainly will."

"It was only one vampire," Ilona said. "And I'm not certain that's what it was. It was stunning and dressed in a lovely robe, and it had fangs and felt like death simmered within it."

"That was a vampire." Tairin skinned her lips back from her teeth, adding a feral aspect to her beauty.

Elliott hooked two fingers into the Romani sign against evil. "See you soon, Ilona. I'm glad you took a chance on us. This is no time for anyone to be by themselves."

She wasn't sure how to respond, so she trotted to the black car and got in. Jamal fired the engine and the car lurched slowly down the rutted track.

She tried out and discarded several conversational gambits. Jamal wasn't one of the gadjos. If she were going to talk with him, it had to be real, not something conjured because she wanted him to trust her.

"Tell me about yourself." He looked at her. "Nothing that makes you uncomfortable. Maybe we could talk about magic and how you learned about your power."

"Gypsies start young," she began.

"I know," he broke in. "I traveled with a caravan for more than a dozen years."

"You did?" Her voice cracked and broke. "When? How?"

"How else?" His deep, rich voice soothed and excited her at the same time. "By pretending to be one of you."

CHAPTER 4

Jamal kept his gaze on the rutted track to avoid staring at Ilona. His first glimpse of her in the clearing had mesmerized him. He'd avoided women since his ill-fated pairing with Aneksi imploded, leaving heartbreak and destruction in its wake. What could he possibly offer any woman beyond his own broken dreams and ravaged heart?

No relationship could survive secrets, and his humiliation and guilt over Aneksi and Tairin had been far too pervasive to gloss over and pretend they didn't exist. Besides, any shifter with marginal magic could have plucked his mind bare of its shame-tinged contents.

Easier to remain by himself.

What was it about Ilona that caught his eye? She was average height for a woman and quite thin, but that went with escape from Dachau where rations had to have been scant. Long, dark hair curled down her shoulders and cascaded to waist level. Her eyes, set in a high cheek boned face, were her most arresting feature. A pure, pale gray, they reminded him of a stormy sky just before a rainstorm. Beyond that, she held herself proud and straight, her chin tilted at a defiant angle.

No matter what she'd lived through, it hadn't quashed her spirit. And her magic was strong. Meara had called that one. Ilona would be quite an asset in the Rom encampment. Elliott's power had rivaled hers before he'd added shifter magic to the mix, but Ilona was stronger than any of the others in Michael's or Stewart's caravans.

Except maybe Stewart, who was an unknown quantity.

Having her so close was intoxicating. She smelled of wildflowers and vanilla. Perhaps she knew he was thinking about her because she looked at him, and her mouth—a beautifully formed mouth with full lips—broke into half a smile.

"Tell me about yourself." He met her

forthright gaze and tried not to get lost in her eyes. "Nothing that makes you uncomfortable. Maybe we could talk about magic and how you learned about your power."

"Gypsies start young," she replied.

"I know," he broke in. "I traveled with a caravan for a dozen years."

"You did?" Her voice cracked and broke. "When? How?"

"How else? By pretending to be one of you."

She crinkled her forehead in concentration. "Was that when you were with Tairin's mother? How long ago?"

"Yes. It's the only time I traveled with a caravan. What I did, deceiving everyone, was wrong. Aneksi and I were thoughtless and self-indulgent. We might have been young, but that was no excuse. Tairin was born roughly two hundred thirteen years ago."

A small gasp whooshed from Ilona. "Oh my. Tairin said long-lived. She even said two hundred years, but it didn't exactly sink in. Did Tairin's mother know what you were?"

"Of course, and we shielded that knowledge from the rest of her kin. And from our daughter." Jamal inhaled sharply. There. He'd actually admitted his sin out loud for the first time since the council grilled him two centuries before. It hadn't been as impossible as he'd feared, but he wanted to stop while he was ahead. Before Ilona asked any uncomfortable questions, like how could Tairin not have known what she was?

"I'd rather have you tell me about yourself," he said. The car sloughed sideways, its springs squealing loudly, and he corrected the steering.

"If I do, will you teach me to drive?" She cast an appraising look his way. "I've wanted to learn for a long time, but our caravan only had wagons."

Jamal couldn't help himself. He burst out laughing.

Color splotched Ilona's weather-stained skin, spreading across her defined cheekbones. "What's so funny?" she gritted out. "If you don't want to, saying no is sufficient."

"It's not that." He reined in his mirth. "Your barter suggestion took me back to my time with Aneksi's caravan. Rom are nothing if not traders. Of course, I'll teach you to drive. I'd do that even if you never told me a word about yourself. You needn't negotiate for everything."

The stiff lines of her face relaxed, and she trained her gaze on her hands. "I was out of line. I apologize. You are right about gypsies, though.

We never miss an opportunity to wangle our way into a better place. It's in the blood."

She clasped her hands together. "You rescued me from surviving on my own. It was rude of me to ask for anything else."

"Rescuing you was my daughter's doing." Words butted up against each other in his head. Words lined with guilt that he hadn't been there for Tairin when she'd needed him, but he pushed them aside. No going back.

"Yes, but the rest of you must have agreed with her. You'd asked about me. There's little enough to tell. I was born in a caravan. My mother was one of our strongest fortunetellers. She foretold the future with a shocking level of accuracy. She also read minds and could twist the strands of time to do her bidding. She taught me everything I know."

"I heard you tell Tairin that she'd died," Jamal said. "I'm sorry. You must miss her."

"I do. I wasn't close with anyone else in the caravan. Valentin is…was…different. It altered the composition of who was willing to travel with us."

"Do you mean he liked men?"

Ilona's face turned bright red, and Jamal figured he'd been too blunt. "Look," he blundered on since he'd already put his foot in it. "I met Valentin and the rest of the caravan leaders. I recognize that energy—when men prefer men. Shifters don't shun same sex pairings like Romani do. We accept them for what they are. Love is a wonderful thing—no matter where it finds us."

It was his turn to feel embarrassed. He'd barely met the woman in his passenger seat. Probably not the best time to launch into a dissertation on sexual mores.

"So you worked telling fortunes?" he asked to move the conversation to more neutral ground.

Ilona nodded. "Yes. And I cast Tarot spreads and astrological charts. I also cooked and did some sewing."

Jamal tightened his hands on the wheel. "Did you leave a husband and children back in the caravan?" Maybe he shouldn't have asked, but he had to know if this woman was spoken for.

She shook her head. "No. I never married."

"Why not?"

"Lots of reasons. Mother said it wasn't wise, that it would dilute our power. And I never met anyone I felt strongly enough about to go against her will."

"Look." Jamal motioned through the windscreen at the collection of horses and wagons milling about beneath a cliff face. "We're almost there."

"I see that. Even though it's not my caravan, it still feels like coming home."

"Did you believe what your mother said about marriage weakening your power?"

She drew her brows into a thoughtful line. "Not really. I always suspected my father abandoned her and broke her heart. She never wanted to deal with that kind of heartache again, so she wove a fabrication about needing to be celibate to keep her power at its peak."

Jamal thought about it. "I'm surprised no one else in the caravan spilled the beans about who your father was. Surely someone would've known, and besides being traders, the Rom are an inveterate bunch of gossips."

A giggle blew past her lips, followed by a full-throated laugh. "You do have our number," she said once she was done laughing. "But, no. No one ever ponied up that piece of information."

"Did you ask?" he persisted.

"Not much. It made Mother very angry, and it was just her and me and my brother Aron." Ilona was still snickering. "Guess Mom had a lapse from her self-imposed celibacy at least long enough to conceive my little brother."

"Did he know who his father was?"

"Oh yeah. One of Valentin's uncles with a penchant for gambling. He ended up with a bullet in his head one morning when Aron wasn't quite ten. He and Mother didn't share a wagon, and he never paid much attention to Aron, so none of us missed him much."

"I'd offer condolences for your loss—"

"Eh, don't waste your breath." Ilona rolled her eyes. "Mom entered her *marriage is bad for my magic* phase again right after Aron was born. He was eleven years younger than me." She closed her teeth over her lower lip. "The Nazis got him too, but he ran before they could drag him into Dachau. I hope he made it out of the city."

Jamal wanted to reach across the car and place a hand over hers, but he held himself back. She might take it wrong, and he had no right to touch her. Instead he settled for saying, "I hope he made it out of Dachau too. Did you try reaching him with magic?"

"No. By the time I escaped the city, my magic was almost drained. And I know less than nothing about vampires. I was afraid if I did anything magical near Dachau, I might draw their attention. If I'd been apprehended and taken back to the work camp, the guards would have flogged me and chained me, and I'd still be there."

Jamal's heart ached for her. She had good reasons for not seeking her brother, but guilt—and responsibility—dogged her just the same. He'd lived with both long enough to recognize them in others. He wanted to say something comforting, but he didn't want to lie to her, either. Both of them knew Aron's chances of escape hadn't been very good.

The ruts that passed for a road finally ended in a large clearing, and Jamal drew the car off to one side. Tairin and Elliott's wagon clopped past, heading for where the other wagons were parked.

"Ready to get out and meet everyone?" Jamal asked.

"Yeah. It will take me a while to keep everybody straight. Just look at all those wagons. Lots of Rom here."

Her words caught him up short. Yes, lots of Rom were here, which meant it made sense for Tairin or Elliott to take Ilona around to introduce her. He may have helped with the vampire nest, but he was still a shifter.

Meara solved the problem for him by striding to his car. She waited until they got out, and then focused her shrewd gaze on Ilona. "How are you doing?"

"Better. Thank you again."

Tairin loped to where they stood with Elliott right behind her. "We've come to take you around to the wagons and introduce you," she announced.

"I thought you were going to do that," Ilona said to Jamal, but then she shook her head. "It's fine. Really. I can make my way to the caravan leaders' wagons and introduce myself. It's not a problem. You've all been more than kind to me, and—"

"I need Jamal for something else," Meara cut in. "We must alert others like us to stand ready. In a perfect world, I'd use Tairin too, but her place is here for now."

"What about me?" Elliott asked. "I'm a shifter now."

Meara rolled her eyes. "A very new one. So new, your credibility with other shifters will be close to nil."

Elliott opened his mouth, but Jamal waved him to silence. "Your wolf just lodged a protest. I heard it growling in my mind. Tell it to stand down. We'll be in the thick of battle soon enough. Plenty of time to prove your mettle."

Tairin wrapped a protective arm around Elliot and trained her dark gaze on Meara. "Have you seen something in your glass?"

"I have, indeed. Once I return, Elliott and I will spend time together. I'm interested if we produce the same future reading."

Discomfort and confusion poured from Ilona, far too strong to ignore. Jamal focused on her. "What's wrong?"

"I can scry the future too." She straightened her spine. "I'd like to help."

"You're a Romani seer?" Elliott sounded surprised. "I thought I was the only one, at least for the caravans here in Germany."

Ilona's nostrils flared. "Valentin never wanted anyone to know. He always thought Mother's magic—and mine—were unnatural. He didn't want it to get around that our visions were real. I figured he thought if the gadjo found out, they'd be too frightened to plunk down coin for Tarot and fortunes."

Jamal sucked in an annoyed breath. No one believed in magic anymore. They might duck into a fortuneteller's wagon, but it was all for sport. For fun. Nothing was serious.

"I'm ready." Meara jabbed Jamal's chest with an index finger.

"Shifted or not?"

"We make better time in our animal forms."

"How far are we going?" Jamal asked. He wanted to remain with Ilona, see she was settled and comfortable, but Meara's commands overshadowed his personal needs.

She drew her silver brows together. "We will split up. We can cover twice the ground that way. Because I fly faster than you can run, I'll return to our settlement where Tairin found us."

"Where do you want me to go? And what message am I delivering?" Jamal kicked off his shoes and pulled off his socks, tossing them into the car. No reason to ruin a perfectly good set of clothes ripping them to shreds when he shifted. He slipped off his jacket and felt Ilona's gaze on him. She was subtle about it, but he knew the feel of her energy.

Part of him was pleased by her attention, but another part felt embarrassed and he stopped after slinging his coat into the front seat.

Meara knelt and drew a circle in the dirt. She marked two Xs within it. "Here is where we are." She pointed at one of them. "And here's Munich." She pointed at the other and drew a long line. "This is the main roadway between Munich and Dachau. I want you to locate all our kinfolk in this area. Be sure to check the small farms on both sides of the main byway."

"When I find them, what shall I tell them? Surely by now everyone knows vampires are a problem."

"I'm sure they do. We have a well-established telepathic network," Meara concurred. "Make certain they know about mingled power being stronger. Tell them I command them to fight the Reich and the vampire threat." She pressed her lips together. "We must meet to plan our next steps, but I'm not certain where would be safest."

"The tunnels beneath that old castle where I'd set up shop might work," Elliott said.

"Not big enough," Meara replied. "If my estimate is close, there will be somewhere around a hundred fifty shifters, perhaps a few more."

A long, low whistle escaped Ilona. "That many. May I ask something?"

"Be quick about it," Meara snapped. "Jamal and I must be gone soon."

"If you're planning to tackle the Nazis with magic, are there other magic wielders who might join with us?" Ilona asked.

"Yes to other people who carry magic," Elliot answered.

"But Druids don't command much power at

all," Meara protested. "No one's seen either dark or light Fae for hundreds of years."

"We could ask Stewart about them," Tairin said. "If anyone would know, he would with his Celtic roots."

"He might know about the other fairy folk too," Elliott said, sounding thoughtful.

Meara made a chopping motion with one hand. "I like the idea of a magical army, but let's start with shifters and Romani. Historically, none of us have played well together. I'm reluctant to mix too many of us, none of whom trust one another, too quickly."

"Probably wise," Ilona said. "I don't know enough to be making suggestions, anyway."

"Of course you do," Tairin said. "We need ideas. So don't be shy about voicing them."

"Meanwhile"—power crackled around Meara —"absent a better location, I will instruct shifters to meet here two nights hence. The moon will be full then, and Arianrhod may well lend us her power."

Jamal swallowed surprise. When had Meara switched from Egyptian deities to Celtic? "What about Khonsu?" he asked, invoking the ancient Egyptian god of the moon.

Meara flashed him a rare smile. "Feel free to

call on him too. The more support we have from all quarters, the better. Now get moving. I'll be back as soon as I can."

The energy sparking around Meara brightened, and her vulture flew out of its center, winging its way to the west.

"Come on." Tairin let go of Elliott and linked a hand beneath Ilona's elbow. "I'm surprised no one came out to greet us, but everyone is likely busy getting settled."

"Thanks again for everything." Ilona smiled at Jamal. "You've been kind to me."

"You're welcome."

He waited while she walked toward the wagons with Elliott and Tairin before stripping off the rest of his clothes and summoning shift magic.

"Finally," the wolf muttered. *"I thought you were going to stand there talking until tomorrow's sunrise."* After a quick stretch where it shook out its paws and arched its back, the wolf took off running. *"Where do we go first?"*

"We're closer to Munich than Dachau, so let's make our way back to the main road, cross it, and finish traversing the last distance to town in the woods. From there, we can work our way back."

The wolf didn't reply, just ran in the indicated direction.

Jamal settled into the wolf's consciousness, enjoying the freedom of claws digging into rocky dirt for purchase and the wind from the dying day ruffling his fur. His wolf form simplified everything. So much easier than being human.

Hours passed. Hours during which they visited many shifters from hawks to bears to mountain lions to foxes. Other wolves as well. Most had heard about the vampire threat, but not everyone. Jamal shifted to converse with all but the wolves.

Dawn found them on the outskirts of Dachau, and Jamal lifted his muzzle, scenting the air.

"It's Ilona," the wolf said, mirroring Jamal's conclusion. *"She must have come this way when she escaped the prison camp."*

Before Jamal could argue himself out of it, he said, *"Let's follow her trail. I'd like to know where she went."*

He girded himself for pushback from the wolf, but it never materialized. They turned hard right and headed up a steep, muddy hillside choked with downed branches and forest debris. With its unerring ability to track, the wolf came to a stop in a small clearing. Ilona's scent was far stronger here than it should be.

Her prison clothes. She must have left them here. Before he could instruct the wolf to hunt for them, it trotted farther uphill to a pile of deadfall and began scratching. Sure enough, a striped prison suit had been stuffed in a crevice. So far, no one else had been here. No people, but more importantly, no vampires. They were exceptional trackers, as skilled as any shifter.

"We can't leave this here," he told the wolf.

"I know, but we can't make it invisible so we can travel with it, either. It's getting brighter with the coming day, and we're miles from the caravans."

Jamal sent power spiraling outward searching for nearby shifter dens. Hidden within cliffs, they deflected discovery by a complex system of magic which kept them concealed from all but other shifters.

"I already thought of that," the wolf informed him. *"Nearest shelter is on the other side of Dachau."*

"I have a better idea."

"Yes?" the wolf's ears pricked forward, and Jamal smiled.

"We drag the prison suit uphill—"

"Brilliant! And lay a false track." The wolf tossed its muzzle back, but stopped shy of howling.

"Hang on. You'll like this even better," Jamal went on. *"It will mean we don't return to the caravans until midday, but we drag the suit well away from here in a direction to fool anyone who might pursue Ilona. Once we're at least a mile—maybe two—from this spot, we hunt down a deer or a coyote or something large. Then we spread its blood all over the suit so whoever is tracking her will believe something killed her."*

"And dragged the corpse off and ate it! Perfect." The wolf bent and tugged the rest of the filthy, stinking heap of cloth out of its hiding spot. Getting a firm hold on it with its teeth, the wolf let the rest of the garment hang between its front legs and bounded uphill.

Jamal wondered why Ilona hadn't taken greater care with something that could lead the enemy right to her. Maybe she had no idea about vampire skills. Beyond that, she'd been exhausted, told him her magic was running on fumes. A surge of protectiveness rushed through him.

He tried to temper it with caution. His last attempt at loving had exploded, the shrapnel from the detonation injuring everyone. Ilona was a gypsy, just as Aneksi had been, and he was still a shifter. It didn't take a Romani fortuneteller to predict treacherous waters from that combination.

Tairin had a foot in both camps, making her relationship with Elliott at least possible. Jamal didn't.

His earlier elation faded, as did the scene he'd imagined where he drew Ilona aside and told her what he'd done to keep her safe. The wolf was privy to all his thoughts. That it was keeping quiet about Ilona spoke volumes. It remembered the disaster with Aneksi, although so far it hadn't reminded him.

As if I need reminding.

Jamal drew a curtain over his emotions. He'd shelved them for so long, it wasn't hard. After being without family for years, he had his daughter back and a son-in-law to be. It was more than he'd ever expected, and it would have to be enough.

Now if he could just get himself to believe that.

The wolf skidded to a stop. *"Far enough?"*

Jamal glanced at rocky, precipitous landscape rich with the scents of game. *"Far enough,"* he agreed, more than ready to lose himself in bloodlust and hunting.

CHAPTER 5

Ilona tossed and turned in the rough, woolen blanket Tairin had let her borrow. She'd joined two other Rom women in their wagon, both of whom were fast asleep and snoring. Tairin and Elliott had offered to let her sleep in their wagon, but they were newly mated, and she hadn't wanted to put a damper on their lovemaking.

It felt right to be back in a caravan. Ilona hadn't realized what a comfort zone it was for her until it was gone. She'd been formally introduced to Michael and Stewart, men she'd seen before when they'd visited Valentin's caravan. Both leaders had welcomed her and encouraged her to make herself at home. Even though the mountainous terrain appeared deserted, no one wanted to take a chance with fires, so they'd cooked the evening meal over kerosene burners.

Her first taste of hot food almost made her cry. The rations at Dachau had been one step up from inedible. While an improvement over prison fare, the raw rodents and greens she'd been living on since her escape had filled her stomach but not her soul.

She stammered through a few teary *thank yous*, but everyone just hugged her and told her she had a home with them for as long as she wanted. Romani were like that—to other Rom. She still didn't quite understand how they'd accepted shifters into their midst, but hadn't wanted to pry the lid off that can of worms for fear of loosing a storm.

Tairin and Elliott had sat on either side of her during dinner. They took such joy in one another Ilona was happy for them. She knew enough about Tairin's story to be furious at the Rom elders who'd ordered her mother into flames for mating outside the blood. Elliott carried his own sad tale. She sensed it beneath his calm exterior.

He hadn't been kidding when he said he wasn't certain exactly what he was now. She felt the Rom in him, but also his wolf bondmate. Still, he had a different emanation than Tairin, who'd been born with both bloodlines.

Trina, one of the women whose wagon she shared, turned over and sat up. Older, heavyset, with long, gray hair that hung in two plaits down her nightdress, she focused her sleepy, blue eyes on Ilona.

"Can't sleep, honey?"

Ilona shook her head. "I'm sure I will, but a lot has happened today."

"You're safe now." Trina's voice faltered. "Well, safe as any of us can be these days, I guess." Twisting, she dug into one of many crates littering the wagon and came up with a small, silver flask that she handed to Ilona.

"Thanks." Ilona removed the cap and took a cautious swallow. Gypsy homebrew was always breath-stealingly strong, and this was no exception. The liquid burned like fire as it tracked down her throat to her stomach. She gave the flask back to Trina, who took a hefty swallow.

"Be right back." Trina hefted her bulk to her knees and crawled to the wagon's door where she let herself out into the night.

The other woman, Marguerite, was Trina's mother. She moaned in her sleep and rolled over.

Judging from her lined face, she had to be in her sixth decade, or maybe even her seventh. Ilona hadn't looked too closely, but illness ate at her, the darkness concentrated in her breasts and abdomen.

Ilona wondered if Trina knew. Neither woman had much in the way of power, but that was true of most of the Rom. If the lore books were accurate, magic was on the decline in their people. Perhaps it was incompatible with modern life. Or maybe it required people to believe in it.

No one did anymore. Not the Rom or their customers, but both made a great show of pretending.

What will become of us?

Ilona chewed on her lower lip. If the Nazis won, it was an easy enough question to answer. Eventually, they'd round up all the gypsies and Jews and other undesirables and kill them. If a few Rom escaped to join their kin in other countries, they might not die out entirely.

If the Nazis lost and Europe's gypsies could once again roam free, they still needed something akin to a miracle to get back in touch with the vibrant, magical people they'd been when they emigrated from India centuries ago.

Trina came back inside, latching the door

behind her, and got under her blankets. "It will be all right." She patted Ilona's arm. "Try to get some rest. Who knows what tomorrow will bring."

"We could look," Ilona whispered, not wanting to disturb Marguerite. "You tell fortunes just like me."

"Ha!" Trina snorted softly. "You bought into that tripe, huh? I make it up as I go depending on who pays me. Sleep now."

"Thanks. You too." Ilona didn't bother crafting a response to Trina. Maybe when your power was as puny as hers, everything did seem made up. Her mind buzzed from the alcoholic homebrew, and she wished she'd swallowed more. When she wasn't vigilant, Jamal entered her thoughts.

Jamal with his intelligent, dark eyes and tawny, chestnut hair. He'd started to take his clothes off prior to shifting. She'd known she shouldn't look, but she hadn't been able to rip her gaze from his tall, broad-shouldered form. He smelled like forests and wintergreen and mystery with a musky undertone that made her want to undress him slowly, savoring every inch of skin as she revealed it.

Ilona wasn't a virgin. Very few grown gypsy women were, regardless of whether they were married. But she'd kept her dalliances brief, private, and outside the caravan. The last thing she wanted was for Valentin to launch into one of his famous, anti-women rages and call her a slut. The next thing after that would be a forced marriage before she ended up pregnant and shamed him and the caravan.

She tucked her mouth beneath the blanket to smother a giggle. Valentin had been a piece of work. His desire to fuck every man who crossed his path had done more to shame the caravan than a whole wagonload of slutty women would have. She'd longed to tell him that, but had the good sense to bite her tongue. No one was supposed to know about Valentin and his boys, some of them barely past childhood. If she'd mouthed off to him, he'd have kicked her out.

Getting through her interviews with Michael and Stewart had been a relief. Elliott may have reassured her that he'd never force her to return to Valentin, but he wasn't the guiding force for either of these caravans. When both Michael and Stewart reinforced Elliott's sentiment, she'd truly begun to relax.

Ilona rolled onto her side, her stomach still pleasantly full from dinner. A few Rom had apologized for what they saw as scant rations, but to her dinner had been plentiful and delicious.

Her mind returned to Jamal.

What was it about him that drew her? His dark good looks? His powerful body? The strong magic that made the air around him sparkle with promise? What would it be like to weave her magic with his?

After her mother died, no one in her caravan commanded power nearly as strong as her own. Sometimes she and her mother had snuck off to practice their trade unobserved. The level of their magic frightened the others. Not that the men would ever admit it.

Even in the midst of a Romani caravan, she'd often felt like a freak and had downplayed her ability. Maybe she wouldn't have to do that in a group of shifters. Ilona's eyes snapped open at the thought. Not that shifters would ever accept her.

Jamal had been kind to her. No more. No less. She'd probably imagined interest hovering in the depths of his remarkable eyes because of her attraction to him. For all she knew, he had a shifter wife somewhere. One thing was certain, he'd never take up with another gypsy. Not after what had happened with Tairin's mother. What Ilona didn't know was why Jamal hadn't raised Tairin. It seemed like an indelicate question to ask, so she'd kept her mouth shut.

What kind of father let his thirteen-year-old loose in the world to fend for herself? Granted, thirteen was considered grown up in the seventeen hundreds, but still.

Maybe he's not the man I think he is.

No. If he were a bad person, a slipshod father, Tairin wouldn't look at him the way she does. Like she's happy he's in her life.

Ilona reached outward with her magic taking stock of the gypsy camp and who was here. She was used to employing power for simple tasks like this, and her touch was light enough no one who wasn't looking would know she'd just taken the magical equivalent of roll call.

Jamal hadn't yet returned, but neither had Meara. Probably a good thing because Meara's power was strong enough to set a Nazi tank on its side—or explode it. Ilona hadn't looked directly because she didn't wish to anger the shifter, but Meara's magic was a force unto itself. Ilona had always longed for that kind of strength. Where she didn't have to conserve her magical well for fear of running it dry.

She closed her eyes and willed sleep to come. The sooner she slept, the sooner it would be morning. Even if Meara weren't back yet, maybe she could sit with Elliott and scry the future. Her power was recovered from her precipitous flight out of Dachau's work camp, and she wanted to help any way she could.

She hadn't given up on finding Aron, either. If he'd returned to Valentin's caravan, he'd moved beyond her reach, but if he were still in this area, she might locate him. Perhaps Elliott could help with that. Or Meara with her ability to fly.

A thought struck her, and she embraced it, reveling in the possibilities it unlocked. Maybe she could become a wolf or a vulture or a hawk. Elliott's transition to wolf shifter was quite new, which argued it was at least possible to augment her magical side.

Her brain was pedaling in crazy circles by the time she released her grip on consciousness and fell into blackness.

ILONA CROUCHED around a camp stove outside Trina and Marguerite's wagon eating boiled grain and raisins. She'd slept well once she'd fallen asleep, and Trina had to wake her to tell her the morning meal was in the cookpot. Marguerite had requested a bowl inside the wagon. Something about the expression on Trina's face told Ilona the other woman knew how gravely ill her mother was.

Ilona huddled deeper into the cloak Trina loaned her. Layered over her shirt and jacket, it was wonderfully warm. "Thanks for making breakfast," she said.

"No thanks needed. It's easy enough, and Mother needs to eat more."

Ilona placed her empty dish next to her and lowered her voice. "How long has she been like this?"

"Months. I took her to a doctor in Berlin. And to others in Augsburg and Munich. They all said the same thing." Trina sidled close and placed her mouth next to Ilona's ear. "She has cancer. It started in her breasts, but it spread. Nothing they can do except give her morphine for when the pain gets bad."

Tears sheened the other woman's eyes. "She's all I've got. I'll miss her so bad."

Ilona hugged Trina. "I know. I lost my mother a year ago. It's still hard. We didn't always get along, but she was my closest friend, the only one in the caravan who understood me."

Trina hugged her back. "I'm glad you're sharing our wagon. I've feared being alone."

"Have your healers looked at Marguerite?"

"She won't have any of it. She wouldn't have gone to those doctors, but I insisted."

Ilona let go of Trina and pushed to her feet. "Your mother doesn't believe in gypsy magic?"

Trina rolled her eyes. "What's to believe in? Once we were strong, but the goddess hasn't seen fit to maintain our magic." She got up from her low campstool. "Now you're strong. Even I have enough power to sense yours, but most of us are like me. We have occasional moments, but for the most part, we're just like the gadjo. Magicless."

Ilona took a chance. "Do you wish it were otherwise?"

Trina frowned, thinking. "Maybe, but I may as well wish for wings like that vulture shifter for all the good it will do me. Best get the wagon together for the day, and I need to see to Mother."

"Can I help?"

"No. Pretty much a one-woman job. Wagon's not big enough for you and me moving around in there at the same time." She turned and disappeared into her home on wheels.

Ilona picked up their empty bowls and ladled water from a bucket to rinse them. Trina and Marguerite's situation was eerily similar to what she'd just lived through. Maybe fortune had led her here. Regardless, it felt like she was where she belonged—at least for now.

Tairin and Elliott strode between the neighboring wagons and walked to where Ilona stood. "Sleep well?" Tairin asked.

Ilona shrugged. "Eventually. What's up? Looks like you came to get me."

"We did," Elliott concurred. "Meara is back, and she and I are going to do what we can to look into the future. If you want to lend your power, I'd welcome it."

Something about how he'd phrased his words caught her attention, and she asked, "Will Meara welcome me too?"

"Probably," Tairin said. "She's hard to read. But she didn't call Elliott back when he said he was on his way to round you up."

"I'd be glad to help any way I can." Ilona looked from one to the other. Meara was back. Was Jamal? She sent magic outward, hunting for his energy but not finding it.

"What was that about?" Elliott quirked a brow.

Heat swooshed from Ilona's chest over her head. She was blushing furiously, but she couldn't do anything about the color she'd just turned. "Um, nothing."

"Let's go," Tairin urged. "Meara's impatient enough as it is."

Ilona could have hugged her for not digging deeper into why she'd just turned the shade of an overripe tomato. She hurried after Tairin with Elliott bringing up the rear. If questions danced in his mind because he recognized Tairin's transparent diversion for what it was, he didn't bring them up.

Meara stood in the center of a circle of leafless oak trees about a quarter mile past the wagons. A creek ran through the grove, forming several pools where the water eddied as opposed to flowing fast. Still swathed in Trina's cloak atop her other clothing, Ilona started to sweat before they reached Meara. She swiped the back of one hand across her forehead before drops could run in her eyes and make them sting.

"I accessed the future while I waited for you," Meara announced. "It's your turn. Once the two of you have gathered your own set of possibilities, we can compare notes."

"What if what we see is different?" Elliott asked.

"It will be," Meara said, "but not so different as all that. Magic comes to each of us by dint of our unique abilities, so our visions will vary. Focus the lens close. We need to get the next couple of weeks pegged down as accurately as we can."

Ilona inhaled sharply. "We can alter what we see if we don't like it."

Meara shifted her unsettling gaze onto Ilona. "Aye. That we can. Have you ever clipped and rewoven the strands of time?"

Looking right at Meara was impossible, so Ilona gave up. "Um, yes. A few times, but the last time I tried, I failed."

"What were you trying to do?" Meara's strident tone softened, but not by much.

"Save my mother."

"Aw, Ilona." Tairin grasped her hand and squeezed it. "I'm sorry."

"You learned a valuable lesson," Meara said. "Look at me, child."

Ilona bristled. No one had called her *child* for a very long time. She raked her gaze off the stone-strewn ground and stared at Meara. "What exactly did I learn?"

"That illness runs its own course. It's one of the few things we can't tamper with. Except to hasten someone's death and spare them suffering. That we can do. So long as your energy is engaged, you go before Elliott. Dig into your gift. Spare nothing. We need precision."

Ilona knelt next to the stillest of the pools and spread her hands in front of her. Chanting softly, she marshalled her power and focused the lens of her third eye. This was familiar territory. Looking ahead, particularly not too far ahead, was easy. Whirlpools formed in the water, running into each other until images took shape.

Tanks rolled down the streets of a city. Maybe Munich. Maybe Dachau. Planes roared overhead. A screaming Hitler spewed hatred from a flag-draped podium. On one side of her vision, a line of gypsies—heads down and covered with black scarves—marched in a sad line, chained to one another. A similar line of Jews marched up the other side of her trance.

Ilona wrenched her attention away from the scene, forcing it closer to where they hid. Would the Nazis find them?

The first images cleared, and mercifully Hitler vanished along with them. Ilona altered the cadence of her chant, hoping for more relevant information. To up her odds of success, she dug a long, sharp fingernail into the ball of her thumb, making a shallow cut. When blood welled, she dipped her hand into the pool, willing her essence to become one with the water.

The next image that took shape held the

wagons. She pushed more power into her working, urging it to yield information. Meara had instructed her to spare nothing, and Ilona dredged power she didn't know she had from her depths. For long moments, nothing disturbed the wagons or the Rom wandering about in the clearing as they engaged in day-to-day tasks. She was about to clear her power, convinced all was well, but Meara closed a viselike grip over her shoulder.

"Stay the course, Romani," she hissed. "You are not yet done."

Power poured from the shifter into Ilona, heady like a rich wine. She let it flow through her, strengthening her vision. Something dark and malevolent tinged one side of the pool black. As she watched, the stain spread. No longer quiet, the water roiled as if the stream resented being used in this fashion.

Scared to keep looking, but unable to wrench herself out of a trance that was anchored by her own power plus Meara's, Ilona's eyes grew hot and gritty. Pressure grew in her chest and her head until she thought she'd explode. Her breath came in little panting gasps. Just when she thought she'd pass out, the maelstrom in the water shattered, and vampires marched through the hole.

Ilona tried to hold it back, but a shriek rose from her gut, and she just kept screaming as she counted ten vampires. Dark, daunting, unbelievably lovely. The lead vampire stared up at her, almost as if he sensed her presence.

Not possible. It's a trance. A vision.

She was still shrieking when Meara waved an arm and the water quieted as if nothing had ever been there.

"Hush." Tairin gathered her into her arms. "It's all right. You're safe."

Ilona writhed in her arms. "No. You're wrong. None of us will ever be safe again." At least talking cut the flow of those other ungodly sounds she'd been making.

"Well?" Elliott asked from behind her.

"She saw the same thing I did," Meara intoned sounding like the death that stalked them. "No reason for a third rerun."

Meara grasped Ilona from behind and dragged her from Tairin's embrace. "Get hold of yourself. We used our gifts to grant us knowledge. Now that we know what we face, we can employ that knowledge to make certain those vampires get exactly what they deserve."

Ilona inhaled deep, shuddery breaths. "How can you kill something that looks like those things do? That one hypnotized me, and he wasn't even here."

"That where shifters come in," Tairin said. "We're immune to their mind control, and we can shield you from it as well."

Ilona shook herself out of Meara's grasp and turned to face the others. "Or you could make me one of you same as you did for Elliott. That way, I'd be stronger. A better warrior. We have a few days before the vampires find us. It's what the quiet time meant at the front end of my vision."

Shock ricocheted through her. What had she just suggested? Where had it come from? "Never mind. I didn't mean it. Not really. I'm ready to work on those plans, whatever they are. Rom magic has always been good enough for me. It still is. I—" Ilona chopped off her flow of words. She was babbling and needed to shut up.

"Come along." Meara beckoned with one hand. "Words that come after vision states are often truer than we suspect."

"Where are we going?" Tairin asked.

"To Stewart's wagon. We will require his and Michael's cooperation. Beyond that, we're allies, and allies share information."

After a final backward glance at the pool that was just a pool now and no longer a bloody battlefield, Ilona plodded after the other three. In the midst of her terror, she'd forgotten about Aron.

"Elliott," she called to his retreating back.

"Yes?" He and Tairin stopped to wait for her.

"I'd meant to cast my net to see if I could locate my brother. Can you help me with that?"

"Sure. As soon as we have the rest of this under better control, I'd be glad to."

Ilona licked dry lips. She'd already made a total ass out of herself with all her shrieking and crying. What was one more thing? "Do you know why your father's not back yet?" she asked Tairin.

"No. And I've begun to worry about him."

"Get moving," Meara yelled from fifty yards ahead.

"We can talk more later." Tairin took off at a trot with Ilona and Elliott right behind her.

CHAPTER 6

Jamal was maybe a mile from the wagons when he heard a woman screaming. Or his wolf did. His senses were more acute than a normal human's, but his wolf had a phenomenal sense of hearing and smell.

"Hurry," he urged, recognizing Ilona's agonized shrieks.

What the hell had happened? He couldn't see Michael or Stewart turning on the magic-laden Rom, but he wasn't so sure about the other inhabitants of the caravans. Everyone was on edge, and after her stint in Dachau, others might believe she was a spy.

If anything happened to her, he'd get to the

bottom of it and—

And what? he asked himself.

It wasn't as if the hundred or so Romani milling about the clearing had suddenly come to terms with shifters as partners. Even Michael, Stewart, and the other Rom who'd fought side by side with him and the group of shifters, had done so because there wasn't any other choice. Centuries of distrust weren't going to evaporate overnight. And him charging into the camp like a raging bull would only serve to get him thrown out.

Quite aside from alienating the Rom, Meara would be furious with him. A cavalcade of the shifters he'd met with over the past several hours filled his mind. Most had been mired in disbelief that Rom would ever be other than sworn enemies. They'd agreed to meet, but only because he'd told them Meara demanded it.

Unlike Rom, who sometimes ignored their leaders, shifters held to a strict chain of command. No one who wanted to remain part of shifter society disregarded an order from one of the first shifters.

Ilona's cries had faded. Did that mean things were better?

She could be unconscious. Or dead... Alarm filled

him, and he pushed the wolf to greater speed.

"Use your magic," his wolf said dryly. *"She's very much alive."*

"Since you know so much, what happened?"

The wolf's muscles flexed in a rolling motion as it ran. *"She was frightened, and now she isn't. It will have to do until we return."*

Jamal glanced at familiar landmarks flashing past. It wouldn't be long now. He angled their trajectory so they'd come to the car first. He wanted his human form, and for that he needed clothes.

Meara stood next to the Mercedes, arms folded beneath her breasts. Before he'd fully drawn to a stop, she narrowed her eyes. "What took you so long?"

"I found Ilona's discarded prison suit. The wolf and I laid a false track and disposed of it in a way it won't lead anyone right to us. Hang on. Let me shift."

Light scattered as he summoned magic to make himself human again. Once he had hands, he tugged open one of the car's back doors and grabbed clothing, dressing as quickly as he could.

"How many of our kin did you speak with?" Meara asked before he could craft a question about Ilona. Something subtle that wouldn't give away his bone-deep longing for her.

"I followed your instructions. By the time we were done, we'd passed the message to eighty-seven shifters. Wolves, bears, coyotes, hawks. Even a pair of foxes."

"Humph. I'm surprised the bears even let you inside. Their animal forms prefer sleep during the cold months."

"Well, they did. Everyone will be here as you commanded." Jamal shrugged into a warm jacket and closed the car door before shoving his hands into his pockets. "What happened here? Why'd you feel the need to intercept me as soon as I returned?"

He turned what he hoped were guileless eyes on Meara, although he doubted he'd fooled her.

"Come with me. We're meeting with Michael and Stewart."

"Did something happen?" Jamal repeated, too anxious about Ilona to wait any longer for information.

Meara rolled her eyes. "You young ones. Always so impatient. Yes, something happened. I scryed the future. So did Ilona. Our visions matched well enough, I didn't feel the need for a third opinion from Elliott."

"And?" Jamal pressed.

"Vampires will attack this location—"

Jamal stiffened. "Why are we wasting time meeting? We need more amulets and a war plan. We must form groups and practice. All those shifters I raised need to show up sooner rather than two days hence." He paused long enough to take a breath.

"I didn't say they'd be here tonight," Meara cut in. "Although once we're done talking with Michael and Stewart, I'll do what I can to hurry up both your group of shifters and the fifty or so I contacted." She took off at a lope for the wagons. All the horses had been unharnessed and were hobbled where they could graze.

Jamal fell into step beside her. "Did Ilona's vision harm her? I heard her screaming."

Meara sent a pointed look his way, and he stared right back at her. "She was more frightened than anything. I suspect she hasn't used her gift for anything serious—until now. Future seeing doesn't just wash over you. You have to plan for it, summon what you want to see." She shrugged. "Since her caravan leader didn't fully understand or appreciate her gifts, she was never called upon to use them."

"Told you," Jamal's wolf piped up.

"Indeed you did," Jamal replied, recalling the wolf's assessment that Ilona had sounded scared.

Meara looked as if she wanted to say something, but she must have changed her mind. Threading her way around the front of Michael's wagon, she led Jamal to where a group hunkered in a tight circle. Magic danced around them, probably to shield their words from the rest of the Rom.

Tairin, Elliott, Ilona, Michael, Stewart, and two other Rom that Jamal recognized from the vampire hunt glanced at Meara and him. Michael made come along motions with one hand. "We waited for you." His dark hair was chopped to shoulder length, and his thickset body bulged with muscle. Black eyes snapped with annoyance—and worry. He wore his usual leather pants and brightly patterned shirt, painted with runic symbols.

Jamal slipped between Michael and Tairin. He wanted to position himself next to Ilona, but she looked nervous, as if shards from her vision still haunted her. He tried to establish eye contact, but she kept her gaze stubbornly on the dirt in front of her.

She had to know he and Meara were there. Why wouldn't she look at him?

Power settled around the circle like a shroud. "Now that we're all here and can chew this through," Stewart said, "I suppose 'tis pointless for us to run."

"The vampires know where we are," Meara said. "If they could find us once, they can find us again. No. We must face them. How many of those amulets from our last skirmish are left?"

Michael frowned. "I might have five or so."

"And I've another ten," Stewart said. "I gathered them from the Rom afore they left the killing field."

"We may need more," Meara said. "It depends how we do this."

"Ye have something in mind," Stewart trained astute dark eyes on her. Dressed in his usual kilt, his long, red hair was braided close to his head.

Meara's sharp-featured, ageless face split into an untamed expression with lips skinned back from her teeth. "Indeed I do, but it has a better chance of success if you'll work with us. Stronger power and all that."

"Ye have to say more," said one of the Rom Jamal didn't know by name. He sounded like Stewart, his brogue thick and soft. He was dressed in loose trousers and a woolen top. Curly dark hair was unevenly cut to shoulder length, and his blue eyes radiated sharp intelligence.

"And you are?" Meara asked.

Color splotched the man's face. "Sorry. My name is Cadr."

"I'm his brother, Vreis," the other man spoke up.

Once he said the word *brother,* Jamal picked up the family resemblance. Vreis had longer hair, but the same lanky build and blue eyes.

"Their magic is potent," Stewart cut in. "'Tis why they're here. They're transplants from the Old Country, just like me."

"Well, Cadr and Vreis"—Meara looked from one to the other—"how would you feel about a wee bit of mayhem in one of the work camps?"

Michael smiled grimly. "You're thinking if the vampires are busy here, we can mete out damage in the camps, perhaps even free some of the poor sods stuck in there."

Meara nodded, but held up a cautionary hand. "I don't believe every vampire will be part of the attack planned for this location, but the numbers I've seen suggest fewer of them will be scattered elsewhere."

"When Tairin and I went into Dachau, we didn't sense any vampires at all. It was only after we were well clear of the prison that we found them," Elliott said.

"I only saw one." Ilona finally looked up. "It

was outside Dachau's gates, and it never returned the few weeks I was inside." A shudder racked her. "I'd have noticed if one were close. Nothing else feels quite as bad as they do."

Meara cleared her throat, nostrils flaring. "The other camps in Germany are Sachsenhausen-Oranienburg near Berlin, Esterwegen near Hamburg, and Ravensbrück near Brandenburg. We must get a jump on this now. I've seen..." She hesitated, probably because sharing material from her visions didn't come easily.

"What have you seen?" Jamal asked, keeping his voice soft.

"Far worse prisons than those already here. Soon the Nazis will begin construction of a place near Oswiecim, Poland. That's not far from Krakow. They will call it Auschwitz, and many Rom will die there. Shifters too, although we will not fare as badly as the Romani and Jews."

"Define many." Michael's voice was strained.

"Hundreds of thousands."

A collective gasp moved through the group.

Meara made a chopping motion with one hand. "We cannot afford to lose ourselves in horror and our own fears. I've been alive for a long time, and if we are cunning and quick, we might be able to defeat the future that's shown itself in my glass."

"Have ye thwarted destiny afore?" Stewart asked.

She nodded gravely. "It's why I know it's possible. Not easy, but possible. The foretold future will fight to have its way, but nothing is absolute."

"How soon will the vampires be here?" Michael asked. "We will need to do the same thing we did before. Form teams and take them on simultaneously."

"Exactly." Meara smoothed the dirt in front of her, picked up a stick, and began to draw something that looked like a diagram. When she looked up, she said, "This is a very defensible position. It's why I picked it. You haven't been here long enough to explore, but this shelf only butts up against a cliff here." She pointed with the stick. "If you move past where you have the horses"—she pointed again—"there's a steep drop off. The area at the bottom is riddled with caves. Once upon a time, they were shifter hideaways, but none of us have used them for years. Rather than burning the vampire remains, we can spirit them into a cave and seal it with magic."

"Will they be dead?" Cadr asked in a surprisingly steady voice.

Meara shrugged. "Dead is relative. Vampires aren't exactly alive, using anyone else's definition. It's why burning them is a failsafe, a guarantee they can't jump bodies."

"Och aye, and such a large fire would draw attention to our location," Stewart muttered. He stretched his hands in front of him, flexing his fingers. "Shouldna be all that difficult. We did it once afore. Second time should be smoother."

"We do have that advantage," Elliott said, "although I'd hoped for a longer break between last time and when we had to face them again. Do you know how many we face?"

"I saw ten," Ilona answered.

"Easier than last time," Tairin gritted out.

"Don't make that mistake," Meara cautioned. "Last time, we surprised them. This time, they'll assume we're ready for them, and they won't be scrambling to mount a defense."

"What's the best we can hope for?" Ilona asked.

"That if we destroy this batch, they'll think twice before targeting us again," Meara answered.

"I'll sign on for damn near anything that discourages other vampires," Michael said.

"But if they're working hand in glove with Hitler as we suspect," Stewart broke in. "We'll end up with the Third Reich breathing down our necks. They've already targeted the Romani for extermination—"

"Yes, you'll have to move from here." Meara raked a hand through her hair. "The best place for your people is in shifter households."

Vreis made a rude, snorting sound. "How do ye see that working, madam shifter? The best place for us is in the British Isles, but it may as well be the moon for how inaccessible 'tis."

"I see it working"—she eyed him—"because we're all committed to maintaining magic in this world. Once it dies out, humankind won't be far behind."

"What about the other ten caravans?" Michael asked. "Will any of them make it out of Germany?"

Meara made a noncommittal gesture with one hand. "At least two have chosen to hide themselves, much as you've done. They may survive. The others will be detained crossing into other countries. Their possessions will be stripped from them, and they'll end up in the camps."

A long, low moan rose from Ilona, but she cut it off fast.

Jamal wanted to go to her, gather her close, but what comfort could he offer? The world had turned into exactly what she feared. A place hostile to gypsies.

"I'm glad Mother's not alive to see this," she muttered. "And she would have seen it—all of it—in water or her glass."

Meara looked from Michael to Stewart. "Talk with your people. See who will fight. I can hide the others in the caves. They'll be safe there. Meanwhile, I'll return to the shifters in the area. I need them here sooner rather than later, and I need to sort who will be the strongest warriors."

"Do ye need us to come up with more amulet material?" Stewart asked.

"It would be helpful, but if it's too risky to go into Munich to the priest who helped with holy water and consecrated earth before, don't chance it."

Jamal felt a change in the air currents and shielded his eyes. For once, Meara's shift didn't catch him unaware.

Cadr and Vreis shot to their feet, eyes trained on the skies. "By Christ and all the bloody saints, I wish I could to that," Vreis mumbled.

"Aye." Cadr nodded. "'Twould be a handy trick to have to hand."

Stewart stood. "Come on, both of ye," he said. "We must do some sorting and see who wants to face down vampires."

"From the sound of things," Elliott said, "it might also go down well if you identified some folk who are game to sneak into the other work camps. What Tairin and I did was simple enough…"

Words flowed around Jamal as he got to his feet and walked to where Ilona crouched. She might tell him to go to hell, but he wanted to offer what paltry emotional support he could. He knelt next to her and asked, "How are you doing?"

After a pause so long he felt certain she wasn't going to answer, she trained her restless, gray eyes on him. Up close like this, he saw silvery flecks dance around her pupils. "Truth?"

"Of course."

She pushed to her feet. "Feel like a walk? Sitting still isn't working for me."

Jamal stood and slipped a hand beneath her elbow. Maybe he shouldn't have touched her, but she didn't shake him off. "Where would you like to walk?"

"Back to where I saw the vampires in trance."

"Not safe," his wolf said.

"What was that?" Ilona darted her gaze from side to side.

"My wolf. Come on. We can talk more when we're a little bit away from here."

"Don't go too far," Tairin cautioned. "My wolf can always find yours, but still…"

"We won't," he reassured his daughter and set off at a moderate pace, still holding onto Ilona.

"What did your wolf say?" Ilona asked when they were far enough away it would be impossible to overhear them without employing magic.

"That it wasn't safe to return to where you'd seen the vampires." He slowed and turned her to face him. "How about if you start by telling me what happened?"

Ilona chewed on her lower lip. "I can do that. Not much to tell. You already know I saw vampires attack this camp, but it didn't happen right away in my trance, which is how I know the attack won't come today or tonight or probably even tomorrow." She straightened her spine. "The creepy part, and what I've never had happen before, is one of the vampires reached through my spell. He saw me, felt me."

Jamal gripped her hands. “Maybe you imagined it.”

“She didn’t,” the wolf spoke up.

“Your wolf just said something, didn’t he?”

“Would you like to be able to talk with it?” Jamal answered her query with one of his own.

Ilona nodded. “Why do you refer to the wolf as it? Don’t you know if it’s male or female?”

“I don’t. The bond animals are genderless. It’s always been that way. If I shift and you meet my other form, then you’ll be able to hear it and even engage it in conversation.” He hesitated. “That might come in useful if for some reason you’re angry or tired of me but need to communicate anyway.”

“Yes. I want to meet your wolf but only so I can hear him, er it, when it speaks.”

“Fair enough. Before I shift, what were you hoping to accomplish by returning to where you had your vision?”

She scrunched her face in concentration. “You asked if I imagined the vampire reaching for me. I’m not sure. I guess I thought if I tried to recreate the scene, and the creature was just a vision and not a malevolent presence—”

“—it might add credence to the first occurrence being your imagination working overtime." Jamal finished her thought and considered it.

"What?" She watched him closely, but stopped shy of digging into his mind.

"It's possible, but unlikely. My wolf agrees with that conclusion." She opened her mouth, but he said, "Hear me out. You said this trance was dissimilar to other ones. You felt the difference. If you truly opened a portal—and I believe you did —next time you do the same thing, the vampire will be waiting. He may even expect you to seek him out again. They're extraordinarily seductive. He might assume you won't be able to stay away."

Ilona narrowed her eyes. "What aren't you saying?"

Jamal soft-pedaled a grimace. She'd caught him dead to rights. "If you open the same portal, and the vampire is there waiting, this time he'll be ready."

"Ready for what?"

"They're very strong magically. Once you open a conduit, he can pull you through to where he is. After you're there, he'll feed from you, probably fuck you, and turn you."

He let go of her hands and looked away. "I apologize. That was coarse."

"Some things require coarse words. No

apologies needed. You're saying I wouldn't be strong enough to fight him."

A place within Jamal that had been locked tight since he lost Aneksi cracked open. He extended his arms, and Ilona walked into them, twining hers around him. He hugged her back. She felt right in his arms, as if she belonged there, but that was dangerous thinking, dangerous ground.

"It's not that you're weak," he said, focusing on her words rather than the tempting reality of her body crushed against him. "No Romani can withstand vampire powers. They mesmerize you, and you lose your will."

"But not you?" She tilted her head back so she could look at him.

"No. Not me."

"Then I want to be a shifter. I said that earlier and my words shocked me, but I've had time to get used to the idea. Kind of. What good it is to be magical if I'm not as strong as I can be? More specifically, if I'm too weak to fight the enemy bearing down on us."

He choked back incredulity. "You don't know what you're asking for."

"We have time. Why don't you tell me?"

CHAPTER 7

Ilona wanted to lose herself in Jamal's embrace. He felt good. Too good. The last thing she wanted to do was talk about vampires and magic. Far better to trace the lines of his chiseled lips with her fingertips or wind her hands into his beautiful hair. His scent rose, surrounding her, wintergreen mingled with the rich, loamy smell of the forest.

"Let's walk some more." He disentangled his arms from around her and laced his fingers with hers.

She matched her pace to his, which was easy since he moved slowly. "Are you going to answer me?" she asked after a few minutes slid past.

Jamal drew his dark brows into a line,

crinkling his forehead. "Contrary to popular opinion, we're not in the habit of making new shifters by any method beyond giving birth to them."

"What about all those werewolf tales?" she asked, adding, "Never mind. Let's bring this closer to home. What about Elliott? I don't have the whole story, but I know enough of it to intuit he used to be full Romani like me. Something happened, and now he's a wolf shifter like you and Tairin."

"The something was he was almost possessed by a very strong vampire. We had to act and act fast. Actually, it was Tairin's wolf who took a chance on biting Elliott."

"Why a chance? What could have gone wrong?"

"Lots of things."

"Like what?" she prodded. "It may be none of my business, but I want to know."

Jamal nodded slowly and tightened his grip on her hand. "I already told you Romani are no match for vampires. In truth, neither are shifters, but at least we have a ghost of a chance to take one on and win. When we destroyed the vampire nest, we killed their master, the one who'd made the others. Something about feeding from another and turning them adds to a vampire's strength. Most master vampires insist on being the ones who turn new recruits. It solidifies their power base and ensures none of the vampires in their group grow powerful enough to challenge them."

"Fascinating." A shudder tracked down her spine. "And chilling. I never knew anything about them, let along suspected they still existed anywhere in Europe."

"None of us did." He raked his other hand through his hair. "They've kept a rather low profile."

"Until Hitler apparently thought they'd be useful to his cause." The bitterness beneath her words surprised her. "Damn that man. I may not have spent long in Dachau, but the experience will be with me for a long time."

"It would mark anyone, which reminds me of something. The reason I was late returning was my wolf and I found your discarded prison clothes. We laid a false track. Even if anyone comes after you, they'll figure you died about a mile up the mountain from where you changed clothes."

Gratitude welled, and her throat thickened with emotion. "Thank you," she choked out, swallowing hard. "At the time, I thought about doing a better job hiding the striped suit, but I was tapped out and figured I'd use the last of my energy to put more distance between myself and the prison."

He turned back the way they'd come, still walking slowly. "It was wise of you. The terrain the wolf and I covered was rough. Besides, there wouldn't have been a way for you to take the clothes somewhere and not leave a scent trail both coming and going."

Ilona inhaled raggedly. Part of her didn't really want to talk about vampires ever again, but the rest of her overruled it. "Back to Elliott and the vampire. It tried to possess him. Then what happened?"

"Tairin's wolf bit him, which injected shifter essence and paved the path for a bond wolf to enter him, but that alone wasn't enough. The vampire fought hard. It knew what would happen if it lost. Meara was with us. She built a magical concentrator and leveraged more power than I imagined existed urging the wolf within Elliott to come out. He had to shift to activate Tairin's sacrifice."

"He must have since he's still here, but why

was that critical?" Her words emerged as a squeak.

"If he hadn't shifted, Elliott would have been lost. The vampire would have completed its possession and commandeered Elliott's body. Unfortunately, Tairin, her wolf, and the newly bonded wolf would have been lost right along with Elliott, sucked into the half-life of those tainted by vampire contamination."

Shit. That's too horrible to contemplate.

Ilona's heart thudded in her chest, but she'd opened this line of inquiry. She had to see it through to its conclusion. "They can do that?" she asked, her voice breaking.

"Do what?"

"Change bodies?"

"Yes. As many times as they need to to ensure their survival, but there's a time factor. They have to jump bodies right away. This particular vampire required a corporeal presence because its last body lay in a smoking ruin."

Ilona pulled her fingers out of his grip and wrapped her arms around herself. The day wasn't particularly warm, but it had turned far chillier because of Jamal's words.

"So," he went on, "the only time our law permits us to break from tradition and create shifters through biting is if need is great and death imminent." A long, whistling breath rustled from him. "If we acted out the werewolf tales, we'd be no better than vampires."

Ilona chewed on her lower lip. "I understand, but Meara said something after I blurted out that I wanted to be a shifter. It was on the heels of my vision where the vampire came after me."

Jamal cast a sidelong glance her way. "What did she say?"

"Something like 'words that come after vision states are often truer than we suspect.'"

"She'd be right about that." Jamal draped an arm around her shoulders. "You look cold."

"I am, but it's the kind of cold a fire can't fix." She looked up, taking her bearings, and understood they'd been walking in a rather large circle. Light was leaching from the day.

"Now that you know a little more, would you still like to meet my wolf?" His dark eyes glittered with something she didn't have a name for. Challenge. Promise. Hope that she still wanted to know everything about him.

Ilona nodded. Anticipation vied with apprehension. What would his wolf look like? Be like? Would it have Jamal's combination of compassion and tenderness mingled with bottomless strength?

"Wait here. I need to undress first." He let go of her and faded into thick tree cover.

In far less time than she'd anticipated, a rustling behind her was followed by a soft bark. She spun around and was confronted by a large black and gray timber wolf with tawny markings. Its eyes were the same as Jamal's, dark and liquid with amber centers.

The wolf trotted to her and nosed her hand.

Delighted, she dropped to her haunches and buried her hands in its thick fur, inhaling its clean, fresh animal scent. It pressed into her touch. "Talk to me," she urged.

"I'm glad he let me out to meet you." Understated humor ran beneath the wolf's mind voice. *"It's a rare enough occurrence for any reason these days."*

"Don't mind him," another voice jumped in. *"He likes to play martyr."*

"Do not," the wolf shot back.

"You're both in there," she said, marveling at what felt like a miracle.

"Of course we are," the wolf replied. *"Just like I'm always inside when we're wearing our human body."*

Ilona continued to pet the wolf shamelessly. In a far corner of her mind, she knew she wanted to do the same thing to Jamal—love him, stroke him, explore his body. Dangerous territory, but when her desire to touch him was translated into scratching the wolf's ears and patting the rough outer hairs that ran along its back and shoulders, the contact felt safe and non-threatening.

"That's wonderful, you can do it for hours." The wolf leaned into her.

"She could, but we need to get back. They may need me as they plan their next moves," Jamal spoke up.

With a whuffly growl, the wolf straightened and licked her fingertips before it trotted back into the thick tree cover.

She was still marveling at the wonder of having an animal as part of you when Jamal rejoined her. "Thank you." She smiled broadly. "Your wolf is an amazing animal."

"Indeed I am," it said into her mind, and her smile grew wider.

"You were right," she crowed. "I can hear him, er it."

Jamal made a snorting noise. "I'd watch it with those compliments, the wolf will become more insufferable that it already is."

"I'll keep it in mind, but I could've petted it for hours."

"We'll just have to make sure Jamal lets me out

again soon." The wolf's voice held a soft, purring quality.

"Ready to go back?" Jamal asked, but he didn't make any move to leave her side.

"Yeah. I guess. I'm grateful to have somewhere to go back to."

Jamal hesitated. "Thanks for keeping an open mind about my animal bondmate. I'm sorry I can't offer you an opportunity to become a shifter—not without breaking one of our cardinal laws. Working next to us, though, potentiates both our magics." He cradled the side of her face in his hand. "You're so lovely. I'm out of line saying that, but I haven't been able to think about much besides you since we found you in that little clearing."

Warmth rose from her chest and swept over the top of her head. She felt tongue-tied, but managed to murmur, "I like you too. You've been good to me when you didn't have to be."

He traced the line of her cheekbone with a fingertip, and then brushed his thumb over her lower lip. She arched against him, wanting him to kiss her. Maybe it was wrong, but she yearned for him, and she infused that hunger into her touch as she wrapped her arms around his broad back.

Jamal groaned, the sound of a man caught

between misgiving and need, and lowered his mouth atop hers. His lips were firm, perfect, and she moved her hands upward, weaving her fingers into his glorious hair. He teased her lips with his. Little biting kisses as he explored her mouth with teeth and tongue. She bit back, latching onto his lower lip and sucking on it.

When she opened her mouth, he sank his tongue inside and she sparred with it. Her nipples peaked where they pressed against his chest, and she felt the swell of his erection prod her belly. Their breathing quickened as they fell into the kiss, offering it a life of its own. He tasted sweet, and his intoxicating scent intensified, swirling around them.

She added a dash of Rom magic and ran her tongue across his whiskered cheek to his earlobe before taking it into her mouth. He strung kisses down her face, settling in the hollow of her collarbone where his tongue did wicked things to her sensitive flesh. The dark, secret place between her legs flooded with heat as lust spilled through her, and she writhed against him.

Jamal lifted his head and speared her with his dark-eyed gaze. The bronze color of his skin was heightened, and he was breathing faster. "You're lovely, *liebchen,* but we must stop. The same reasons I had for returning to the wagons haven't gone away." He twined a lock of hair behind one of her ears.

Desire thickened behind her breastbone, rising into her throat. She wanted to tear off his clothing and ride the erection that still pressed into her belly, but she recognized the wisdom in not giving in to the lust that held her captive.

"Probably wise." She pulled away from his embrace. The place he'd been pressed against her body felt cold and empty, and it took self-discipline not to make a grab for his penis. She felt his indecision and his yearning. Calling a halt to their passion hadn't been easy for him.

Jamal held out a hand, and she clasped it. Together, they walked back toward camp. Her heart and mind were full, so full words felt inadequate at least until she'd sorted through her confused welter of thoughts and feelings. He was a shifter. She wasn't. That should have been the end of things, but she wanted to make love with him.

More than that, for the first time she'd met a man she might want to make a life with.

I can't possibly know that. It's too soon. We just met.

"I feel the same way." His deep voice buzzed

low. "Forgive me for helping myself to your thoughts. It was cowardly of me, but I had to know if you sensed the attraction as keenly as me."

She angled her head so their gazes met. Tenderness and yearning blazed from his eyes, but beneath it all lay resignation and sorrow. "Why are you sad?" she asked.

"Tairin's mother was Rom. It didn't end well. Her caravan burned her alive for the sin of mating outside her blood."

Ilona closed her teeth over her lower lip. "I knew that part, but hadn't considered exactly what it meant. Where were you when it happened? Oh my God." She slapped a hand over her heart. "They made you watch, didn't they? It's something I can see Rom elders doing."

Shame joined the mix on his expressive features, and he looked away. "I wasn't there. Aneksi and I had quarreled. I knew Tairin's first shift was imminent and that we had to flee. Aneksi didn't agree. She hoped Tairin would never shift. I knew otherwise. Our last words weren't pretty."

Ilona stopped walking, but didn't let go of his hand, so Jamal came to a halt too. "Look at me."

When he did, she almost wished she hadn't

asked. His eyes had darkened to midnight and reflected guilt and torture. "You've blamed yourself for a long time." Ilona gripped his hand harder. "What would you have done if you'd been there?"

"Become my wolf and taken down as many of those murderous Rom as I could. At least it would have given Aneksi a chance to take Tairin and run."

"Would she have?" Ilona tilted her chin upward. She knew the answer because she knew how Romani thought.

The harsh, desperate look left Jamal's face, and it crumpled into a painful expression that broke her heart. "No." His voice was scratchy with suffering. "I begged her to leave before Tairin shifted, when we could have slipped away with very little notice. She refused. I'd even found us a small oasis where we could have lived a quiet life."

"Rom are nomadic, but they're also wedded to their caravans." Ilona kept her tone soft, soothing. "None of us leave unless we're kicked out. Take my brother for example. Aron. If he's still alive, he probably hooked back up with Valentin's caravan. Never mind associating with other Rom has turned into a death sentence."

"I didn't smell anyone else when I came across your prison garb. Did he escape Dachau with you?"

She shook her head. "No. I told you before. He ran away the day we got there. Before they even dragged him through the gates. That's when I saw my first vampire. The SS sicced it on Aron after he gave them the slip."

"You do know that's not good news."

"Yeah, I know, but my magic was still strong then, and I probably would have sensed it if that thing had killed him. Until I find out otherwise, I'm choosing to believe Aron is still alive."

"My brave gypsy. Your spirit was one of the things that drew me to you from the moment I saw you. You might have been scared—"

"Might have been?" she cut in. "Nothing like one Rom against four shifters, two of whom turned out to be part Rom."

"Regardless," he insisted. "You stood your ground. I admire that."

Ilona gazed at him, drinking him in. "What are we going to do about us? About wanting to know one another better."

"It goes against both of our laws and customs. I fell into that trap long ago. I want you, but that's not the issue."

Anguish seared her. He couldn't walk away. Not before they'd fully explored their attraction for one another. "But you're drawn to me. I feel it."

He let go of her and squared his shoulders. "Oh yes, my dear. I do want you. More than is good for me—or for you. But now is the only time we can cut our losses. If we get in any deeper, it will be much harder. One of us has to be strong."

Her eyes flooded. She didn't want to be strong. She wanted Jamal's arms around her and his mouth on hers. She wanted to bury her hands in his wolf's rough pelt and feel its hot tongue lick her fingers and chin.

She should've keep her mouth shut, but words tumbled out anyway. "Tairin and Elliott found a way to make it work."

"She was half Rom, and now he's a shifter too."

Ilona wanted to shriek that he hadn't been when he and Tairin chose one another. Anger and frustration swept through her. "You're a coward." She spat the words. "Either that or you were just in it for cheap thrills when you kissed me."

Not trusting herself if she stayed, Ilona took off at a blind run heedless of where she was going. It didn't matter. She'd finally found a man she could love, but he didn't want her and for the lamest of reasons. This was wartime. If Rom and shifters could fight side-by-side, why the hell couldn't they love one another?

She stuffed a hand in her mouth to stifle the tortured sounds that wanted to bubble past her chest.

I'm being stupid, she lectured herself.

I barely know him. I can't be this upset over losing something I never had.

Words didn't quell the ache in her soul, though. She understood he'd lived through hell and carried a boatload of guilt, but that happened centuries ago. People got over things. What was wrong with him?

Ilona cringed. More to the point, what was wrong with her? She'd thrown herself into his arms like a bitch in heat. Maybe he'd decided she was a loose woman and that whole Aneksi explanation had been nothing but a smokescreen to not hurt her feelings by calling her a slut.

"It doesn't matter." Her voice sounded dull and dead.

When she finally looked around, she was back in the clearing with the pools where she'd fallen into trance earlier that day. A shudder racked her, followed by several more. There was a reason she'd ended up back here. Her feet hadn't just randomly carried her to this place.

She'd been a seer long enough to recognize that being here was far more than mere synchronicity. The question was if she had enough determination to act on it. Ilona fell into a familiar pattern and checked her magical well. If it were depleted, that would make the decision for her.

If not, she'd at least have the option to gather her resources and go after the vampire who'd marked her with his disturbing energy.

CHAPTER 8

Jamal gazed after Ilona's fleeing form. He'd handled things badly and hurt her feelings. And he felt like the worst kind of cad. He never should have given in to the temptation to kiss her, except he had. Which made the scene that just played itself out—and her justifiable anger—harder to bear.

"You have to go after her," the wolf urged.

"No. That will just make things worse. I can't offer her anything."

"Why not? She isn't Aneksi. Besides, times have changed, or haven't you noticed?"

Jamal plodded back toward the wagons. Arguing with the wolf was pointless. Ilona might not be Aneksi, but she was still Romani.

"Your daughter had the courage to follow her heart," the wolf continued, relentless as always when it wanted something.

"She was half Rom to start with," Jamal argued back. *"I'm not. Besides, she lived with gypsies, traveled with them. Passed herself off as one."*

The wolf's words made him feel worse and worse. Boosted by her shifter side, Tairin's magic was far stronger than any other Romani's was. Her innate ability had made it easy for her to draw wards, so the caravans she traveled with never looked too closely at what she was.

She'd been alone a very long time when she dropped her barriers and took a chance on loving Elliott. Jamal was glad for her, grateful to the bottom of his heart that his daughter had found a man to love her.

"You've been alone for a long time too," the wolf said.

"Not the same."

"Why?" The wolf adopted a sly tone. *"Because Tairin's not doing penance for your sins?"*

"Something like that. Leave me alone."

"Hard to do when I know you're making a mistake."

Jamal clamped his jaw in a tight line and

shuttered his roiling thoughts. No reason to give the wolf more ammunition to challenge him. Ilona was young, beautiful, fearless. She needed a man to match her forthright spirit, not one who came with a tarnished past—and a whole lot of baggage.

"Stop." The wolf's command was harsh.

At first, Jamal thought his bond animal was referring to the downward spiral of his thoughts, but when his body moved of its own accord into the shadows between two enormous trees, he realized the wolf must sense danger. It was rare for it to commandeer their shared form when it was human.

"What is it?" Jamal breathed the question in shielded telepathy, hoping no magic would leak out to reveal their location.

"From the smell of things, Nazis."

Thank Christ it wasn't vampires, although Nazis were scourge enough. Since the SS held zero magical ability and couldn't detect him, Jamal sent his own power zinging outward and cast a wide net.

"Two. Is that what you came up with?" he asked the wolf.

"Yes. They're following the wagons' tracks, but on foot."

"Mmph. Probably had a vehicle and it broke down or split an axle or something."

Jamal kicked off his shoes and stripped off the rest of his clothes, not stopping to think about his next move. He'd shift and then kill those Nazi bastards. Before they could radio any information back to whomever had deployed them.

Maybe they were working on their own.

Possibly deserters, but that wasn't likely.

Shift magic spilled through him. Taking care to be quiet, stealthy as only a wolf could manage, he scented the air and circled behind the men moving toward where the wagons were parked. Something about their smell gave him pause. These men weren't regular Nazi officers. They carried an infusion of power from vampires.

Not that it would help them much. If they had magic that was worth a Reichsmark, they'd have noticed him. He closed from behind. If he were quick, decisive, he could leap on one, close his jaws over the spot where carotid and jugular lay and rip out the man's throat before the second soldier could react. Both men had rifles slung over their shoulders and sported sidearms strapped to their hips, but their hands were empty.

Good. Meant precious seconds. Time when he could strike without dealing with bullets aimed for his heart.

The hunting cry of a vulture drew his gaze skyward, and his jaws parted in a lolling grin.

Meara.

Sure enough. *"Take the one nearest you,"* she instructed just before she plummeted from the sky, talons extended.

Jamal broke into a hard run, no longer quiet.

One of the Germans looked up, pointing at the large black vulture. "What the fuck?" he demanded in German and reached for his pistol.

"*Nein,*" the other man shouted. "Vultures are Hitler's bird."

"*Ja,* but this one's headed right for us."

"Eh, you must be mistaken. They only feed on the dead. Not so unlike our Fuehrer." He spun, no doubt because he finally heard Jamal behind him. "If you're going to shoot something, shoot the wolf," he shouted at his companion, not knowing those would be his last words.

Meara buried her talons deep in the other man's neck. Blood geysered everywhere, and Jamal leapt atop his target biting sure and deep. More blood, hot, coppery, viscous, showered him, and he lapped it up. Once it slowed, he ripped the man's uniform aside and dug his teeth into his gut where the stomach and liver were. Heart too. Still warm and trying to beat.

A flurry of German blatting from the radio strapped to the man sliced through Jamal's blood fever. He lifted his bloody muzzle from his feast and stared at the radio's dials trying to make sense of it with his wolf's brain.

Meara raised her beak from her own feeding frenzy, holding an intact eyeball aloft. *"What are they saying?"* She sounded as caught up in the hunt energy as he was.

Jamal licked blood from his snout and coaxed his human intelligence back into ascendance. The radio was still spitting German, but it wasn't set to transmit, only to receive.

"Luck is with us." He nodded at Meara. *"Whoever's on the other end can't hear us."*

"Can you disable that thing?" She flapped her way over to him, the eye still clamped in her beak.

Instead of answering, Jamal called shift magic with his wolf's protests loud in their shared mind.

"We weren't done eating. There's more..."

Jamal flexed his newly forming fingers and pulled the radio out of its leather case. Once he had it, he peeled the back off its metal casing.

Inside, he pulled wires at random until the thing was silent. A flash of brilliant light told him Meara was human again too.

Blood streaked her face and hands, but her smile radiated grim satisfaction. She chewed quickly, likely the pilfered eyeball. "We need to get rid of the bodies."

"No. What we need to do is round up the wagons and move our location. It's only a matter of time before more come after these two when they don't return. It might foil the vampires for a short time too, if we relocate."

"Speaking of vampires. These two had some vampire essence. Not enough to ruin feeding on them, but I wonder how many of the SS have been contaminated by Hitler's pets."

"Hard to say." Jamal shrugged. "For all we know, fucking a vampire is a requirement for joining the SS."

Meara wiped the back of a bloody hand across her mouth, but all it did was smear more gore. She spread her arms wide. "This. All of it is such an affront to the goddess. We cannot let them win. They'll destroy the Earth and everything living on it."

Jamal narrowed his eyes and surveyed the two SS officers. Absent the destroyed radio, it looked as if they'd been the victim of animal attacks. Maybe he could add to that impression by resurrecting the radio. He coaxed the missing plate into place and tucked it back into its carrying case.

"There." He straightened. "This almost looks accidental."

"I'll fly to the wagons," Meara announced. "This is damned inconvenient since I spent the last several hours telling our kinfolk to show up at this location as soon as they could."

"Not the end of the world." Jamal headed for his clothes and switched to telepathy. He wasn't done talking, and Meara had taken her bird form again. *"We tell whomever we can reach with mind speech about the new location and have them pass it on."*

Meara didn't reply, but she had to have heard him.

Jamal wiped his bloody hands on vegetation. He needed water to clean himself better, but didn't want to take the time. He was leaning over his clothing pile when his wolf asked, *"If we leave here, who will tell Ilona?"*

The question rocked him. *"How do you know she didn't return to the wagons?"*

"She was headed the opposite direction. I'd have sensed her if she'd retraced her steps and passed us."

As always, the wolf's logic was impeccable. Jamal didn't waste time sparring with it. *"Do you know where she is?"*

"Not precisely, but we can track her easily enough."

Jamal set his jaw in a tight line. The wolf's argument had merit, but Meara was expecting them. He raised his mind voice. *"Meara?"*

"Why aren't you back yet?"

Jamal inhaled raggedly. Now wasn't the time to beat around the bush. *"Ilona and I quarreled. I have to find her so she'll know it's not safe to remain here and that the wagons are moving."*

"Fine. I'll locate one of the Rom who knows how to drive. They will move your car from this place. I will mask us ever having been here with magic, but we cannot leave anything behind."

"I understand. Keys are in it. Don't worry about us, we'll find you."

Jamal dressed fast and ceded their shared consciousness to the wolf, trusting its superior hunting skills. They took off at a lope. After a mile or so, the ground grew progressively boggier, and he stopped next to a sluggish stream to clean the gore off his hands and face.

"I don't like how this is shaping up," the wolf said.

Jamal straightened from where he'd been crouched next to the water. *"Why not? This was your idea."*

"Look where we are. When you turn me loose, you often don't pay attention."

Jamal let his gaze rove over ancient trees festooned with moss. Sick knowledge sucker punched him. "Goddammit!" He fisted one hand and punched a nearby tree trunk not bothering with mind speech. "She went back to where she raised the vampire. The place she had her vision."

"My take too. Hurry," the wolf urged.

Jamal took off, water dripping from his hands and face. Branches cracked and snapped beneath his shoes. Why would Ilona do something so rash and ill-advised? He'd been abundantly clear she wasn't strong enough to take on a vampire. Had even told her the one who'd broken through her spell would probably be lying in wait for her.

She'd been hurt, angry, but surely those two things wouldn't have undermined her common sense. When he cut to the meat of things, he didn't understand how women viewed the world. The same helpless fury that had filled him when Aneksi steadfastly refused to leave the caravan returned with a vengeance.

"How would you feel if someone told you that your

magic wasn't strong enough to do something?" The wolf's question came out of the blue.

Jamal winced. "But I'm a man."

"So?"

"So, indeed. It reinforces my insight about not understanding—"

"You stopped even trying to understand anyone—including yourself," the wolf cut him off midstream. *"First, you were devastated about Aneksi not obeying you. You hadn't come close to recovering from that when you let our blood kin bully you into not going after your daughter."*

Jamal ran harder. Ilona's scent was growing stronger. She couldn't be much farther away. "Are you done lecturing me?" he asked the wolf.

"No. After you chose pack over your daughter, you abdicated from everything. You lived day to day, month to month, year to year, not caring what happened. Until Tairin's wolf found us and told us about the vampires and that she needed our help."

"If I was such a son of a bitch, why didn't you break our bond?" Bitterness left over from Aneksi's abandonment ran beneath his words, still outrageously strong. Her stubbornness had cost her life, but she'd taken a chunk of his along with it.

"If I had, it would have removed your last reason for living."

Jamal bristled. "I'm stronger than that."

"Are you? I wasn't certain. I love you, just as you love me. Would you have deserted me if I lost my mind?"

"Of course not, but I didn't—"

"Poor choice of words. You changed. Nothing reached you. There were times I was surprised you—"

The wolf had stopped talking for a reason. Jamal halted abruptly, his nostrils twitching. Ilona's wildflower and vanilla scent flooded with the sharp overtone of adrenaline, fear. He inhaled harder, and his heart twisted wildly in his chest.

Vampire. She'd recreated her trance and the vampire was waiting, just as he'd predicted.

He dropped his jacket into the dirt. No time to save the rest of his clothes. The harsh sound of fabric ripping pelted him as he summoned shift magic. Jamal bolted for Ilona's scent before his paws were fully finished forming. Pain shot through his half-human, half-wolf form, but he ignored it. The only important thing was that he was fully a wolf before he located the vampire. One facet of their magic was they could suspend his kind mid-shift until the lack of connection to either side spelled their death.

He passed a band of oak trees with thick, heavily burled trunks. Light flashed on the far side, so bright he squinted against its brilliance. What was that? Some new brand of vampire malfeasance?

Jamal burst into a small clearing dotted with pools, runoff from a stream pounding down the mountainside. Ilona stood with her back to him, cloaked in multihued brilliance. Power danced around her, sparking from her hands as she chanted in Coptic, the Rom's Egyptian spell language.

Beyond her, a vampire wavered, insubstantial and then not. Clearly, it had shot through the connection when Ilona established it. Just as clearly, she'd trapped it and it was stuck. So far, both were so intent on each other, neither had noticed him.

"Is enough of it on this side for us to kill it?" the wolf asked, keeping its mind voice very quiet.

Jamal shuffled pros and cons quick as any card shark. *"Worst thing that could happen is it will try to drag us back with it. Of course, if we kill it in this plane, it won't have enough power left to do anything. It should die everywhere."*

"What happens if it gets stuck between the rest of its body and here?"

"I don't know." He also wasn't certain about the addition of Ilona's magic to the equation. He didn't want to have it snare him by dint of proximity and weaken his attack on the vampire.

"I'll get you for this, gypsy bitch," the apparition snarled.

Ilona shrugged. "If you can't do any better than you are right now, I'm not worried."

A sly expression played over the vampire's features. "Your magic is strong, but you're a neophyte. You can't let me go because I'll spirit you back with me. You've already figured that out. Sooner or later, your magic will falter. When that happens, I'll win."

"You're wrong, vampire. If I loose my spell, you'll fall back through the ether and rejoin the rest of you."

It was as good an entry as Jamal was likely to get, and he sauntered toward the tableau. *"Don't turn around, Ilona. I'm just behind you,"* he said to not break her concentration—or her spell—when she discovered his presence.

"Thanks, but I'm good," she replied.

He detected an off note to her bravado, but didn't mention it. She'd be a fool not to be frightened, with the situation she'd gotten herself into.

"You are holding your own, which is impressive, but how about this?" he suggested brightly and took a step toward where the vampire wavered about eight feet away.

"How about what?" Power crackled around her turning the air silvery.

"On my count of three, you sheathe your power and I kill that piece of shit."

"Sounds good to me." She didn't bother to mask the relief in her voice. "Except it's my count of three. You need to get close enough to make certain he doesn't escape."

"You're on."

"No, we're on," the wolf corrected. Jamal sensed its excitement. Two kills in one day would make his bond animal ecstatic.

"One," Ilona began.

Jamal bounded toward the vampire, trusting Ilona to time two and three to coincide with his attack.

She didn't let him down, shouting out numbers. The word three barely left her mouth when Jamal's wolf closed its powerful jaws around the vampire's neck. Because he wasn't fully corporeal, the wolf's teeth clacked together. Still, they held enough flesh for black, stinking ichor to stream over his fur.

"Don't let go," he cautioned his wolf. *"We want to make good and certain it's dead."*

Ilona ran to where he grappled with the vampire. Drawing a dirk from a thigh sheath, she ran it through both the vampire's eyes, one after the other, taking pains to twist the blade once she hit bottom in brain tissue. A thin, high shriek burbled past the vampire's lips, followed by a flood of black blood tinged with red flecks.

Ilona moved behind the creature and sank her dagger into the base of its neck. She began chanting, urging power with hands and mouth. Jamal wondered what she was doing, and then he knew.

The vampire grew heavier in his jaws as she forced all of it through her portal. Jamal shook it hard, once, twice, until he heard its neck snap.

Ilona's voice rose to a screech, and the hole in the earth beneath the vampire sealed over as if it had never existed.

"There." She was breathing hard when she slipped her knife back into its scabbard after stabbing it into dirt to clean it. "I closed my gateway. No one can follow. If I did what I hope, no one will even know it was there."

Jamal dropped the vampire. Now that the creature wasn't split between locales, he knew it was well and truly dead. He shook his head spitting out the rotten taste of vampire blood. There'd be no feasting on this corpse. He wanted his human body so he could talk more easily and think with his human mind, but first he padded to one of the other pools and rinsed stinking ichor from his mouth and paws, slurping down water to kill the taste of vampire.

"We did good," his wolf crowed. *"I want to kill something else. Let's hunt our dinner tonight."*

"Don't you want to talk with Ilona first?" Jamal asked.

"Did you change your mind about her?"

The wolf's question caught him by surprise.

Had he?

An image of Ilona, her hands raised like an Old World goddess while power sheeted from her, filled his mind. His heart ached with wanting her. He was a long way from his clothes, but he called shift magic anyway. Her seeing him naked wasn't the worst thing in the world.

When his human body returned, he felt her gaze on him and desire ignited. Before he ended up with a full-blown erection, he rounded on her. "What would you have done if I hadn't shown up?" he demanded. "No, back up. What were you thinking in the first place? I told you the vampire would be waiting, and he was."

Her features developed a closed off aspect, and she looked away. "I was doing all right before you got here," she said defiantly. "Speaking of that, why are you here?"

"Nazis were tracking the wagons. Meara and I killed them, but the caravans have to move. By now, they're likely gone. I wanted to make certain you knew not to return to where they'd been. It's possible other SS came after the two we killed."

"Fine. You told me. I'll figure things out from here." She held her body ramrod straight.

"You didn't answer me," he countered. "Why the hell did you reconstruct a spell after I told you it was a bad idea?"

"I don't answer to you." She crossed her arms beneath her breasts.

He narrowed his eyes. How could she be so exasperating and desirable at the same time? "No, you don't, but humor me because I don't understand why you'd put yourself at risk like you did."

"My magic's never been tested. Mother and I, we experimented, but the stakes were never particularly high. Mostly, we were trying to escape Valentin's detection." She tilted her chin. "I wanted to see what I could do if I ran my magic wide open."

He wanted to shake her. Just before he crashed his mouth over hers and buried himself in her body. Damn his cock, anyway. It was thickening again. He pushed the sexual imagery of her long legs wrapped around his hips to a distant part of his mind and resisted an impulse to cover his cock with his hands.

"Magical practice is essential," he began, decided he sounded insufferably patronizing, and changed his approach. "Maybe you might want to run those practice sessions when the odds aren't quite so high."

"Why do you care?" she countered and transferred her gaze to his face before raking it down his body.

He took a deep breath and blew it out. "Because I care about you. I don't want anything untoward to happen to you."

"Like being turned by a vampire?" She quirked a sarcastic brow.

"Yes, like being used and turned by one of those bastards."

A complex array of emotions played over her features. Hope and caring mingled with resignation. "Caring's not a good idea," she gritted. "Not unless you become Rom or I find some way to change into someone like you."

"But you were the one who argued that didn't matter." The words ripped from a place deep inside him, one that left shards of pain in their wake.

"Yeah. I had a chance to rethink that." She shook herself from head to toe. "Go recover your clothes, and then we need to figure out where the caravans went."

He nodded. At least she hadn't taken off without him. The dull ache in his chest pushed his lust aside, and he turned back the way he'd come. "Not much left of my clothes, I'm afraid," he said. "When I knew what you faced, I didn't take time to undress."

"We'll recover what we can," she replied. "I'm handy with a needle and thread. Maybe I can repair the worst of the damage."

"You don't have to—" he began.

"I want to," she cut in. "Even though we've danced around it, you and your wolf saved my life. The vampire was right. I was holding my own, but eventually, my magic would've faded. He wasn't expending any power at all, and he knew I didn't have enough extra magic to finish him off."

Her level of openness seared Jamal. He wanted to touch her, at least take her hand, but he held back. “Some experiments have a higher price than others.”

“Yeah. You saved me from myself. This must be what’s left of your clothes.” She knelt and gathered his shirt, trousers, and jacket into her arms, examining them. “Jacket’s fine. I can mend the shirt and pants.”

He bent and slipped on his shoes and socks. They always survived a shift.

She handed him the jacket and he tossed it over himself, welcoming the warmth of the rough woolen fabric. The earlier tension between them —tension he’d precipitated by his harsh questions —had dissipated.

“I’m sorry.”

“For what?” she asked. Power shimmered around her.

“Coming off like a Nazi commandant with my questions. What are you doing?”

“What else? Figuring out which way the wagons went. It’s full dark. I’m hungry, and I bet you’re cold.”

That she cared enough to be concerned made the raw places in him ache all over again. “If I get really chilled, I'll turn into the wolf." He kept his voice gruff to mask his emotions.

"Wish I could do that."

Jamal held silence. More than anything, he wished she could too. For once, his wolf had nothing to say.

CHAPTER 9

An hour earlier

Ilona stumbled back into the clearing where she'd confronted the vampire. What in Isis's name was she doing testing her magic like this? She'd ascertained she had plenty to play with, but maybe she was being the worst kind of fool. She and her mother had pushed their boundaries, but the dangers had never been quite this daunting.

Yeah, and we always had each other—in case something went horribly wrong.

She swallowed around a dry throat. Either she did this, or she left. Which would it be?

Her thoughts crept to Jamal and how much she wanted him. She shut that line of reasoning down fast. He didn't want her. He'd made that clear as glass—after they'd kissed. Rejection sat like a physical ache behind her breastbone, and she pulled herself together.

She was used to keeping her emotions buried behind bulletproof walls. No reason to let them out to play now.

Before she thought things to death, she knelt before the pool she'd used earlier and began a brief purification ritual to make certain any traces of her earlier summoning were eradicated. She didn't want to make it easy for the vampire—the one Jamal was certain lay in wait—to snatch her and pull her through to where he was.

They congregated in nests. In her vision ten of the horrid things had marched into the gypsy camp. What if the one who'd seen her was surrounded by his kin? If he was, and he captured her, she'd wish she were dead a thousand times over.

Ilona rocked back on her heels and stood. Maybe this wasn't such a good idea. Fear licked at her, and her mouth flooded with the acrid taste of adrenaline. She paced from one side of the clearing to the other and back again, arguing with herself.

Was she going to spend the rest of her life jumping at every shadow?

She'd been trapped in the caravan, forced into hiding her power so she didn't intimidate the men, none of whom had anywhere near her level of ability. Even her mother, the original brassy broad, kowtowed to Valentin. When Ilona asked her why she put up with him, she'd replied that gypsies needed caravans. They provided history, purpose, and friendships.

People who always stood up for you.

Ilona sputtered. Tairin's mother hadn't had that experience. Her caravan had turned on her. Killed her. Ilona didn't recall anything quite that Draconian in modern times, but caravans kicked miscreants out on a regular basis. Since Romani had a reputation as thieves and scoundrels, finding work was usually a problem.

And now we have the Nazis...

They'd begun rounding up gypsies along with Jews. Meara had predicted hundreds of thousands of Rom would die in the camps.

Ilona squared her shoulders. Some of her people had to survive. Otherwise no one would remember the magic and mystery of the Romani. In an arcane way that she didn't totally understand, her people were tied to the making of the world. If their magic died out, humankind wouldn't be far behind. She might be afraid, but that wasn't a reason to hide her head in the sand.

A quick glance told her she didn't have much time before sundown. Vampires were stronger at night, at least according to myth. If she were going to challenge one, she needed to move now. Her purification ritual was done, and magic hummed through her.

No reason not to face her fears.

She stomped to the exact spot she'd stood earlier and chanted to summon her vision magic. Power streamed from her, swirling in the day's fading light. Visual evidence of her ability heartened her. Surely the goddess wouldn't abandon her and her people.

The water bubbled and churned before its surface quieted, turning glassy. Ilona watched intently. At the very least, she'd glean information from her spell. She wound wards about herself to be on the safe side. Would something so simplistic hold a vampire at bay?

She had no idea.

Ilona urged the water to yield images. It was how her magic worked. How she pried information from a future that hadn't yet occurred. Nothing happened, so she pressed harder.

Minutes ticked past. So many she was on the verge of reeling in her magic and leaving this place. A keening howl rose out of nowhere in a cacophony of discordant minor notes, and the water formed a vortex, spinning downward.

She'd never seen anything quite like it and focused power on the pond, instructing it to respond to her command. Instead, the vortex deepened. Eyes formed in its depths. Fear clawed at her like a live thing, and she chopped the flow of her magic, but it was too late.

The portal was open. Nothing she could do would change that.

She beat back horror and dread. She'd asked for this. Welcomed it. Now that it was here, she'd damn well better meet the challenge as something other than a simpering ninny. Ilona let power flow from her outstretched fingertips and strengthened her warding.

A vampire—maybe the one from earlier, she couldn't tell—took form in the still, cold air. A quick check with her magic told her it was maybe only a quarter corporeal. How was the rest of it anchored? And where? If it wasn't too far away, maybe she could push the damn thing back where he came from.

Long dark hair, thick and luxuriant, fell down his shoulders and back. Eyes the color of a turbulent sea met hers. The creature was stunning, so beautiful it was impossible not to look at him. A creamy, silk robe sashed in deep blue hung from his broad shoulders. Sharp cheekbones suggested Mongol or Asian blood.

She kept magic flowing, relieved beyond words when it seemed to keep the thing at bay. If he could have seized her and vanished back through the now still water, he would have.

The vampire smiled lazily showing elongated fangs. "I knew you'd be back. Women can't resist me. Neither can men."

He pushed the robe back, displaying a muscled chest and copper nipples, all the while watching her closely.

Ilona tried not to stare, but she had to maintain her focus on the vampire to keep it contained. As he pushed the robe farther back, revealing more of his perfect body, sexual heat kindled in her. He wasn't saying anything, but the invitation streaming from him was impossible to misinterpret.

Part of her wanted to see more. Another part

was afraid she'd be lost if he exposed the ridged flesh she glimpsed through his robe. His penis was engorged, ready. He wanted her. All she needed to do was drop her magical protections and that body and cock could be hers. Her nipples turned into aching points of sensation, and need slicked her thighs.

Jamal had started this when he kissed her. She'd been aroused then, but this ratcheted up the game by a factor of a hundred or better. Her desire for Jamal was normal. What she felt now was sick and perverted. She told her body to stand down, but the throbbing between her legs intensified.

The vampire's hand strayed to his crotch and he cupped himself through his robe, mouth opening suggestively as he licked his perfect lips.

Ilona wrenched her gaze above his waist. If she saw that cock, she'd be lost. Her resolve would shatter.

Yeah and that bastard will turn me. I'll be nothing better than a sex slave. Or worse, I'll become like him and feed on blood and fear.

"Nice try," she gritted. "Keep your private parts covered. I'm not interested."

"Not my take, human, and I'm a most excellent judge of such things. I could force you with my mind, but it's ever so much better when women come to me of their own free will."

He was probably still touching himself, but she'd stopped looking. Ilona forced a magical barrier between their bodies—one created from cool, rational thought. Her lust abated as if someone had turned off a switch, and she exhaled sharply. She could stay on top of this. Not give in.

"I'll get you for this, gypsy bitch," the apparition snarled, no longer playing at his seduction charade.

Ilona shrugged. "If you can't do any better than you are right now, I'm not worried."

A sly expression slithered over the vampire's features. It shrugged, displaying still more skin. "Your magic is strong, but you're a neophyte. You can't let me go because I'll drag you back with me. You've already figured that out. Sooner or later, your magic will falter. When that happens, I'll win."

"You're wrong, vampire. If I loose my spell, you'll fall back through the ether and rejoin the rest of you." It was a bluff, but maybe the vampire wouldn't know that.

"Don't turn around, Ilona. I'm just behind you," flashed into her mind.

Jamal! How the hell had he ended up here?

And then she remembered the way they'd parted, and her gratitude that she wasn't alone anymore evaporated.

"Thanks, but I'm good," she replied, keeping to a neutral tone.

"You are holding your own, which is impressive, but how about this?" Jamal suggested brightly. The wolf passed her, moving toward where the vampire wavered about eight feet away.

"How about what?" Power crackled around her, turning the air silvery.

"On my count of three, you sheathe your power and I kill that piece of shit."

"Sounds good to me." She didn't bother to mask the relief in her voice. "Except it's my count of three. You need to get close enough to make certain he doesn't escape."

"You're on."

"No, we're on," the wolf corrected, and Ilona could have hugged it.

"One," Ilona began.

Jamal bounded toward the vampire. Ilona timed the wolf's approach carefully, shouting out numbers. The word three had barely left her mouth when Jamal's wolf closed its powerful jaws around the vampire's neck, and black, stinking ichor streamed over its fur.

Ilona ran to where the wolf grappled with the vampire. She could help, wanted to make certain the hell-spawned thing was dead. Drawing a dirk from a thigh sheath, she ran it through both the vampire's eyes, one after the other, taking pains to twist the blade once she hit bottom in brain tissue.

A thin, high shriek burbled past the vampire's lips, followed by a flood of black blood tinged with red flecks. Up close like this, it reeked of death and rot. The stench made her gag, but the thing's misery egged her on, and she moved to where she could sink her dagger into the base of its neck. Wanting to make certain her efforts weren't in vain, she chanted, urging more power with both her hands and voice.

She'd drag the thing across the veil separating where he lived from this glade. He was too weak to fight back.

Her chant rose to a screech, and the hole in the earth beneath the vampire sealed over as if it had never existed. Exultation was heady, like a rich wine. She'd done it. Pulled the bastard through. Once it started dying, she'd had plenty of magic to spare.

"There." She was breathing hard when she slipped her knife back into its scabbard after cleaning it in the dirt. "I closed the portal. No one can follow. If I did what I hope, no one will even know a gateway was there."

Jamal dropped the vampire. He shook his head spitting out vampire blood before padding to one of the other pools where he rinsed ichor from his mouth and paws, slurping down water once he was done. Magic bubbled around him. She'd felt it before and knew he was shifting back to human. Ilona waited, feeling grateful to him. They'd fought side by side. Would that change how they'd parted? She hoped so.

She tried not to stare as his body emerged, but it was arresting. Marks cut through bronzed skin, running across his torso and shoulders thick with muscle. How had he gotten all those scars? His arms and legs were shapely and strong, radiating power and danger. Her gaze tracked to where his cock was beginning to swell from its nest of dark curls. She shouldn't look. It wasn't right, but she was having a hell of a time looking at anything else.

Jamal rounded on her, his face like a thundercloud and his brows drawn into a single, thick line. "What would you have done if I hadn't shown up?" he demanded. "No, back up. What were you thinking in the first place? I told you the vampire would be waiting, and he was."

Shock ricocheted through her at his tone, and she looked away. He didn't sound any different from when she'd run from him earlier, and his rebuke stung. "I was doing all right before you got here," she said defiantly. "Speaking of that, why are you here?"

"Nazis were tracking the wagons. Meara and I killed them, but the caravans have to move. By now, they're likely gone. I wanted to make certain you knew not to return to where they'd been. It's possible other SS came after the two we killed."

"Fine. You told me. I'll figure things out from here." She held her body ramrod straight.

"You didn't answer me," he countered. "Why the hell did you reconstruct a spell after I told you it was a bad idea?"

Barely controlled fury spilled through her. "I don't answer to you." She crossed her arms beneath her breasts.

He narrowed his eyes. "No, you don't, but humor me because I don't understand why you'd put yourself at risk like you did."

She gritted her teeth against one another. He had rescued her, which meant he deserved at least some explanation. "My magic's never been tested.

Mother and I, we experimented, but the stakes were never particularly high. Mostly, we were trying to escape Valentin's detection. I wanted to see what I could do if I ran my magic wide open."

"Magical practice is essential," he began, but his voice trailed off. When he started over, he said, "Maybe you might want to launch those practice sessions when the odds aren't quite so dangerous."

"Why do you care?" she countered, still battling anger. Despite that, she returned her gaze to him and his naked body. How could she hate him and want him all at the same time? This wasn't the sick desire the vampire conjured, but something clean and pure.

He took a deep breath and blew it out. "Because I care about you. I don't want anything untoward to happen to you."

"Like being turned by a vampire?" She quirked a sarcastic brow.

"Yes, like being used and turned by one of those bastards."

Hope speared her, mingled with resignation. She couldn't open the door to him again. Not if he were just going to slam it on her foot a second time.

"Caring's not a good idea," she gritted. "Not

unless you become Rom, or I find some way to change into someone like you."

"But you were the one who argued that didn't matter." His words held harsh edges, as if they cost him.

"Yeah. I had a chance to rethink that." She shook herself from head to toe. They had to get moving. Now. Before she threw herself into his arms and dove into his nakedness with her fingers and mouth. "Go recover your clothes, and then we need to figure out where the caravans went."

"Not much left of my clothes, I'm afraid." He shrugged. "When I knew what you faced, I didn't take time to undress."

"We'll recover what we can," she replied and followed him out of the boggy area where the pools lay. "I'm handy with a needle and thread. Maybe I can repair the worst of the damage."

"You don't have to—" he began.

"I want to," she cut in. She made a grab for her earlier ire, but it eluded her. Driven by a need for honesty, she said, "Even though we've danced around it, you and your wolf saved my life. The vampire was right. I was holding my own, but eventually, my magic would've faded. He wasn't expending any power at all, and he knew I didn't have enough extra magic to finish him off."

"Some experiments have a higher price than others."

"Yeah. You saved me from myself. This must be what's left of your clothes." She knelt and gathered his shirt, trousers, and jacket into her arms, examining them. "Jacket's fine. I can mend the shirt and pants."

He bent and slipped on his shoes and socks. She handed him the jacket and he tossed it over himself.

"I'm sorry."

"For what?" she asked and sent power outward, seeking the location of the caravans.

"Coming off like a Nazi commandant with my questions. What are you doing?"

"What else? Figuring out which way the wagons went. It's full dark. I'm hungry, and I bet you're cold."

"If I get really chilled, I'll turn into the wolf." His tone was gruff as he began walking.

"Wish I could do that," she muttered wondering why he sounded so out of sorts.

"May I take a look at your dirk?"

His question came out of nowhere, but she

dug it out of her thigh sheath and handed it over. "Sure, but why?"

He turned it this way and that before handing it back to her. "Explains a lot."

"What exactly does that mean?" Ilona battled exasperation. She was exhausted and too hungry to figure out riddles.

"I wondered why we managed to kill the vampire. I'd expected it to retreat to where its body was. Your blade solves that mystery. It's an alloy, but silver is part of it. That metal is lethal to vampires. According to the lore, they need to be stabbed through the heart, but apparently it's just as effective in other locations. Good to know."

She tucked the dirk back into place. It had belonged to her mother and her grandmother and goddess only knew who else in her family. Had they used it to defeat vampires? If they had, her mother never mentioned it.

They lapsed into silence. The wagons were still on the move, so she selected a trajectory to intercept them. Jamal was a solid presence next to her. She wanted so many things, wished their lives could be simpler, different.

"Tell me about the Nazis," she said, mostly because she wanted to hear his deep, musical voice. "How do you think they tracked the wagons so quickly? From what Michael and Stewart told me, they figured they'd have at least a couple weeks before they had to move on."

"Vampires helped."

"Vampires were with them?" Fear twisted her empty stomach into a hard, painful knot.

He shook his head. "No, I wasn't clear. Let me backtrack. Vampires can interact with humans without turning them. They can drink human blood without killing their victims, and they love having sex with anything alive." He hesitated. "From what I've seen, the SS have some kind of unholy alliance with vampires. They fuck them and feed from them. In the course of both, the SS absorb some level of unnatural magic."

"So that's how those Nazis you killed were able to track the wagons?"

"Maybe. I'm not certain. Either that, or they had vampires providing more direct help."

Hopelessness crashed through her. "If that's true, we won't be safe anywhere. It's not that I didn't know that—especially after I ended up in Dachau, but I figured once I escaped I'd find somewhere to wait out the war."

Jamal laced his fingers with hers, and she grasped his hand. "We could run, seek safe haven for ourselves," he said, "but it's not the right thing to do."

"We could never run far enough to escape Shifter or Rom law." Resentment at the injustice of edicts forcing shifters and Rom to never mate bit deep.

"Even if edicts prohibiting congress among our two types of magic wielders didn't exist," he went on, "we must face our enemy. If magic dies out of the world, chaos will ensue. Beyond that"—he stopped walking and turned her to face him—"am I right that you're not angry with me any longer? I acted like a jerk, and I apologize."

She met his gaze as moonlight filtered through leafless branches. "I'm not angry. Mostly I was hurt."

A crooked smile lit his even features. "I don't know if we can find our way together. Hell, I don't even know if we'll both live to see tomorrow's sunrise, but I vow I will do my damnedest to try to figure things out." He cupped the side of her face. "You fascinate me, Ilona Lovas. My wolf gave me grief after I turned away from you, reminded me you weren't Aneksi. Just because my world turned to shit two centuries ago is no reason to expect the same thing will happen twice."

"The world is a different place."

"Yes, the wolf said much the same." He bent and kissed her once lightly, before recapturing her hand. "Which way?"

A quick check with her magic surprised her. "They switched direction," Ilona said.

"Which way?" he repeated. "I could look for myself, but since you've already opened a magical channel, there's no reason for me to draw more power."

"Higher into the mountains, and from the speed they're traveling, they've abandoned at least some of the wagons."

"Or else a cadre of my shifter kin caught up with them, and they've added magic to the mix. Let's hurry."

Ilona trotted next to him. The world didn't feel nearly as bleak with Jamal next to her.

Nothing changed. Not really, she reminded herself. *Danger still hovers. I feel it every time I deploy my power.*

"Maybe so." Jamal answered her unspoken thoughts. "But we're stronger together than we are apart. You have to believe we'll survive."

She wanted to, but her earlier fear that linking her fortune to any gypsy caravan would be her undoing cast a pall over everything. She needed to scry her own future, something that wasn't unheard of, but was frowned upon.

Next chance she got, she'd take a peek. Knowledge might not change her actions, but at least she'd have some sense of what lay before her.

And if Jamal would be part of her path.

CHAPTER 10

Jamal strode next to Ilona, grateful she'd relented enough to give them a chance to explore what flowed between them. He gave himself a good, mental shake. They'd actually taken turns spelling out all the reasons their relationship would be doomed from its inception, but maybe they'd each traded pessimism for hope.

The path steepened. Half the time, he had to use one hand to steady himself, and he kept the other laced with Ilona's to make sure she was safe. Shifter magic could probably coax horses and teams up a grade this abrupt, but it would take a hell of a lot of power. He had no idea how his car could manage—unless maybe there was a track on the other side of this hillock. When he reached outward, testing, he sensed a surfeit of magic not far above them.

"They're close," he observed.

"Either they located a stopping place," Ilona agreed, "or they're resting."

Jamal switched frequencies, employing different magic. "Interesting. Someone, probably Meara, guided the group to what feels like a cluster of shifter shelters. I've never actually sensed quite so many in close proximity before."

"What exactly are they?"

"Usually large, commodious caves carved into cliffs. Magic hides them from everyone. We need to employ a particular brand of tracking to locate them ourselves. And to get inside."

"Are they safe from vampires?"

He shrugged. "I have no idea. In Egypt, vampires were plentiful, but so were a phalanx of priests and priestesses who devoted their lives to holding the vampire population at bay. They never bothered us back then. In truth, I mostly forgot about them until Tairin showed up on my doorstep requesting help."

"Fascinating. Whew! All that magic above us is overwhelming. Where we're going can't be much farther." She let go of him and used both hands to work her way through a particularly steep section.

Jamal scrambled up behind her. They emerged onto a broad mesa dotted with evergreens and berry bushes studded with thorns. He looked around. The place held an otherworldly feel, as if it didn't quite belong in twentieth century Germany.

Beside him, Ilona frowned. "I've been through this country so many times, I've lost count, but this place wasn't here."

"Are you certain of that?" Jamal sent magical feelers out, sorting impressions.

"Quite." She nodded once, sharply. "Mother and I would play hooky from the caravan whenever we could. This escarpment isn't far from Munich. I recognized the approach, but where we are now—" she spread her arms wide "—didn't use to be here. No plateau. The hillside butted into those cliffs dead ahead."

The sharp scents of shifter magic, rife with animal musk and electrical byproducts, stung his nostrils. If Ilona were right, someone had altered the geography. Not an impossible task, but far from commonplace. Before he could set off to explore where everyone was, Meara broke through an invisible barrier and walked toward them. One minute she wasn't there, and then she was, accompanied by the sucking sound of a vacuum being broken. He squinted against brightness surrounding the vulture shifter.

"There you are," she announced. "I've been waiting for you to arrive. You took far longer than you should have, given your earlier location, but never mind that. Follow me. So far, we've pulled this off, but you're a loose end."

"We killed a vampire," Ilona announced.

Meara focused her unsettling gaze on Ilona. "I don't care if you killed Hitler. You're still late."

Jamal sucked in a tight breath. "Killing the vampire was my idea."

"Fine." Meara rolled eyes that appeared far more avian than human. "That's why you're half naked? You shifted first and thought later?"

"Not exactly," Jamal said through clenched teeth. Why was Meara treating him like a halfwit? It wasn't like her to be overtly rude. Direct, maybe, but not supercilious.

"Give me those." Meara snatched his pants and shirt from Ilona. Power flared, gray with red edges, and she handed them to Jamal. "They're patched enough to wear. Dress and dress fast."

Jamal pushed off his shoes and hustled into his trousers. He dropped his jacket on the ground and slid into the shirt, still warm and prickly from its go round with Meara's power. His jacket and shoes came last.

Ilona looked from one to the other of them, confusion plain on her face. At least she wasn't peppering Meara with questions.

"Come on. This will be uncomfortable, but the pain doesn't last." Meara spun and ran back the way she'd come, vanishing once she hit the barrier he couldn't see.

"What is that thing she went through?" Ilona asked, her voice higher than usual. "And why was she so…abrupt?"

"I have no idea why she was such a bitch. The answer to your first question is she disappeared through an alteration in the weave of the time-space continuum. That spell requires a very complicated type of shifter magic, which is probably why I mistook it for multiple shifter shelters. Don't ask any more because that's all I know." He extended a hand, and she gripped it. "Don't let go. If Meara felt the need to caution us about the transition being rough, gird yourself."

"One more moment won't hurt," Ilona countered. "I know you're a shifter, but shifters aren't like gypsies. You don't travel in caravans casting Tarot spreads and sharpening knives and telling fortunes."

"You want to know what I did to earn my way." At her nod, he went on. "Most recently, I taught ancient and medieval history at the University in Innsbruck, Austria, a post I'd held for almost thirty years. I went on sabbatical a few months ago, but my plan was to fade out of everyone's memory—again. Living as long as we do is inconvenient." He tugged on her hand. "It's not wise to anger Meara. Patience was never her long suit."

"Convenient to teach what you lived through." She smiled.

Jamal chuckled. "Oh I'm not as old as all that." He moved toward the barrier, gathering momentum. Having watched Meara go through, he figured speed would ameliorate the pain.

He was wrong.

He entered blackness so deep, it was endless. Once he got close, a vacuum took over, sucking so hard escape wasn't possible. It felt as if a million hot needles penetrated his flesh, flaying it from his bones while the vacuum tried to turn him inside out until bone pierced flesh. Ilona's hand clamped around his, and a hissing shriek rose from her. He bit down hard, determined not to shame himself by crying out.

"Goddammit!" Ilona gasped between words. "Where are we?"

"Transiting some kind of void. It guards the demarcation between the plateau and the world beyond the obstruction."

"What do you suppose it does to outsiders?"

"Not sure." Talking was a struggle, but he forced a few more words. "I hope far worse than what it's doing to us."

"This is amazing," the wolf spoke up. *"We're viewing one of the mysteries. Other bond animals have spoken of them—described invisible walls just like this one—but I never believed the stories."*

It took all Jamal's energy to keep moving. This might be shifter magic, but it was so potent it made him want to fall to his knees and call on all the gods for strength. He hunted for words to ask the wolf for clarification, but they eluded him.

Ilona started to fall back. He dragged her forward and clamped an arm around her waist. He wanted to reassure her this would end, but his lungs burned and he understood another problem with this in-between zone was it lacked oxygen.

"Keep going," the wolf urged. *"I sense others—Rom and shifters—very close."*

Rom. If Ilona were struggling, how the hell had they managed this barrier? On the heels of that thought came grim satisfaction that Meara had discovered something to stymie both Nazis and vampires.

Not discovered. Merely leveraged and employed.

Was that his thought, or had Meara been inside his mind, answering him?

His lungs seized painfully and he inhaled, desperate for air. Maybe it was his imagination, but it seemed as if he could breathe a little better. The iron band that had wrapped around his temples wasn't quite so tight, and his lungs didn't burn as much.

As quickly as it had formed, the airless vacuum spit them out with a loud, sucking *thunk*. He glanced at a mesa, twin to the one they'd left behind except the sky held three moons, suspended mid-heaven.

"What is this place?" Ilona asked, still panting from their sojourn through the barrier.

"There you are." Tairin ran lightly to them with Elliott right behind her. She scooped Ilona into a hug. "We've been worried about you."

A chorus of wolf howls rose from ahead.

Jamal tossed his head back and let his wolf's voice emerge in greeting. The howls were invitation to join the pack, and he gestured to Tairin, Elliott, and Ilona.

"We know," Elliott said. "Everyone is gathered around a council fire. You two were the last." He lowered his voice and spoke near Jamal's ear. "Other first shifters are here. It's how they manipulated enough magic to move all of us to wherever we are."

Excitement coursed through Jamal, and he named the ancient Egyptian wolf deity. "Is Anubis among them?"

"My wolf says so," Tairin cut in and let go of Ilona.

"Mine too," Elliott concurred. "It hasn't shut up since we fought our way through the void."

"I've never felt this much power concentrated in one place," Ilona murmured, her gray eyes luminous with wonder. "The air is so rich with it, just breathing will make me drunk on magic."

Her wonder was infectious, and Jamal took her hand. He moved toward where the other wolf voices had hailed him. As he got closer, others of his kind called his name, and he greeted them in turn.

"It's a big family, kind of like gypsies," Ilona said into his mind.

"Yes, it is. I recognized the similarity during the time I lived and traveled with a caravan." Jamal didn't say any more. When he'd suggested to Aneksi that their peoples weren't really all that different, she'd shut him out.

"Now is a time to forget all that," his wolf suggested. *"Long past time, actually."*

It wasn't the first time the wolf had harped on that, but Jamal vowed to take its advice to heart. He'd done everything in his power, and Aneksi hadn't listened to him or to reason. Her intransigence had spelled her death. He couldn't have prevented it. What he could have done was make a different choice regarding Tairin, but the goddess had seen fit to offer them a second chance to be a family.

An enormous circle with a fire in its center came into view. The Rom wagons were bunched off to one side sans horses, which meant they had to be hobbled somewhere out of sight. Wagons and horses were one thing since they were part of the natural world. Jamal was almost certain his Mercedes wasn't within the vacuum-protected enclosure. It didn't matter. The car had been an indulgence, and possessions could be replaced.

Money had never been a problem or a motivator. It wasn't for most shifters because they had centuries to accumulate wealth.

The gypsies sat in a large group between their wagons and the fire, conversing among themselves. Shifters, sorted by the animals they'd bonded with, spread around the blaze like spokes in a wagon wheel.

Meara stood near the fire with two other figures, their heads bent in conversation.

Jamal focused his magic and recognized wolf energy from one of them, so it had to be Anubis. The first wolf shifter was cloaked in black with his back to Jamal. The other man was probably a first shifter as well, but Jamal didn't know whom he might be.

He squared his shoulders. "Take Ilona with you," he instructed Tairin and Elliott. "I will join you in the wolf group as soon as I've offered my obeisance to our leader."

"Should we do that too?" Tairin asked, looking uncertain.

Jamal smiled at his daughter. "I have no idea what the proper protocol is with our primary ancestor. For all I know, he'll turn me into a tower of dust for having the temerity to approach him."

"We'll wait and see how you do." Elliott started toward the wolf group with Tairin, but Ilona held back.

"I should sit with the Rom," she said.

Jamal gazed at her. She was so striking—her beauty harsh and stark—he could have looked at her forever. He wanted her by his side, but not if she felt out of place. "Is that where you'll be most comfortable?"

She nodded. "Of course. It's what I am. We can catch up with each other afterward."

He watched her skirt the edges of the circle for a moment before he followed the initial part of her path, veering toward Meara and the two men.

Meara turned toward him. Her long silver-gray hair gleamed with energy, and her amber eyes were pure vulture. Nothing human about them. "Jamal."

He bent his head in a show of respect. "Meara, first of the bird shifters."

The cloaked man twisted so quickly his body blurred. By the time he faced Jamal, his cloak had slipped from his head. Coal black hair streamed down his shoulders and back to knee level. Keen dark eyes with golden centers bored into Jamal's soul, and he fell to his knees.

"Sire. It is an honor to meet you."

"Get up. I do not require slavish devotion."

Jamal scrambled upright. "Yes sire. Of course."

"What about me? Do you recognize me as well?" The other man, dressed in formfitting hunting leathers, looked like an ancient Viking with white-blond hair, ice-blue eyes with silvery centers, and slabs of muscle from shoulder to calf.

Jamal shuffled through possibilities. "Are you the first bear shifter?"

The man's roughhewn features broke into a broad grin. "Good guess, Jamal wolf shifter. I am Nivkh."

Jamal opened his mouth to say he was glad to meet the other first shifters, but Meara beat him to the punch.

"Sit!" She pointed toward the wolf shifter group. "We are late because of you, and time is precious."

Jamal bolted for the wolves, selecting a spot on the ground near Tairin and Elliott. This might be a type of parallel universe, but the ground on this side was dry, sandy, whereas what he'd left in the other world had been wet and muddy.

Meara paced around the circle, projecting her voice with magic. The fire burned behind her with a life of its own since no one fed tinder into it. “I have heard you talk among yourselves,” she began. “The question I heard most often regarded what this place is, yet I cannot answer that without some background.”

Jamal leaned forward, listening intently.

“It became clear to me,” Meara went on, “that we had to have a safe place, a staging area if you will, from which we could launch a coordinated attack against the Nazis and their pet vampires.”

Anubis elbowed her and said, “If you were to ask the vampires, they’d say the Nazis fiddled for them, not the other way round.”

Meara cracked a rare smile. “True enough. I had thought the last spot I selected for two gypsy caravans that have joined with us would be safe from discovery. I was wrong. It was then I knew I had to split the worlds and create a place no one could find us. A place we can come and go as we undermine the Nazi war effort and their hideous work camps.”

Nivkh stepped forward. “I am Nivkh, first of the bear shifters. Every shifter here understands our cliff dwellings. They’re sheltered from the rest of the world with strong magic. This place—” he spread his burly arms wide “—is an extension of the magic that formed our shelters. They don’t fully exist in the world, and this tiny slice of land doesn't, either. Although, I must admit I've never seen triple moons before."

Meara stood even straighter. "My hope is they signify that Arianrhod, Artemis, Khonsu, and every other moon god or goddess blesses our efforts."

Anubis paced around the fire pit until he faced the Rom. "I am Anubis, first wolf shifter. We welcome you into our midst. I, for one, wish more than two caravans were represented here. You strengthen our magic, and the reverse is also true. Just as you found when you entered the vacuum sealing this place off from the rest of southern Germany, magic is required. It will be easier for you to both leave and return when you have a shifter or two with you."

Stewart stood and bowed before Anubis. "How long can your magic maintain this place?" he asked in his pronounced Scottish brogue.

"As long as we need it to," Anubis replied. "The gateway will require some maintenance, but any shifter could see to it, now that it's here."

"And without this *maintenance* ye referred to?" Stewart persisted.

"Then it reverts to what it was before we altered the warp and weft of space and time."

"Thank ye for accommodating me and my questions." Stewart returned to his place.

Meara raised her hands to quell the many conversations that had broken out. "Silence. Hear me. All of you. From this day forth, the enmity between shifters and Romani ceases. We are allies. Not just until this war ends, but forever. Do all of you understand me?"

A chorus of yesses and ayes rose from every group, but Jamal sensed a definite lack of enthusiasm. It would take far more than a command from a first shifter to overcome millennia of distrust and wariness.

"Good." She dropped her hands to her sides. "Now that we have that out of the way, we must forge ahead. No time to waste. Some of us will team up to hunt down vampire nests. Others will sneak into the Nazi work camps and do maximum damage. When you are between assignments, you will return here to rest, eat, and recharge your magic."

Michael stood and approached her. "Anubis said he wished for more Romani caravans. Perhaps an additional assignment could be locating others that have chosen to go into hiding. I fear the caravans that chose to flee Germany have been apprehended."

"Are you volunteering?" Meara raised a silver brow.

Michael's nostrils flared in his swarthy face. "Since I've already fought vampires, faced down my fears, that is where I should focus. But many Rom here could work at finding others to add to our ranks. Much as you did earlier when you flew off to alert shifters."

"We will leave you in charge of that project," Anubis broke in. "Do any of you know the location of vampire nests?" He paced around the fire, moving from group to group, but no one spoke up.

"I can probably get that information via scrying," Meara said. "Meanwhile the rest of you will sort out who infiltrates which prison camp. My thought was we'd focus on the primary ones in Germany. Once we have them well in hand, we can branch out."

"Name the locations and I will head up that effort," Nivkh said, his pale eyes gleaming with anticipation.

"Sachsenhausen-Oranienburg near Berlin, Esterwegen near Hamburg, Ravensbrück near Brandenburg, and of course Dachau just a few miles from here."

"Got it." Nivkh raised his voice to a roar. "All

who wish to volunteer join me. I require sixteen to begin, four for each prison."

After a long pause, shifters and Romani moved toward the first bear shifter. Was their hesitation because of risk or because they were hesitant to work together? Jamal suspected it was a little of each.

Meara snapped her fingers. "Elliott. Ilona. Come with me. We must be on the far side of the barrier for our seeking ability to utilize the full extent of its magic."

"Wolves who didn't heed Nivkh's call, join me," Anubis commanded. "We will strategize how to best deploy our ability."

Jamal had planned to at least try to join Ilona and Meara. He hadn't been certain if Meara would allow it, but Anubis's orders took precedence. If shifters understood anything, it was line of command.

Elliott grimaced. "It's not that I don't want to lend my magic to Meara's scrying gambit, but I'm not looking forward to another trip through that hellish blockade. See you both soon." He jumped to his feet, reaching Meara and Ilona seconds before the trio vanished in a flash of white light.

"Now, people!" Anubis punctuated his words with a snarl.

Jamal shot upright and extended a hand to Tairin, helping her up. She was grinning. *"Not so different from a caravan leader,"* she said into his mind.

"Not different at all," Jamal agreed, and they hurried toward where Anubis stood, waiting to command his shifters.

He wanted to be with Ilona, making certain she got through the barrier unscathed, but he smothered his desire to protect her. She'd been taking care of herself for a long time. Her independence was one of the things that attracted him.

Self-sufficiency.

Spirit.

Courage.

Determination.

He'd do well to nurture all those things. And tell her how deeply they touched him.

Tairin closed a hand over his lower arm. "My wolf is really, really excited. Is yours?"

"Probably, but it hasn't said much."

He focused on his bondmate. *"What are you thinking?"*

The wolf didn't answer. It was there; he felt its presence, and its silence weighed heavy. The wolf knew something, something it wasn't willing to give voice to. It was much older than Tairin's wolf, which meant it may well have come across Anubis while bonded to an earlier wolf shifter.

Jamal fought through uneasiness and joined the other wolf shifters in the second of four ragged rows with Tairin by his side.

"You belong to me," Anubis began. "That means my commands take precedence—over everything. Are we clear about that?"

Amidst a chorus of howls, Anubis smiled. Something about the expression, cocky and arrogant, sounded an alarm, but Jamal buried his reservations. Anubis had to be skilled at reading minds. The last thing Jamal needed was for his thoughts to sound a sour note that alerted the first of them that he might not be fully on board with whatever came next.

CHAPTER 11

Ilona shook herself once Meara led them back through the barrier and into the encampment. Its energy still felt strange to her, a reminder that it existed in a place that wasn't quite part of the world. Maybe because she was weary, this last journey through the vacuum hadn't been as excruciating as her first two trips.

Or maybe she was getting used to the barrage of odd sensations.

Elliott bid her goodnight and hurried away, presumably to find his wagon and Tairin. Meara vanished back through the barrier once she'd herded them through. The vulture shifter definitely marched to her own tune, answering to no one beyond herself. Ilona had no idea where she was off to this time.

Meara had called a halt to their joint scrying after they located a nest. When Ilona asked why they didn't find all of them and be done with it, Meara replied they'd been lucky so far that their magic hadn't alerted the vampires.

"Better to do this in stages," she'd gone on. "Once we take on the nest we found, if there are others, they'll be on the move."

It made sense as Ilona thought about it. Vampires didn't live in anything as permanent as a house. They did have coffins, though. Elliott had described the lineup at the nest he and Tairin stumbled across.

They probably don't need those exact coffins. Or even coffins at all. Any dark, enclosed place that protects them from daylight hours would likely do.

A thought slapped her hard. The vampire who'd come through the gateway from her spell didn't seem to be suffering because it wasn't full dark. And the attack she'd seen in her earlier vision had occurred in daylight too. Taken in aggregate, it had to mean they might prefer to retire to their caskets to wait out the sunlight hours, but they sure as hell didn't need to.

Jamal's unique energy approached, and she moved toward him.

"There you are," he said softly. "I was waiting with Tairin for Elliott to return. I figured once he was back, you would be too. How'd it go?"

She walked into his extended arms and wrapped hers around him. "If finding another nest means it went well, then we succeeded."

He tightened his hold on her. "Where is it?"

"Right outside Berlin, which makes sense since that's where Hitler is most of the time."

"That's over three hundred miles from here. It will take some planning to pull off the same type of raid we did in this region."

"Meara didn't seem overly worried, but she's hard to read. Plus, she left as soon as she saw Elliott and me safely back."

He kissed her forehead and let go of her. "Want me to walk you back to Marguerite and Trina's wagon?"

Under normal circumstances, she'd have acquiesced. The other women would likely be asleep, but Ilona would take care not to disturb them. These circumstances were anything but normal, though. Who knew when she and Jamal might have a few hours alone again? Once assignments were parceled out, they might be separated. One—or both—of them could die.

She tilted her chin and latched her gaze onto his. "I'd rather be with you."

A shadow crossed his features. If she hadn't been looking right at him, she wouldn't have seen it. "What? Did you rethink us again?" Weariness crashed through her. She couldn't do this back and forth game with Jamal much longer. Either they moved their attraction forward—or they settled for being friends.

Allies as Meara had called it earlier.

She remembered the wolf's invitation—or maybe it had been Jamal's—that she could always engage it in conversation, so she switched to telepathy.

"What's going on?"

"Listen carefully. It's probably not safe for me to say much, but this isn't about you."

Ilona waited, but the wolf was done talking.

"The less we say out here in the open, the better." Jamal threaded an arm around her and led her through a space between two of the Romani wagons. From there he kept moving until they were about fifty feet from the wagons. Neighs, whickers, and the fresh scent of horse dung told her they had to be close to the impromptu corral.

Where were they going?

Ilona squeezed her eyes shut. She was so tired they burned. When she opened them, he gestured with one hand, and she followed his directions around the horses to a place she actually recognized.

This was where the steep hillside intercepted cliffs. Did that mean the vacuum-driven spell didn't cover every side of the encampment?

"That's exactly what it means," he said, speaking low. "And yes, I've been inside your head. Since an attack can't very well come from this quarter, there was no point in extending the perimeter—which requires a great deal of magic to maintain—in this precise location. It's here, but it's weak. Step through just ahead, and we'll be on the other side."

A mild, tugging sensation buffeted her, and then she was through. Ilona turned to Jamal. "I thought safety lay within. Not without."

His dark eyes bored into her. "Do you trust me?"

Well, do I?

Ilona nodded.

"Then follow me another few feet. I've made us a bed. I wasn't certain you'd want to join me, but you said you did." He pulled gently on her hand and led the way through a thicket and into a place where boulders and trees formed a small, flat area not much larger than the blankets lying on sandy earth.

She sank onto the soft wool and crawled between its folds.

Jamal lay next to her and cradled her in his arms. She tucked her head into the hollow of his shoulder and listened to the steady beat of his heart. Not much point in asking again about why they were here and not within the first shifters' magic. Jamal would tell her—or not.

He traced the line of her cheekbone with his fingertips, and she leaned into his touch. "I have a dilemma." The faintest smile played over his mouth, but his words were heavy, serious.

"What is it?"

"I want to make love with you, but we need to talk too. I'm afraid if we talk first, neither of us will feel like making love."

"It sounds as if you're offering me a choice."

"I suppose in a way, I am."

Ilona thought about the man in her arms. His scent. His warmth. His overpowering maleness. Desire speared her. While she could still think, she asked, "This thing we need to talk about, is it why we're out here?"

He nodded. “And even that may not be entirely without risk, but if we open that door, we must follow the path to its end. If we’re discovered, it may mean my death, but there are things you must know.”

She turned in his arms until she lay atop him. Fierce protectiveness beat a path through her. “No one will hurt you. I won’t let them.”

“Ilona, my brave darling.”

Jamal hooked his arms beneath hers, grasped her head, and pulled her mouth down to his. The kiss took off like a wildfire fanned by restless winds. She opened her mouth to his tongue and sucked on it, teasing his mouth with her tongue as well. Little nibbling kisses turned into soul-searing exploration as he bit her lower lip, sucked it, and then bit some more. She wove her hands beneath his head, wanting him just as close as they could be.

The muscled planes of his body merged with hers as their kiss extended, drawing them into a place outside time, not unlike the magical world just behind them. Her breathing quickened, and her heart thudded against her ears. Her breasts felt heavy, the nipples sensitive peaks where they were crushed against his chest.

The dark, magical place between her legs

exploded with desire, sharper and more intense than she'd ever felt before. Without lifting his mouth from hers, Jamal rolled them onto their sides and reached between them to cradle a breast, twirling the nipple between his fingers. Sensation shot through her, straight to her crotch, and she writhed against him, desperate for more.

She wanted to undress him, eat him up with her eyes and fingers and mouth. She wrenched away from their kiss long enough to assess what she'd have to do to undress him, but she didn't want to wait that long. Pushing his jacket aside, she unbuttoned his shirt, opening it to reveal hard, muscled flesh.

"So many scars." She followed one with a fingertip.

"So many battles," he countered. "Times used to be much bloodier than they are now and war far more personal."

He let go of her breast long enough to slide a hand beneath her tunic. The shock of his skin against hers took her breath away, and she pressed into his touch. The outline of his cock, straining against his trousers, drew her, and she fumbled with the buttons holding them closed. Even though they'd covered miles with the bottom half of his body naked, she hadn't been focused on his raw masculinity.

One more button, and she pushed the front of his pants aside and drew out what lay beneath. His cock almost leapt into her hand, and she cradled it, stroking its hot, heavy length. He groaned and twisted in their embrace until he closed his mouth over the nipple he'd been teasing.

The feel of his teeth grazing her sensitive tissue and the heat of his mouth surrounding her made her belly tighten with hunger. No longer modulating her actions, she thrust her nub against his thigh. She wanted the man in her arms. Wanted to do everything to him and with him.

His cock bucked beneath her fingertips, and liquid slicked its velvety head. Ilona bent and took him into her mouth. It meant he couldn't suckle her breast, but she needed to feel his cock in her mouth, had to lick up those salty drops. She ran her hands up and down his shaft, while teasing the tip with her mouth.

Groaning, he jackknifed his body until he could pull her skirts up and out of the way. Hot breath settled over her nub, followed by his mouth sucking on her. She squirmed beneath his touch as an orgasm spooled deep within her. Shrieks wanted out, but she held them back. No reason to alert anyone that they were out here, and she had no idea if sound carried through the barrier.

Sentient thought fled as Jamal sank fingers inside her body. She convulsed around them before he hit bottom. Release crested and raced through her, turning her body to quicksilver. Before the spasms had fully quieted, he pulled himself from her mouth and knelt between her legs, one hand wrapped around his cock.

She threaded her legs around his waist, opening herself for him, and he let himself sink slowly into the mystery and magic of her body.

Magic. She hadn't used a twit. Usually she needed power—and heaps of fantasy—to drive herself into orgasm, but not with Jamal.

"You're smiling like a vixen—or a siren." He plunged the rest of the way inside and stopped moving.

"If I am, it's because this feels so right. You're wonderful. We could do this forever."

A bittersweet shadow darkened his eyes. "Darling. I'm grateful we're able to be together once. Hush. Talking is soon, but not quite yet."

She opened her arms, and he fell into them,

murmuring her name and stringing kisses across her face. He flexed his cock and it jumped inside her, doing wicked things to her nerves. Rocking against him, she encouraged him to move.

He withdrew and drove into her, the rhythm and tempo increasing with each stroke until their bodies crashed together. She came again, but he only moved faster, his cock swelling harder still. Just when she thought she couldn't hold any more lust, any more sensation, he shuddered inside her. Scorching heat from his semen pushed her over the edge one more time, and she lay gasping and panting in his arms.

He held her close as their breathing quieted and repositioned them so they lay on their sides. "No matter what happens next," he said, "thank you for tonight. I haven't had a woman since Aneksi. You reminded me what it means to be a man, what it means to be alive."

Ilona basked in his words. She wanted to be everything to Jamal. Wanted to soothe the wounds from his past and throw herself into creating a future for them.

"What you did for me is special too. I hate to ruin any of it, but you have to tell me what happened here tonight while I was gone. What isn't safe to talk about inside the barrier?"

"It may not be safe out here, either," he cautioned.

"I don't understand. Meara made a huge point of saying there wouldn't be any more enmity between shifters and Rom."

"That was her opinion. Not necessarily one shared by the first wolf shifter."

Ilona digested that. "If he doesn't want anything to do with us, why is he here? Didn't he say he wished more than two caravans were present?"

"He loves both battle and glory," the wolf spoke up. *"I remember that one from long years past. From a time eons before I bonded with Jamal. I only met him once, but stories about his bloodthirstiness were widespread."*

So long as the wolf had made its presence known, Ilona said, *"This may not be the best timing, but I want to make certain you know I welcome both you and Jamal into my life. I'm looking forward to spending more time with you too."*

"Thank you." The wolf woofed its endorsement.

"That was kind." Jamal's dark eyes gleamed with approval.

"No," she countered. "It was true. What exactly do you believe Anu—?"

Jamal clamped a hand over her mouth. "Never, never say his name. No matter what magic is in play, it will draw his attention."

Ilona nodded, and Jamal moved his hand. "I'm sorry. Did I hurt you?"

"No, you didn't. What can he do that worries you? He sounded so sincere when he said he wished more Rom were here."

Jamal exhaled briskly. "A lot. He gave tacit permission for his wolves to sabotage the Rom on shared missions. And maybe he truly does wish more gypsies were here. Easier to create chaos if he doesn't have to hunt them down first." He hesitated and looked away.

"What else?" she demanded. "You've told me this much."

"There's always been bad blood between him and Meara. I fear he'll take advantage of this situation to kill her."

Ilona's eyes widened. She hadn't believed such a thing were even possible. "He can do that?"

"Yes. Firsts are close to immortal, but another first can take them down."

She closed her teeth over her lower lip. Meara could be a high-handed bitch, but Ilona respected her intelligence and ability. Her own scrying skills would be stronger for having worked alongside the vulture shifter.

"I can see why you didn't want to have this conversation before we made love. That's terrible. So we'll be out there, putting our lives at grave risk in prison camps and destroying vampire nests. All the while, we'll have to watch our backs if we're working with any wolf shifters."

"It's not quite as bad as all that. I know many of the wolves here, and they're decent folk. There are a few, however, who cheered when An—er he, all but offered permission to do maximum damage so long as they were subtle about it."

She stroked hair back from his face, laying its clean lines bare. "If you could come up with a list of names, I'll make certain Michael and Stewart know."

Jamal creased his forehead into a mass of worried lines. "I'd come to that conclusion myself, but it feels twisted. Like no matter how I play this, I'm doing someone wrong. My loyalty to my kind runs deep, but it doesn't extend to shielding them when what they're doing is wrong.

"The first should have died millennia ago," the wolf spoke up.

"Do you know why he didn't?" Jamal asked.

"I do. He entered into an alliance with a powerful vampire."

Breath hissed from between Jamal's clenched teeth. *"When were you going to get around to telling me that?"*

"When you needed the information. It's not as if the first has been anywhere around lately."

Jamal's body went rigid in her arms and she pulled him close. "It's all right. Your wolf told us in time." She ran her hands up and down his back until the tension bled out of him.

"That explains a whole lot," Jamal muttered. "Like why the first wolf is here."

"Maybe," Ilona said, marshaling her thoughts. "You're assuming he's something like a double agent, and that he'll sabotage all our efforts. I can understand him hating Romani, but would he sacrifice his own wolf shifters in the same vein?"

"Humph." Jamal set his jaw in a harsh line. "There's a lot we don't know."

"Indeed," she replied. "We have no idea if the vampire he got cozy with is even still alive."

"The odds are good," Jamal muttered. "Those fuckers live forever."

"We've also established they can die," she cut

in and switched to telepathy focused on the wolf. *"Do you know anything else?"*

"No. The first has been absent for centuries. Many of us, the bond animals, thought it strange and there's been much conjecture regarding why that is. Insofar as I know, though, no one's spoken about this for a very long time. Either no one knows anything, or the truth is so unpalatable, no one wanted to give voice to it."

Jamal disentangled his arms and legs from hers. "I don't want you to think I'm ashamed of you or that I don't want people to know about you and me. This is nothing like my relationship with Aneksi where I kept things hidden from my blood kin. Until we know more about what we face, though, it would be best for you to sneak into Trina and Marguerite's wagon while there's still some of the night left. That way, it will at least appear you spent the last part of your evening there."

"I agree, but I don't want to leave you."

He smiled crookedly. "I don't want you to leave, but it's too risky otherwise."

"Where will you go?"

"Michael's wagon. He offered me a spot beneath it. Before I do that, though, I'll see if I can't neutralize the scent of our lovemaking that's clinging to these blankets."

She pushed her clothing back into place and realized she'd never even taken off her shoes. After leaning in for one more sweet kiss, she got to her feet. "See you tomorrow."

He nodded. "Take care of yourself, Ilona. I don't want anything to happen to you."

A cold tongue of fear sliced into her heart, and his earlier caution about danger slammed into her. "You too."

A grim laugh escaped him. "I'm not worried about tonight or tomorrow. It's when we're away from here that we're vulnerable."

"We'll just have to make certain we're assigned to the same project." Once she heard the words, they made perfect sense. "We'll protect each other. Don't forget that list of names."

"You'll have it by morning."

Ilona hastened back the way they'd come, covering her presence with magic. Not much point in him cleansing the blankets if her scent was all over this place. Moving past the barrier was almost a non-event, and she slipped past the horses and made her way to Trina and Marguerite's wagon.

Neither woman woke as she crept past them to where they'd laid her pallet and blanket for her. Trina's thoughtfulness touched her. The woman had enough on her mind with her dying mother. An unpleasant thought struck as she settled herself to sleep for what was left of the night.

What if the weak place in the barrier had been placed there on purpose? All Anubis had to do was tell his vampire pal about it, and their otherworld location would be ripe for attack.

Tomorrow, she'd have a chat with Michael and Stewart. After she got the list of names from Jamal.

Jamal. Just the sound of his name in her mind warmed her. When she shut her eyes, the feel of him surrounding her, inside her, kindled desire all over again. She said a quick prayer to Isis to see him safely through the night and welcomed sleep when it claimed her.

CHAPTER 12

Jamal didn't want to erase Ilona's wildflower scent from his blankets, but he couldn't very well cart them to Michael's wagon, either. The Rom's magic—and his nose—were sharp. He inhaled a few more times before putting his clothing to rights and getting to his feet. Once there, he summoned power, instructed the blankets to release the molecules trapped in their weave, and tossed both over a shoulder.

His body hummed with the aftermath of their lovemaking. He felt alive in a way he never had before. Within him, the wolf was joyful too. He felt its approval and its relief he'd finally moved beyond his past.

He thought about the weak place in the barrier as he stepped through it. He'd discovered the fault quite by accident as he hunted for a place to bring Ilona. Why was it here? Was it a way to save a bit of magic as he'd originally suspected, or did it serve some darker, more nefarious purpose?

He wondered which of the first shifters had constructed the barrier, or if they'd tag-teamed it. Surely, there'd be a way to find out without putting anyone in an uncomfortable position. Or clueing Anubis that he wasn't a willing participant in the intentional and focused harm the first wolf shifter had laid out earlier that evening.

Jamal had seen some of his kin exchanging looks. Particularly the women. But everyone hid their reactions from their first. It was how they'd been trained. He started a mental list of the wolves he knew beyond any doubt were fully behind Anubis and his stated goals.

Wolves were superior. They should be at the head of any decisions regarding all shifters. If any disagreed, they should be banished—or destroyed. Anubis hadn't actually spelled that last out, but he didn't have to. His meaning had been clear enough.

Jamal winced. He'd been raised on tales of the first wolf shifter, had deified Anubis as a young man. To have the reality fall so far from his ideal was harsh, but he was grateful the first had been so vocal. Easier to fight what you knew than something you had to guess at.

He slipped beneath Michael's wagon to where he planned to lay out the blankets, but before he had a chance to spread them on the ground, the wagon's door opened, and Michael let himself outside. Without saying a word, he gestured for Jamal to follow him. After tucking the folded woolen coverlets next to the wagon, Jamal crossed to Stewart's wagon and followed Michael inside.

Stewart sat cross-legged in a corner, wrapped in the folds of his kilt. For once his red hair hung loose, rather than snugged into braids. He nodded and the door, encouraged by a jot of magic, swung shut silently on well-greased hinges. The air thickened with the scent of Rom magic as Stewart—or perhaps Michael—spelled the small enclosure.

Michael dropped into a crouch across from Stewart and patted the floor next to him. Jamal knelt too, waiting. They'd tell him what they wanted soon enough.

"What we have to say may put you in a compromising position," Stewart began.

"You fought alongside us before," Michael added, "although Stewart and I were of two minds about speaking frankly with you."

Jamal looked from one man to the other, still waiting.

"First, where were ye tonight?" Stewart asked. "'Tis as good a place as any to begin. If ye'd rather not answer, ye can leave since it means ye willna answer any of our other concerns, either."

Jamal hesitated, unsure if implicating Ilona was wise, but if he lied, the two Romani would know.

"Tell them," the wolf urged. *"Silence perpetuates the unrest between shifters and the rest of the magical world."*

"Was that your wolf?" Michael asked.

"Aye, and if 'twas, what did he say?" Stewart cut in.

"Yes, it was my wolf urging me to tell you the truth. Bond animals are wise, and I've never gone wrong listening to it."

"So, where were you?" Michael prodded.

"With Ilona. I'd be with her still, but I feared causing problems between our two peoples. Meara may have pronounced that we're now partners, but it takes more than words to overcome fear and distrust."

"I'd add hatred to that list," Michael said sourly.

"Beyond the point," Stewart muttered and focused his astute dark eyes on Jamal. "Do ye care for her, or is this merely a passing fancy?"

"I can only speak for myself, but I believe I'm falling in love." Jamal rocked back on his heels. "That's not why you brought me here, nor why you shrouded the wagon in spells. Spells, by the way, that shifter magic can probably penetrate except most everyone is asleep right now."

"We're all too aware that our magic doesn't stack up well against yours," Michael said. "It's one of the reasons for my concern. We've come to trust Meara, and Nivkh has a good heart." He paused, and a muscle flinched along the side of his face.

Jamal saved Michael the trouble of hunting for politically neutral words. "You are right not to trust the other first. And it's far better if you don't use his name."

Stewart narrowed his eyes to slits. "Is this knowledge ye've always held, or something new?"

The question cut so close to home, it gave Jamal pause. "New. Why would you ask?"

"I sense something in him. Something beyond shifter energy, and it disturbs me. 'Twas why I questioned him about the magic sustaining this location. Not because I dinna already know, but because I wanted an excuse to get closer to him."

Breath hissed through Jamal's teeth.

Michael gripped his forearm hard. "If you know something, tell us. My people are here. I agreed to bring them across the barrier, and I must know if it was a poor decision."

"As are mine," Stewart said. "They are my life. I'm sworn to keep them safe as best I can. 'Tis how caravans have always operated."

Even though it might not keep the conversation any more private, Jamal switched to telepathy. *"The first wolf shifter is both a bigot and a racist. He would put his shifters before all others, and he encouraged his shifters to harm Romani if they could do so without attracting attention."*

"So his story about wanting to work with Romani was bogus—something crafted to lull us into trusting him," Michael replied in kind.

"'Twould seem so," Stewart muttered half aloud.

"Beyond that," Jamal went on, *"the one of which we speak has been absent for centuries. Before his*

disappearance, he entered into an alliance with one of the old, powerful vampires."

Michael inhaled sharply and made a hooked sign against evil. Stewart made the sigil as well. Both chanted a few words in Coptic.

"Did ye ever meet him afore?" Stewart asked.

Jamal shook his head.

"Mmph." Michael frowned. *"So you'd not have the feel of him—or know if what's here is real or an imposter."*

"How about your wolf?" Stewart asked.

It was a good question, so Jamal turned it inward. The wolf knew about the vampire, and it had said it met Anubis while bonded to an earlier shifter.

"I wish I knew more," the wolf said after a lengthy pause. *"I was within a bondmate when the first was present, but it was only once, and hundreds of us were there. I wasn't paying that close attention since we had no idea it was the first and last time we'd ever see him."*

"What did he say?" Michael asked. "Your wolf. He was just talking with you."

"It's not a he or a she," Jamal replied. "It didn't have useful information."

"Let me do this," the wolf spoke up. *"I can retreat to the other place and see if any of the bond animals*

know more. Like I said before, it's been a long time since the topic came up."

"Do it, but don't be gone long."

"What was that about?" Stewart asked and resettled himself so he leaned against a wall.

"The short answer is the bond animals have a place that's not part of this world. It's where they roam when they're between bondmates. It's also where they go to take breaks from us. My wolf is there now, attempting to gather information from others like it."

"Thank him, er it, for us," Michael said.

"I will."

A soft tap on the wagon door snapped Jamal's head around.

The power eddying around Stewart pulsed with blues and greens, but his grim expression softened. "'Och aye, 'tis Ilona."

The door snicked open, and she stood framed in it. "May I enter?" she asked softly.

"If the answer were nay, the door wouldna have opened for ye," Stewart replied.

Her gaze settled on Jamal, and she started. "What are you doing here?"

"Talking. Come in so we can close the door, and Michael and Stewart can resurrect their spell. Did you know we were within?"

"I felt the magic, but I had no idea who was here." She stepped inside, pulling the door to behind her. "I—I'm sorry to intrude like this," she went on. The wagon was just tall enough for her to stand upright, and she didn't make any move to sit.

Jamal heard a tremor beneath her words and wanted to draw her against him, but didn't. These were her people. Any display of affection between them had to come from her.

"I sense need in ye, lassie," Stewart said. "What happened?"

"I fell asleep, but a vision snared me. It was harsh and real and frightening, especially when I tried to escape, and it held me captive." Her rushed flow of words trailed off, and she closed her lower lip over her teeth. "It was almost like when the vampire rose through my trance and looked at me as if it truly saw me."

"Were there vampires in this sending?" Jamal asked as alarm sluiced through him, tightening his muscles into rocks. They may have killed one, but others could have tracked its energy. Even though Ilona thought she'd closed off the portal, maybe she'd missed something. Left a sliver of energy behind. Vampires were notoriously competent trackers.

"Yes, but much more than that." She looked from the two Romani to Jamal and back again. "Did you tell them anything?"

He nodded. "Everything except the list you and I discussed."

"What list?" Michael asked and then waved a hand. "Never mind, we'll get to that. I want to hear about Ilona's sending. Her seer ability is strong, as powerful as Elliott's."

Her eyes widened. "How could you possibly know that?"

He shrugged. "If it weren't, Meara wouldn't have taken you with her to scry the location of vampire nests."

She made a face. "That's a better answer than my power is bleeding out all around me, easy for anyone to notice."

"Close your eyes," Stewart crooned, compulsion strong in his voice. "Start at the beginning, and tell us what ye saw."

Jamal felt the magic snare Ilona. She sank into a crouch between them and the door. When she looked up, her gray eyes held a glazed, otherworldly look, and he figured she couldn't see him or the wagon anymore.

He glanced sidelong at Stewart. The spell he'd just cast didn't feel like any Rom magic Jamal had felt before, and he'd been exposed to a whole lot of it during his years with Aneksi. What was the man? Romani, but maybe something else as well. He almost asked the questions spilling through his head, but Ilona began to talk.

"At first, I thought it was a dream," Ilona murmured. "I was walking by myself through clouds. Sometimes they snagged me, but it wasn't painful, just made me watch where I was going."

"Day or night?" Stewart asked in a hypnotic, singsong-y voice.

"The in between place. The one where time fades and is meaningless."

"Aye, go on, lassie."

She clasped her hands in front of her. "Mother floated out of the ether. I was so glad to see her. I'd been hoping she'd come to me in a dream since she died a year ago. I smiled and floated to her, holding out my hands. When I got close, I took a better look, and she was frantically waving me back. Her mouth was open, but I couldn't hear her.

"She must have known I couldn't hear because she carved *Turn Around* into a cloud." Ilona swallowed visibly, and her knuckles whitened where her hands were clasped in her lap. "This is where it starts to get strange. I made a grab for Mother. Needed to hug her and tell her how much I missed her, but she vanished as soon as I put my arms around the place where she'd been. The words she'd carved turned red and started to bleed, dripping onto my feet."

Ilona took a shuddery breath. "The blood—or whatever it was—burned like crazy, and I bent, trying to rub it off, but I just smeared it. And made the pain worse."

Michael leaned forward. "Let me see one of your feet."

Ilona dropped onto her butt and extended a leg.

Jamal bent closer. Sure enough, pale red streaks marked her shoe, but disappeared above it. He reached forward, trying to get a feel for what kind of magic it was.

Stewart shook his head and cautioned, "Doona disturb the marks until we understand them better."

As if inspection made them gun-shy, the streaks faded, growing lighter by the moment. If Jamal hadn't known they'd been there, he wouldn't have believed they'd ever existed.

"What the holy hell?" Ilona stared at her shoe.

"'Tis nothing," Stewart said. "Marks from the

dream world rarely survive translocation into ours."

"These did," Jamal said.

"Aye, but not for verra long. Go on, lass."

Ilona cleared her throat. "I'm not sure how the next part happened, but I was moving through the clouds again, except now they felt heavy, ominous, as if danger lurked behind each one. I knew by now I was in trance, that it wasn't a normal dream."

"Your mum told you to retreat, why didn't ye?" Stewart probed.

"I don't know. I asked myself that later when I was doing everything I could to escape, but I'm getting ahead of myself. All at once, whatever I was walking on cracked. It made a horrible racket, and I turned around, thinking I'd go back, but there was nothing behind me. When I turned in a circle, the only place that didn't drop off into nothingness lay ahead.

"It didn't feel right. My skin prickled in warning, and the fine hairs on the back of my neck stood on end. I cast magic to stop the trance, figuring I'd end up back in Trina's wagon, but I started to fall. My legs and arms windmilled, and I think I screamed.

"I expected to crash into something and

break every bone in my body, but somehow I ended up on my feet." She licked her lips, and Michael pushed a flask into her hands. When she drank, the pungent reek of raw alcohol filled the wagon.

Ilona handed the flask back, but the vacant look hadn't left her eyes. "Where I'd been alone before, there were others with me, and we were inside someplace that reminded me of Dachau, except it wasn't."

"Did ye know the people with you?" Stewart's question was so soft, Jamal almost didn't hear him.

"Yes. Jamal and two other wolf shifters and two Rom from Michael's caravan and the first wolf shifter, An—"

"Do not say his name," Jamal cautioned, worried it might draw his attention.

Stewart said something in Gaelic, and Ilona replied, "I understand."

"Did you ever figure out which prison camp you were in?" Michael asked.

"Yes. I saw a sign. It was Sachsenhausen-Oranienburg, the one near Berlin."

"What happened then?" Stewart pressed.

Daylight was leaching through the wagon's windows and around its door. Soon the camp would be awake, and the surfeit of power pulsing around Stewart's wagon wouldn't escape notice.

"We were invisible. No one in the camp could see us. I worried about running out of magic, but no one else seemed to care. The first held some type of curved blade, and he sliced off heads right and left. Blood was everywhere, but no one reacted. Prisoners and other guards walked right by headless corpses spewing blood."

"What were the rest of us doing?" Jamal asked.

Her eyes sheened with tears, but she kept talking. "Everyone was killing including you and me. We killed so many, but more showed up. It seemed like for every German we killed, three sprang up to take his place. I knew it was wrong—not a clean sending. I recognized I was caught up in something perverse, but I didn't see a way out.

"Vampires rose out of the ground then. Maybe a dozen. One walked to An—er, the one I can't name, and sort of disappeared into him. First there were two, but then only one, and it was the vampire."

She drew a deep, ragged breath and tears spilled over, but she didn't brush them away. "The other vampires ranged around it. The rest of us drew back. Everyone wanted to get away. I felt the horror in them, but there was nowhere to go. All our power was tied up in being invisible. If we'd run, the guards would have seen us and mowed us down with their machine guns."

"You're almost to the end," Stewart encouraged her. "Not much more."

"It's true, but how would you know that?"

"Doesna matter, lass. Keep going."

"The lead vampire started shouting in a language I've never heard before. The others turned on us. They killed the other Rom—both of them. They killed one of the wolf shifters. By the time they got to me, I was ready. I dug deep and cast the destruction spell—the one we're taught and told never, ever to use because it damages the way Earth is anchored to the universe."

Ilona trained her cloudy gaze on Jamal. "I had to do something." She spread her hands beseechingly. "I couldn't let them kill you. I couldn't."

He didn't care what Stewart thought. Jamal moved to Illona and gathered her against him. She clung to him, sobbing.

"Ssht. Hush," he crooned, holding her.

"The trance shattered after that," Stewart said. It wasn't a question. Somehow, he knew.

"Yes. I ended up wrapped in my blankets.

They were hot and sweaty as if I'd never left the wagon." Ilona's voice was muffled against Jamal's shoulder.

"Let go of her." Stewart's voice was mild, but it left no space for dissent.

Ilona turned toward Stewart, blinking back tears. Her sobs had quieted, and the vacant, disoriented aspect had left her eyes. Now they just looked haunted. "What happened to me? Do you know?"

"Aye, lass, that I do. Come close. Listen carefully, for I willna repeat myself."

Ilona knelt in front of Stewart. Even though he hadn't been invited, Jamal did the same. If there were secrets to be revealed, he wanted to know them too. Michael grunted ominously and spread his arms wide, sheeting power around them all.

Stewart gripped Ilona's hands. "'Twas prophecy, though not as ye normally experience it. The blend of future seeing with a dream where ye're trapped tarnishes the purity of seer magic. Yet it doesna make your vision any less true."

"But how can the shifter be a vampire? Out of everything, it was the one thing I didn't understand." Ilona kept her troubled gaze glued on Stewart's face.

"Because it's not a shifter. 'Tis just a form the vampire can wear." Stewart squeezed Ilona's hands. "Ye did good work this night. Because of it, we have knowledge that may well prove invaluable."

"Dawn is here," Michael said in a gravelly voice. "Tone down the power before we attract undue attention, and I'll do likewise."

"I will," Stewart replied. "Ilona. Ye must find a way to let Meara know about your vision. No one else. Just her."

Jamal spoke up, aiming his words at Ilona. "That thing I told you earlier about one first being able to destroy another doesn't apply here, since the first wolf isn't what he appears."

"Got it." Ilona clamped her jaws together.

"In the meantime," Jamal murmured, "it's business as usual. We're still settling in here. Maybe today we'll team up for the work ahead. We cannot let even a breath of what we know escape. It's going to damn near kill me, but I can't even tell Tairin—or Elliott. The more who know, the better the chances the first will catch wind we're onto him."

"Elliott was with Meara, but wasn't Tairin there when your first outlined his plan last night?" Michael asked.

Jamal shook his head. "She sat through the first part of his speech, but then slipped away. The first was so caught up in the sound of his own rhetoric, he didn't notice. I almost ordered her back, but didn't want to draw attention to her leaving. Once he launched into his other agenda, I was glad I'd left well enough alone."

"Do we just let the next part play out?" Ilona brushed tears from her cheeks. "Go out on missions with people we don't trust?"

"I'm hoping it willna come to that. Find Meara as soon as ye can. She will know the tarnished prophecy was true-seeing." Stewart flexed his fingers in front of him, cracking the knuckles.

"I'm still reeling from that bastard saying he wanted more caravans here," Michael sputtered. "That would make it mighty convenient since all he wants is to thin our ranks."

"I'm back!" the wolf cried. *"I have news."*

Jamal held up a hand. "Just a minute. The wolf has returned. Let me listen to what it discovered."

The wolf snarled long and low before saying, *"It's rumor, but the vampire alliance with our first went bad, and the vampire took over. No one is certain how long ago it happened, but everyone I asked believed it was true. The worst part is the vampire maintained the ability to shift."*

"Why didn't any of the animals bring this to light before now?" Jamal asked and bit back a stern rebuke. For such a critical piece of information to remain hidden was unconscionable.

"They all hoped the first wolf would never show up again. I believe they felt deeply ashamed of him. The animal who was his bondmate has been absent for hundreds of years. No one knows where it went."

Michael raised questioning eyebrows. Clearly he'd felt the energy, but couldn't make out the words and wanted to know what they were.

"My wolf corroborated Ilona's prophecy. The only mystery is why more vampires haven't targeted shifters since they somehow preserve our ability to alter forms."

Stewart moved his hands in a complicated pattern, and the power throbbing around the group fell away. His face settled into worried lines. "Just because one could manage it doesn't mean others could. Mayhap they tried and found the price too high. My guess is your first invited possession."

"He did, at least according to my wolf."

"Every group has a few that are corrupt," Michael said. "Some start out that way, others choose depravity after the fact. I've gotten rid of my share of blackguards to keep my caravan strong. We face enough problems, though. We didn't need this one."

"Mayhap not," Stewart agreed, "but I'm not convinced we canna leverage things to our advantage even now. Return to your wagons afore the camp wakens. Part of my casting was a sleep spell, so ye have a wee bit of time yet."

Jamal turned to him. "What are you?" The words ripped out of him.

"Does it matter, lad?"

Before he could answer, Ilona moved toward the door, saying, "I sense something too, but he'll never tell us that. Come on."

"She's right," Stewart said.

Jamal pushed his questions aside—for now—and told Ilona, "I'll meet you at Tairin and Elliott's wagon. Because we're the ones who rescued you, it's a logical location and one unlikely to rouse suspicion."

"Be there in half an hour. I want to make certain Trina doesn't need me to help with her mother."

Emotion raced through Jamal, tightening his chest as he watched her leave. She was such a pure and decent woman. He'd have spared her pain and suffering if he could.

"'Tisn't how it works," Stewart said. "We all

have a part to play. Not all of us will survive, but if we listen to the goddess and heed her instructions, magic won't die out of the world."

Jamal turned to face the other man. "How much do you know of our future?"

"Ye know better than to ask such a question. If ye had the gift of foreseeing, ye'd realize that altering actions to avoid a future event rarely works the way we hope it will. Even though things appear uncertain, we are all exactly where we are meant to be. Now might be a good time for that list."

He pushed a tattered scrap of paper and a pencil into Jamal's hands, and Jamal scribbled names of the treacherous wolf shifters onto it before making his way into a dank, gray dawn. He hadn't been set upon in Ilona's vision. And she'd been able to save herself. Both had to be good omens.

"Don't you see?" the wolf chimed in, barking excitedly.

"See what?" Jamal set a course for Tairin and Elliott's wagon.

"The first finally came out of hiding. Now that we know what he is, we can do away with him once and for all."

"I love your enthusiasm, but we're talking about a

crafty vampire who's been alive since something like the dawn of time."

"Everyone makes mistakes," the wolf insisted. *"When he does, we'll be there to make him pay."*

Jamal smiled. *"I'm glad you're mine."*

"No. We're each other's. Can we hunt before breakfast?"

The wolf sounded so hopeful, Jamal said, *"Sure. We stop at four mice, though. We have a date to meet Ilona in half an hour."*

"You're on. Hurry."

Jamal trotted to a distant side of the mesa and stripped off his clothes. Shift magic ran through him like rich, heady spirits, and he ceded their shared consciousness to his bondmate.

CHAPTER 13

Ilona hurried toward Tairin and Elliott's wagon. More than her estimated thirty minutes had passed, but Marguerite hadn't been doing well this morning. Her breathing had been labored, and Trina needed help settling her over a brazier fragrant with herbs to ease her chest. The women had shared a bowl of boiled grain thick with dried fruit before Trina shooed her away.

"Go on. I know you're anxious to see that beau of yours." A fond smile wreathed Trina's face.

"I haven't said one word about Jamal. Why'd you call him that?"

Trina's eyes had sparkled knowingly. "I'm

Romani. And a fortuneteller. We know these things."

Ilona had laughed. "Hard to hide anything in a caravan."

"Indeed it is." Trina's smile had turned wistful, and she sighed. "I had me a fellow once. Thought I did. Turned out he was one of those with a gal in every caravan. Soon as I found out, I told him no more, but it still hurt."

"Aw, I'm sorry. There were a few like that in my caravan too." Ilona stopped short of saying most of the ones in her caravan were inclined toward men and had been total players.

As she wove through the tightly packed wagons, her thoughts turned to Meara. She sent power zinging outward, hunting for the vulture shifter, but didn't find her. Probably meant she hadn't returned from wherever she'd gone last night.

Jamal, Tairin, and Elliott sat on three-legged stools around a small camp stove. The stove was cold, and they were nursing cups of what smelled like herbal tea.

Jamal sprang to his feet, relief streaming from him in waves. "There you are. I was getting ready to hunt for you."

"Sorry. Trina needed my help." Ilona smiled,

wanting to hug Jamal, but uncertain with his family present. How much had he told them? Or had he said anything at all?

"Would you like tea?" Tairin asked.

"That would be nice." Ilona unfolded another stool from where it leaned against the wagon and settled onto it.

Tairin poured from a small, dented, metal teapot and handed Ilona a ceramic mug. "Not sure how hot it still is," she said.

"Doesn't matter. It smells heavenly." Ilona inhaled appreciatively and took a sip of tepid liquid, sweetened with honey. "Thank you."

"Welcome." Tairin sat back down. So did Jamal.

"What do you suppose happened to Meara?" Elliott asked, keeping his words quiet.

"I was wondering the same thing," Ilona replied, all too aware of her assignment to clue Meara in. "She went back through the barrier last night."

"I'm sure she'll return soon," Tairin said. "She's come this far with us. No way she'd abandon the project now that things are heating up."

"Say." Elliott looked at Ilona. "Did you ever figure out where your brother is?"

Ilona shook her head and drank more tea. In

truth, with everything else that had transpired, she hadn't thought much about Aron. Guilt pricked her.

"Looks like we'll have a spot of time this morning," Elliott went on. "Want to see if we can join forces and scry his location?"

"I'd love to." Ilona leaned forward. "When would you like to do that?"

"No time like now." Elliott pushed to his feet. "Hard to say exactly what this day will bring, but we have time and we're both here. I can chase your blood markers with my magic. We might not be able to talk with him, but we should be able to locate him."

"How much magic will that take?" Jamal asked.

Ilona stood too. "Ask that a different way. What exactly are you trying to find out?"

"If it's possible to mask your magic from all the shifters here. I'm not concerned about the Rom discovering a seeking spell."

Elliott shrugged. "It's kind of the other way around. Most Rom don't have enough power to sense expended magic, but almost every shifter does. Do you want us to conceal our efforts?"

Jamal nodded. "It would be wise."

Elliott exchanged a pointed glance with

Tairin. In turn, she leveled her gaze at her father. "What aren't you saying?"

"Those aren't words I can speak out here in the open."

"Telepathy?" Tairin raised an eyebrow.

"Won't help. I can't say anything in any form."

"Mmph." Tairin drained her tea and stood, joining the others. "Maybe we'll all take part in the seeking spell for Aron."

"Bad idea," Jamal said. "The more of us throwing magic around, the harder it will be to hide."

Elliott rummaged in a chest and withdrew a small box and a leather pouch. "I have what we'll need here. Come on, Ilona. This shouldn't take long."

As she followed after Elliott, who was heading toward the horse corral, she heard Tairin interrogating her father. "What the fuck is going on? My magic was activated during the night, but I don't know why."

If Jamal answered, he swathed it in spells because she didn't hear his reply.

"Where are we going?" she asked Elliott since he walked like a man with a firm destination in mind.

"The far side of the horses. More private and

less competing magic. It might be easier to project our seeking spell beyond the barrier." He hesitated for a beat. "I'm worried about Meara. I felt her energy dissipate when she moved beyond the barrier, but I was expecting her to return last night."

"Any particular reason?"

"Not really. More intuition than anything else."

"Men aren't supposed to be driven by intuition." Ilona considered leading them through the place she and Jamal had crossed the previous night.

"Funny, I've always put great stock in mine. Where are you going?"

"We can cross beyond the barrier just over there." She pointed.

"Really? Without a heap of fanfare—and discomfort?"

Ilona didn't say anything, just turned sideways to slither through the break in the magic surrounding the camp.

"Wow!" Elliott's eyes widened as he joined her. "How'd you discover that?"

"It wasn't me, but Jamal. The barrier should shield what we're doing from the rest of the camp, though."

Elliott trotted to a flat rock at the base of a cliff and opened the box he'd carried tucked beneath an arm. He spread a worn piece of leather with runic markings over the rock and placed two candles atop it. Next he opened the leather pouch and sprinkled rosemary, fennel, cowslip, and garlic around the candles.

"Do you have preferred herbs?" he asked without looking up as he arranged the accoutrements of the spell he was planning.

"Never use them."

He did look at her then. "Really? They make opening gateways much easier, and your magic lasts longer."

"I'm a woman. We're not supposed to have magic strong enough to worry about conserving it."

Elliott rolled his eyes. "I wasn't looking for a lecture." Bending, he snapped his fingers and both candles caught fire. "We can debate this later. Give me one of your hands, and then lend your power to this casting. We won't be long at this."

Ilona offered her left hand.

He drew a small blade from a pocket and made a quick, clean slice in the meaty part beneath her thumb. Stepping close, she turned her hand and urged her blood to flow into the smoking candles. The air turned first yellow, then orange, and then a flickering red.

Elliott chanted, summoning spirit guides to follow the blood trail.

She wove her power in with his. He was strong, much more so than Michael, the man whose caravan he'd been part of. Ilona closed her eyes, urging a vision state. It was how she accomplished most magic.

No candles. No herbs. No rune-studded artifacts. Just her innate power and trust in her ability.

The blackness behind her eyes yielded to a caravan. Dust rose around horses and wagons. Smells buffeted her. The gypsy scents of herbs and living things mingled with the unmistakable sweet rot of death.

Aron, his dark hair tangled and falling to his shoulders, stared at her through gray eyes that were twin to her own. *"Ilona?"* His mind voice was a ragged whisper. *"Is that really you or am I dreaming?"*

"Yes, it's me," she said quickly. *"Where are you?"*

"You escaped. Tell me you escaped." His face contorted into a sob, but he got hold of himself.

"I did. Be quick, Aron. I sense the caravan. Did you return to Valentin? Where are you?"

Elliott's magic pulsed and throbbed. She had no idea how much she was burning through. How much was his versus hers, and she couldn't take her attention away from her brother to ask.

"You're too late," Aron said. *"We've been captured. We're on our way to a camp. Some of us are already dead, but the Nazis won't let us stop to bury them."*

"Run! Just like you did before." Ilona bit so hard on her lower lip, she tasted blood.

He raised shackled hands and shook them until rattling chains reverberated in her chest. *"My feet are bound too. Do not come after me, Ilona. You got away. Stay free so I have something to believe in."*

The reflection holding her vision shattered outward in a flash so bright it seared her corneas. Elliott's candles guttered and died.

"Ilona?" He gripped her shoulders. "Did you sever the connection?"

"No. It was Aron." She blinked spots away from her visual field until Elliott's face came into clear focus.

He frowned. "That's almost unbelievable. He supplanted my spell with his own. What kind of magic does your brother hold?"

"Good question. I never knew. He's just sixteen, and he and I had different fathers."

"Well, he's amazingly powerful for one that young. Hell, for a Rom of any age." Elliott poured wax that had pooled atop the candles into the dirt and began packing his accoutrements away.

Ilona inhaled raggedly. "Were you able to tell where he was?"

"No. I heard what he said and sensed Rom all around him, though."

"I figured it out." Jamal strode into the small area where they'd launched their spell.

Ilona fell back a pace. "I left you back at the wagon. Were you spying on us?" She shook her head hard. "Sorry. I didn't mean that. I'm still disoriented from how abruptly the spell ended."

"It's all right. We understand. We felt the casting implode too." Tairin hustled past her father and joined Elliott, wrapping an arm around his waist. He hugged her back.

"Tairin and I shielded your casting from the rest of the camp by strengthening the barrier while you were occupied," Jamal explained. "Because I didn't have to focus on maintaining your gateway, I was able to look past the caravan, and I recognized a few landmarks. The caravan is on the main roadway south of Hamburg."

"Must mean they're headed for the prison camp there." Ilona raked her hands through her hair, culling through her memory for its name. "Esterwegen."

"My guess too." Jamal held out his arms and she walked into them. "That's a long way from here. Maybe five hundred miles."

"Through country that's not easy to move across undetected." She wound her arms around him, grateful for his solid presence.

"That's true even for shifters. Cities are thick in northern Germany and wolves less common."

"We might pull it off if we traveled at night," Tairin said from the shelter of Elliott's arms.

"We can add it to the list," Ilona murmured. Sorrow and fear for her brother sliced through her, but she couldn't do much from such a distance. "We have bigger worries that are much closer."

"Yes, like where Meara is." Elliott let go of Tairin and tucked his box back beneath one arm. Tairin picked up the leather pouch.

The beat of wings drew Ilona's attention aloft. Breath whooshed from her. "Look!" She pointed at the sky and moved out of Jamal's embrace.

Meara plummeted earthward, wings furled to soften her landing. Somewhere between fifty feet in the air and where they stood, she shifted in a blaze of pure white light.

Her body may have been human, but her eyes radiated feral displeasure. "Why are all of you out here?" Light still pulsed around her shifting form.

"Elliott and I were hunting for my brother." Ilona squared her shoulders.

"Father and I helped," Tairin spoke up.

"Before we go back into the camp, I must speak with you privately." Ilona started toward Meara.

The shifter made a chopping motion with one hand. "I already know. It's why I was gone last night. Back inside, everyone. So far, you've escaped notice, but that will never last."

"But I promised Stewart." Ilona tried another tack. "You may not know this particular thing, and—"

"Go!" Meara raised one arm. A talon-tipped finger pointed at the barrier. "Not another word."

Elliott and Tairin hurried away.

"Come on," Jamal dropped a hand on Ilona's shoulder and pushed gently.

"Meet me in the same place we gathered last night," Meara called after Elliott and Tairin. "Half an hour or so." She turned her disquieting gaze on Jamal and Ilona. "Goes for you as well." The air around her shimmered, power crackling. When it cleared, she was gone.

Ilona made a grab for Jamal's hand and switched to telepathy. *"What do you think?"*

"We need to trust Meara, which means doing as she says."

"Could she possibly know about An—?" Ilona stumbled over not saying the first wolf shifter's name and started over. *"The problems with him?"*

"I wouldn't put it past her. She's very wise."

Jamal reverted to spoken speech. "How are you feeling about finding Aron?"

Ilona licked dry lips. Events were happening at such breakneck speed it was hard to keep up with them. "Grateful he's still alive. Worried sick he won't remain that way."

"He has youth on his side. And he's resourceful and very resilient magically."

"All that's true," Ilona agreed. "He's also bound with iron, which will mute his ability."

Jamal snorted. "Didn't mute it that much. He blew right past Elliott's blood casting which, by the way, was strong enough to anchor an elephant."

She smiled in spite of herself. "Thanks for trying to make me feel better."

"No thanks needed. I'm just stating what's true. We should get moving. It's not wise for the one who shall remain nameless to see us together. I need him to trust me."

"I know. Thank you for helping Elliott and me."

"Ilona." His liquid gaze captured hers. "I'd lay down my life to keep you from harm."

In one fluid motion, he angled his head and closed his mouth over hers. She fell headlong into the kiss, savoring the feel of his lips. It brought back memories of their passion from the night before, and her blood heated with wanting him.

He licked the seam between her lips, and she opened her mouth to his tongue, sparring with it. Reaching behind him, she closed her hands over his high, tight ass and pulled him against her. Sandwiched between them, his cock lengthened against her belly, and she squirmed against it.

Jamal tore his mouth from hers. "I'd like nothing better, but there's no time."

"Nor can we sneak into a group of shifters, who have noses like bloodhounds, and hope to escape detection."

"There is that." He cradled her head in a hand. "We will find a way to make this work. Do you believe that?"

"I want to believe it." Driven by a need for honesty, she kept talking. "But there's so much rocky ground between where we are and a future together, I'm taking it slow. If I get in too deep and something bad happens—something that means we can't ever be together—both of us have to find the will to keep going."

"You're wise as well as beautiful, but I'm not letting love escape me a second time. No matter what it takes, I will tackle every single roadblock —and find a way around it."

She tilted her chin upward. "Because you have to win?"

"No. Because I want you. More than I've ever wanted anything, and I won't rest until we have a life together."

"What was it you said a while back?"

"Which thing?"

"The one about it being our duty to do everything we can to fight the Nazis."

He smiled sadly. "I haven't forgotten, but I'm not putting my feelings for you on hold until this war ends. It will be years. I don't need scrying ability to know that."

He leaned close, breathing words near her ear. "This current wrinkle won't last long. Once we've dispatched it, we can go back to attacking the Nazi problem."

"How can you know the…wrinkle will be

short-lived?"

"Because my kind won't tolerate double-dealing. Even the ones who agreed with his message won't once they know the truth." He drew her alongside him and they walked back into the encampment, separating as soon as they came to the corral.

Ilona wanted to stay by his side, but understood the wisdom of not rubbing salt into not-yet-healed wounds. She stopped by Trina's wagon to check on Marguerite.

"How is she?"

"Better, I think," Trina whispered back. "Let's let her sleep. I understand we're supposed to gather again. I hope they'll excuse me from anything that takes me away from Mother for longer than a few hours."

"I'm sure they will. Or they'll find someone else to watch over her. Want to walk with me?"

Trina joined her, and they made their way to the front of the wagons. Once there, they sat with other Romani, who chatted among themselves. Unlike last night, the fire pit hadn't been kindled.

Meara strode to the Rom group, stopping near Stewart. "Ready?"

"Never readier." He moved to her side.

"If you need me, I'm here," Michael said.

Ilona narrowed her eyes to slits. Something was up. What was it? Last night, Meara had stood with the bear and wolf firsts. The Rom caravan leaders had kept to themselves. Meara's question presumed she and Stewart had discussed their next moves.

Trina leaned close. "Even I picked up on something. Do you have any idea what's about to happen?"

Ilona was grateful she didn't have to lie. "Not a clue. But I bet we're going to find out."

Meara raised both hands. "Attention, everyone. We have serious business before us."

Nivkh ran lightly to her.

Anubis stalked to where she stood. "What's this about? Why wasn't I consulted before you called this gathering?"

Nivkh prodded him. "For once in your life, get over yourself."

Ilona smothered a satisfied smile. Apparently, Anubis had never been well respected among the other first shifters. It was bound to make whatever unfolded next interesting. When Jamal had mentioned the bad blood between Anubis and Meara, she hadn't thought to ask if it extended to the other first shifters.

When you cut to the heart of things, she had

no idea how many firsts there were—or how many varieties of shifters beyond the ones represented here.

Lots of questions. Hope I get a chance to find answers.

"Look." Trina nudged her.

Ilona's skin tingled, and her heart beat faster. All the shifters were on their feet, and magic jetted from them forming a whirling vortex.

CHAPTER 14

Jamal surged to his feet along with the other wolf shifters present. All around the circle, shifters readied themselves—and their magic. A dizzying cascade of power whirled through the air, making it crackle with potential—and risk.

"We must help our first," a wolf shouted.

"Why?" another yelled. "He's not under attack."

"Not what he just told me," the wolf who'd spoken first countered.

Jamal moved fast, spinning until he faced the forty or so wolf shifters. "Stay back. I outrank all of you by dint of age," he cried.

"So? Move out of my way," the wolf who'd

announced Anubis needed help said and doubled up a fist. Jamal caught it one-handed before the man landed a punch.

"Calm your bondmate." Jamal bypassed the man, speaking to his wolf.

"I'm trying. He's out of control."

"Remind him we do not attack one another."

From behind him, Meara's harsh, strident voice carried. "Look well, shifters and Romani. Anubis is not what he appears."

A roar rose from the crowd and the swirling energy intensified.

"See," the wolf who'd tried to hit Jamal screeched. "She maligns our first. It's just as Anubis said. She's out to discredit not just him, but every wolf shifter."

"Not true!" Jamal thundered.

Meara and Stewart joined in a guttural chant that chilled Jamal to his bones. He wanted to watch, but he couldn't risk turning around and taking his eyes off the wolf shifter who'd challenged him.

A collective gasp pounded his ears, and the other wolves edged forward. Jamal watched the man he'd faced off against. His pupils dilated, and his breathing grew shallow. He fisted both hands but didn't direct them at Jamal.

"Tell me what you see," Jamal demanded.

"I— I'm not sure."

Jamal took a chance and turned his back on his adversary. The other man might jump him, but he was young, untried, and it wouldn't be much of a contest. Besides, he sounded more stunned than angry.

Shifters ringed Anubis, Meara, Stewart, and Nivkh. Anubis's form slithered, growing insubstantial around the edges before solidifying again. He raised a fist, punching the air, and shouted in Coptic.

"Respect me! I am the first wolf shifter. Stop trying to force me from my body."

"Nice try," Meara retorted in German. A wave of brown and green magic flowed from her and Stewart, washing over Anubis's robed form. The cowl fell back from his head and his face, already striking, took on the unearthly beauty only vampires possessed.

"We seek your true form." Nivkh bit off each word, stopping after each one for emphasis. "What you pretend to be affronts not just our natural laws but every shifter who walks the earth."

A muffled shriek from behind Jamal spun him back around.

"Help us," the man's wolf bondmate pleaded.

The wolf shifter was on his knees, gripping the sides of his head and howling in agony. Blood dripped from his eyes and ears. Pity for the young shifter filled Jamal, and he marshaled power to see what he faced. Mesh wound around the other man, magical netting that drew tighter by the minute. Once it was visible, Jamal sliced through the spell wrapped so tightly about the other shifter that it cut off his air.

Jamal knelt next to the man, whose eyes had rolled upward in their sockets showing white all around. He gnashed his teeth, and foamy spittle flew from his clenched jaws.

Gripping his shoulders, Jamal shook him hard enough to get his attention. "Fight back, man. Build a ward."

"Dark. Everything is dark," the man moaned.

"I've got this," the man's wolf cut in. *"I'm coming out."*

Jamal didn't wait. He shot magical darts to clip the remaining strands of the net. The shifter would be vulnerable in between forms. He might die trapped between wolf and man. Time slowed to a crawl as Jamal snipped strands, and the mesh first parted and then fell to the ground.

Clothing ripped and a dark gray wolf

emerged, gasping and panting as if it had just run miles. *"Thanks,"* the wolf nudged Jamal's hands still settled on its shoulders.

"I broke the spell," Jamal told it. *"You should be fine now."*

"I know. My bondmate was terrified."

"How'd you shift?" Jamal asked.

The wolf's jaws lolled. *"Told him if we were going to die, we needed my form to fight back. He was so grateful I wasn't going to abandon him, he summoned shift magic."*

"Quick thinking." Jamal stroked the wolf's rough outercoat. *"You saved your bondmate."*

"No. You did." Snarling, the wolf jerked its muzzle toward the press of bodies between them and whatever was playing out in the middle of the circle. *"What happened to Anubis? Even though I can't see through all those people, I sense that he's not a wolf anymore. He smells wrong, evil.*

"What is he?" the wolf persisted.

"Vampire." Jamal's wolf spat the word. *"We need to get up there."*

"Go," the other wolf urged. *"We're fine now. We'll join you very soon."*

Jamal bounded upright and worked his way through the tight press of bodies. Some had shifted, but most were still human. Light flashed from the center of the circle, but he couldn't see anything. Not yet. Horrified cries pushed him to move faster. He drew magic to force his way past shifters who shouted angrily.

At least he'd called this one right. There might be competition among different types of shifters, but they stuck together when confronted by anything outside their particular brand of magic. That dynamic explained the antagonism between shifters and every other type of magic-wielder. Beyond that, Meara was more than just another first shifter. She was close to a god in their circles. Mother to all the varieties of bird shifter, she may have been the very first of them.

Panting and sweating from effort, Jamal finally broke through to where he could see what was going on.

Stewart, Meara, and Nivkh stood shoulder to shoulder with Meara in the middle. The sand-baked smells of Egyptian earth joined the cool, ocean-washed scent of the northlands. Anubis had dropped any pretense of being the first wolf shifter—or more likely, the others had forced an end to his charade.

What stood in his stead was pure vampire, elongated fangs and all. Jamal sucked in a hasty breath. How could they be so beautiful and brandish such evil?

"I'll be on my way now." Anubis—or whatever his name was—sneered. "You haven't seen the last of me. I was here long enough to know what you plan. I'll mobilize my brethren. If I were you, I'd think again about attacking one of our nests—or waging war on our Nazi chums."

"Chums is it?" Nivkh roared. "No wonder you've been absent for centuries. Had you spent much time around another first, we'd have seen right through you."

Anubis shrugged. The motion made his silken robe ripple around his perfect form. "You weren't all that quick on the uptake, brother." His dark gaze burned with barely suppressed censure.

Fury battered Jamal. He dug through his jacket pockets and closed his hand around one of the silver stakes from their last vampire skirmish. He'd ended up with it after Elliott's near brush with death. Luck—or the goddess or something he didn't have a name for—made certain he hadn't put it away.

Masking his movements with magic, he stole around behind Anubis. Stewart saw him, and perhaps intuited what he was about, because when Nivkh stopped peppering Anubis with commentary, Stewart picked up the banner, baiting the arrogant creature.

Jamal clutched the spike and judged his distance. He wouldn't get a second chance. Anubis, or the vampire, or whatever the fuck stood there, possessed more than enough magic to flatten him.

"We can do this," the wolf spoke up. *"Told you he'd make a mistake."*

"His only error so far has been conceit."

"Let's see if we can't change that."

Jamal focused the entirety of his attention on the vampire's silk-clad back, judging where to strike. He cut the flow of his magic, not wanting any stray thread of power to alert Anubis to the death stalking him.

The distance between them shortened from fifty feet to thirty to twenty. When he passed the ten-foot mark, Jamal launched himself at Anubis. The vampire started to turn at the last moment, but he was too late. Jamal buried the silver stake in his back, sliding it through ribs right into his heart. The weight of his body drove the vampire to the ground.

Nivkh raced forward. So did Meara and Stewart. All three laid hands on the writhing vampire and shot pure, clean deathblows into it.

They wouldn't have been enough by themselves, but coupled with Jamal's silver stake, they hastened the vampire's death.

Noxious gas joined with black ichor spewing from the ancient creature, stinking of dead things left too long beneath a hot sun.

"Watch it!" Meara pinched a large, black beetle crawling out of the dying mass of protoplasm and ground it between thumb and forefinger.

Jamal rocked back on his heels. After what had happened to Elliott, he recognized those bugs. They were the dying vampire's last-ditch effort to reestablish itself in another body. He moved back a foot or two. So did the others.

Smoke rose from the remains, and tissue sloughed from the corpse as the thing's true age asserted itself.

"Nice work." Meara cast an approving glance Jamal's way.

Ilona raced out of the throng of people and threw herself into his arms, heedless of the ichor staining his clothing. "Thank the goddess—all of them and the gods too—that you're unharmed. Once I realized what you were doing, I was frantic to get to you. I threw my magic ahead, urged it to hold your stake in place. But I was scared for you."

He held her close. "It happened too fast for me to be scared. My wolf said we'd win. Told me Anubis would make a mistake—"

"How did you know about Anubis?" Nivkh rounded on Meara. "And why didn't you tell me before this morning?"

She angled her head to one side in a typically avian gesture. "I didn't return until just before we spoke today."

The bear shifter leveled his ice blue gaze on her. "How did you know?"

"I saw it when Elliott, Ilona, and I were locating vampire nests last night. While my Rom helpers were pinpointing locations, I eavesdropped on vampire conversations."

"Which would explain why you left right after we got back," Ilona said.

"It would." Meara nodded sharply. If she'd had a beak, she'd have clacked it shut.

"You returned to the nest and did more sleuthing?" Nivkh furled blond brows.

"Indeed I did."

It didn't explain why Stewart was part of the greeting party to take Anubis down, but maybe this was enough information for one morning. Jamal let go of Ilona and walked to the Celtic caravan leader.

He held out a hand. "Thanks for keeping him busy. How'd you know what I was about?"

Stewart winked. "I sensed the silver, lad. How'd ye come by it on such short notice?"

"Sloppy housekeeping. It was still in my clothing from our last vampire battle."

Stewart eyed Ilona with mock severity. "Women like a neat house, but do not drum that out of him."

She grinned. "Don't worry."

Tairin and Elliott joined the group milling about. Cadr and Vreis strode to Stewart, their faces stamped with grim satisfaction. Elliott slugged Jamal's shoulder. "Excellent demonstration of vampire destruction techniques. We should build on it so long as you kicked that door open—and everyone is here."

"All my shifters are exceptional warriors. Practical too." Meara purred her approval.

"Maybe the others." Elliott waved a dismissive hand. "Being a warrior doesn't come naturally, and I was practical when I was just a garden variety Rom."

Meara eyed him with asperity. "Give yourself time. You'll warm to your shifter magic."

"I already have. On a more serious note, I

counted twelve in that nest we located. Did you discover more when you returned later?"

Meara nodded. "At least fifteen. So we'll need about forty-five of us to take them out."

"Last time we used five man groups," Tairin protested.

"True enough," Meara agreed, "but we're stronger now—and wiser. We only need three. Besides, it will be hard to cover the territory between here and there without drawing undue attention."

"We can shift." Elliott looked pleased with himself.

"Oh my but you're green." Nivkh crossed his arms over his broad chest.

"I'm not sure I catch your meaning." Elliott bristled. "The shifter part of me might be naïve, but the Romani part isn't."

"Think about it," Nivkh said. "A herd or pride or pack or flock of fifty animals is damn hard to hide. Particularly bears. We're supposed to be asleep this time of year, not running through the countryside."

"More than a dozen or so birds would draw attention as well," Meara agreed. "Not in the spring, but now they'd look out of place."

"What do ye have in mind?" Stewart asked, his dark eyes gleaming with something untamed.

Meara strode to the pile of bones, all that was left of Anubis. She bent and extracted the silver stake, handing it to Jamal. He wiped it on a clump of gorse grass and dropped it back into his jacket pocket. Stinking smoke still rose from the ruin. Chanting a few words, she flicked her fingers and flames ran the length of the pile of bones. The fire smelled clean after the reek of rot.

Once her fire had taken hold, she turned to Stewart. "Make certain we have fourteen more stakes. Amulet bags would be helpful too. Pick fifteen Romani, one for each vampire. I will select thirty shifters. Once we have our people, we'll divide into groups and practice for the remainder of today and perhaps tomorrow.

"When we're confident we're as good as we can get, we'll set a path for Berlin. Rather than going right for the nest, though, I believe we should raid Sachsenhausen-Oranienburg first. It's close enough, it should draw the vampires away from their nesting ground. It may well be easier to kill them that way." She hesitated long enough to draw breath. "They'll spread out coming after us, which gives us an advantage over storming their nest."

"Ambitious." Nivkh whistled long and low.

"May as well aim high," Meara countered.

Jamal bent his head close to Ilona's ear. "Would you like to volunteer? You don't have to, but I should go. I've faced vampires before, and I'm not afraid of them."

She gripped his hand. "If you're going, I'm coming too."

"Excellent." Elliott walked over to them. "I heard that. Tairin and I will be part of the mission too."

Meara focused her discerning gaze their way. "Looks as if we have three shifters and one Romani."

"Three Romani." Michael stood straight. "Stewart and I will be there."

"Us too." Cadr jerked his chin at Vreis.

"Aye." Vreis grinned, but it wasn't a warm expression. "Wouldna miss it for the world. I hate those unnatural bastards."

Meara clasped her hands in front of her. "Nivkh and I will be part of this as well, so he and I will locate twenty-five more shifters."

"And we'll come up with ten more Rom," Stewart said. "Meet back here in an hour."

Meara's magic-driven fire was burning itself out as the crowd began to disperse. Trina hurried to Ilona, fanning herself. "Oh my goodness. Wait until I tell Mother. She'll be sorry she missed all the excitement. It's like tales she's spun about her wild girlhood in the Middle East before she moved to Germany." Trina was still chattering to herself as she strode back toward her wagon.

"We have a little time." Jamal tucked his hand beneath Ilona's elbow. "Want to get away from everyone for a little bit?"

"Away from everyone is it?" Tairin closed from one side. Her eyes shone with approval and happiness. "If you two are a couple, let me be the first to offer my congratulations."

"I'm second." Elliott smiled broadly.

The dark gray wolf from earlier loped to Jamal and nosed his hand. *"I can't thank you enough for saving my bondmate."*

"No thanks needed," Jamal replied. *"I'm glad I was there."*

"Me too." The wolf nodded enthusiastically. *"We're going to hunt. Anyone want to join us?"*

Elliott looked at Tairin. "What do you think?"

"My wolf thinks it's a grand idea."

Elliott dropped a hand on the wolf's head. Not bothering with telepathy, he said, "We'll meet you on the southern side of this mesa just outside the barrier. There's a weak spot right past the corral. Make sure you don't spook the horses."

"See you there. I'll be careful." Tail pluming, the wolf took off at a lope.

"What'd you do to save his bondmate?" Tairin asked.

Jamal drew his brows into a thick line, low on his forehead. "That shifter is young. Anubis, or the vampire, sensed he was weak and tried to coopt him. When I intervened, ordered the shifter to refuse, the vampire grew angry and sent magic to kill the wolf shifter. Its human part was so terrified, it was powerless, but the wolf asked me for help."

"Thank the goddess for our animals," Tairin said.

"Mine glommed onto the hunting suggestion," Elliott said. "Let's go."

Jamal watched them race away.

"If you want to join them, it's all right," Ilona said. "I understand. Or I think I do."

"We'd rather be with you." Jamal slipped an arm around her and started walking toward the perimeter of the encampment.

"Is that true?" Ilona asked his wolf.

"Most definitely," the wolf replied.

Jamal smiled. "Didn't believe me, huh?"

"You might have had a difference of opinion."

"We sometimes do, but not over something as important as my future mate."

"Is that what I am?" Spots of color bloomed high on her cheeks.

"I hope so." He stopped at Michael's wagon and let go of Ilona long enough to snap up the blankets he'd laid next to it hours before.

"On a more serious note, I had a thought."

"Dangerous waters." He set a path for where he hoped they wouldn't be disturbed for a little while.

"My vision, the tarnished one, happened in Sachsenhausen-Oranienburg. Maybe it validates Meara's suggestion of us targeting the prison camp rather than the actual nest. Might be an omen that we'll have clear sailing disrupting the prison."

"It's a good thought." He spread the blankets on a dry, sandy patch of earth beneath a leafless elm tree.

"Looks perfect." She sank onto the blankets and stretched out her legs. The red marks had totally disappeared from her shoes. Ilona pointed. "That's just creepy and not much bothers me."

"You mean the red being gone?" When she nodded, Jamal went on. "Stewart said the magic powering visions like the one you had was different. If the only fallout is shoes that change color—"

"Yeah," she cut in. "I got off cheap, huh?"

"Do you really want to talk?" He laid down next to her and held out his arms.

Instead of answering, she lay next to him, folded her arms around his back, and angled her face for a kiss.

Savage protectiveness raced through him, and he cradled the woman pressed against him. He'd make certain nothing harmed her. Not now, not ever. He brushed his thumb over her full lower lip, delighting in her nearness.

"You can't protect me like that."

He smiled crookedly. "You were in my head."

"Always. Until I run out of magic."

"I like the sound of always. And I will protect you, Ilona. Whether you want me to or not. My wolf will too. What's between us may be new, but you're ours now."

Her expressive gray eyes grew soft and dreamy. "This does seem right. It sounds hokey, but it feels like I've been waiting my whole life for you."

Joy streamed from her, and he lapped it up. "It feels right because it is. Let me love you, darling. This might be the last privacy we have for days."

She snaked a hand between their bodies and cupped his erection. "How can I refuse an invitation like this?" She tightened her grip, and he groaned as sensation shot through him. Someday, they'd have time and privacy for elegant. Right now, urgency trumped everything.

He rucked up her skirts and curved a hand around her vulva. She undid the buttons on his trousers. By the time he knelt above her, her legs were open, body spread before him, waiting.

Jamal plunged deep. Heat closed around him, and he savored the exquisite feeling of being surrounded by her warmth. He let himself down atop her, feeling the firm points of her breasts press into his chest. Just before he closed his mouth over hers and need drove him to thrust hard and fast, he said, "I love you, Ilona."

"I love you too." She locked her legs around his hips. "Now move, goddammit. Before I change my mind."

"Vixen."

"Only for you."

Her words were sweet, and they ran through him like a mantra as he brought her to orgasm. For the briefest moment, he thought he might be able to ride out the crest of her passion so they could keep on fucking, but his balls tightened and semen juddered from him.

She snugged her muscles around him, heightening his pleasure as she ground her body against his. Mouth still locked against hers, cock still deep in her body, he held her close, treasuring their connection.

"We need you back here now." Meara's voice blasted into his mind.

Ilona laughed. "Even I heard that. Playtime's over, huh?"

"Apparently so."

"I suppose we're lucky she didn't hunt us down."

Jamal disentangled arms, legs, and let himself slip from Ilona's body. "She'd only have interrupted us in person if something dire happened."

Ilona sat up and ran fingers through her tousled hair. "You know her pretty well?"

"Let's just say that I've spent more time with her than with Anubis over the years. Ready?"

Ilona nodded. Color was high on her face, and she was so lovely it tugged at Jamal's heart. He stood and then extended a hand to help her up. "I'll leave the blankets here. Maybe we'll get lucky and have another break before we leave for Berlin."

"I'll keep my fingers crossed." She bit her lower lip. "Maybe we shouldn't return together. Particularly since we both smell like sex."

"Maybe so, although you made our relationship pretty clear when you threw yourself into my arms after I killed the vampire."

The color across her cheekbones deepened. "Uh yeah. Guess I did. Okay." She extended a hand. "If you're game to flaunt us to the world, I am too."

"Not just game. Proud. You're an amazing woman, Ilona. How could I be anything but proud to have you by my side?"

"Hush. You'll spoil me."

"That's the idea."

He took her hand and walked back to where they'd find the others.

CHAPTER 15

Magic hammered Ilona from both sides. Her head throbbed, and she was so tired her hands ached from channeling power. She held fast, though, focused on doing her part as she, Jamal, and Gregor, another wolf shifter, grappled with Meara, who pretended to be their vampire adversary. Meara and Nivkh were taking turns circulating among the fifteen groups.

No one was worried about killing SS and camp guards. No need to practice for that, but vampires were a daunting adversary.

Ilona had no idea how the other groups were finessing the job, but she and Gregor immobilized the vampire so Jamal could stake it.

They'd practiced scenarios from every imaginable angle as the first shifters challenged them. Their initial attempts had been fumbling, and the mock vampire declared victory more often than not, but this past hour they'd begun to click as a team.

They'd been at it for a while. So long, night had fallen hours ago.

"Got you!" Jamal howled his triumph.

Meara feinted to the side before bowing low. "Indeed you did." The vulture shifter drew her lips back from her teeth in a show of approval.

"Can't go into this anything other than running wide open." Gregor, a powerfully built Hungarian with black hair and hazel eyes dropped his hands onto his knees, sucking air. He was swarthy like Michael, and thickset through the shoulders.

"Glad you figured that out," Meara muttered. "You may well face more than one vampire, though, so take care not to run your magic dry."

"What if we have to help one of the other groups?" Jamal asked. "It happened last time, and it's a likely enough scenario we need to plan for it."

"We will," Meara said. "We're done for tonight, though. Get supper and a decent night's rest. If practice goes as well tomorrow, we'll leave tomorrow evening. I figure it will take a week to reach our destination."

Gregor straightened. "We won't be in our animal forms. That's fifty miles a day."

Meara looked askance at him. "You won't be shifted, true enough. I plan to fly. The other birds here will too. It's by far the safest means of travel."

"How many birds are there?" Ilona asked.

"Eight."

"All right, so we have to transport thirty-seven of us," Jamal said. "Horses and wagons are out of the question. We could squeeze into eight or nine cars. Fewer if some of us rode motorcycles."

"We'll work all that out before we leave," Meara said. "Speaking of cars, you never asked, but yours is at the very tail end of a passable road on the north side of this hill." Reaching into a pocket, she tossed him a set of keys. "Good night."

Ilona watched her walk briskly into the darkness. "She's amazing. You're lucky to have her. Once long ago, if the old tales are true, we had powerful Romani to lead us, but our magic has waned."

"You're strong for a Romani." Gregor's

comment held a grudging edge. He nodded and started to walk away.

"Would you like to have supper with us?" Ilona called after him. They were a team, after all, and it didn't seem right not to share provisions.

Gregor turned and raked his hands through his hair. His astute hazel gaze settled first on her, and then on Jamal. "You two are a couple, eh?"

Jamal stalked toward him. "Watch what you say. She will be my wife. My mate."

"It's not our way."

Ilona hurried to where they stood. "If you'd rather be reassigned—" she began, feeling uncertain.

"No need for that. I can fight next to you, but we're not going to break bread or become friends." He moved his attention to Jamal. "We mate with other shifters for a reason. So our blood doesn't grow diluted. You heard her." He pointed at Ilona. "Rom magic is on the decline."

"Not because we married outside the blood," she cut in. Defensiveness for her people ran hot, and uncertainty ceded to growing anger.

Gregor transferred his extended finger to Jamal, thumping his chest. "Why do you want feeble children? What does your wolf say about all this?"

"I'm not going to dignify either of those questions with a reply. Leaving now is a good idea," Jamal growled. Tension spiked from him until Ilona feared he'd shift and leap on the other shifter.

"It was what I was doing when the Romani asked about dinner."

"I was being polite," Ilona hissed. "A skill that you lack."

"Would you rather I lied?" he countered. "Manners have nothing to do with this. I don't believe in mixed matings. Nothing either of you can say will change that. And it's not just me. Very few shifters here would bless such a union. Many would be unwilling to work side by side with you. Jamal may not want to admit that, but he knows. He lived among us for centuries. Long enough to understand our laws and customs."

Heated words sat just on the inside of her throat, but Ilona held them back. They had to work with this man—or another shifter who'd likely hold the same views. She ground her teeth together while Gregor stalked into the night.

"I'm sorry." Jamal's voice was low, edgy.

"What are you sorry about?" She circled until she faced him.

"He was rude to you. Insolent."

Ilona drew in a deep breath. "No. He was rude to both of us, but he was also correct. He's not the only one who feels that way. Hell, if we polled the Romani here, they'd mostly have the same reaction. Meara may have decreed that we're allies, but old conceptions and beliefs will take time to fade."

"A very long time." Jamal drew her against him and cradled her head against his chest. "I'd hoped since we face a bigger enemy than our own bigotry and in-fighting, our people would be more willing to open their minds. Particularly in light of Anubis's deception."

"It will happen." She wriggled out of his embrace. Jamal was still furious, and it would be wise for them to do something other than standing there stewing. "Let's find dinner. It must be past midnight."

He laced his fingers with hers and they walked toward Tairin and Elliott's wagon. It was a good choice, since Trina and her mother had probably retired long since. Ilona wanted to soothe Jamal, but lies had never come easy to her. If they managed to survive the Nazis, their next hurdle would be finding an enclave where they'd be welcome.

Most caravans wouldn't want them—if

caravans even existed when the war was over. From Gregor's words, it appeared shifters were just as close-minded as Romani. They had more to protect, though, because their magic was stronger.

An unpleasant tingling twitched at the edges of her magical senses. At first, she thought it was because she was tired from hours of practice. The faint discordance pricked harder, and she stopped walking.

"Did you feel that?"

Jamal's features looked like an angry thundercloud, and fury still sheeted from him. "Feel what? Sorry. I'm afraid I'm buried in resentment about what an ass Gregor was."

"Would you like me to talk with his wolf?" the wolf spoke up.

Ilona's heart melted. *"It's kind of you to offer, but probably better not to."*

"Why not?" the wolf asked.

"Because we don't want Gregor to feel like any of us are ganging up on him. The wolf is his best friend, just as you're Jamal's. Even if it believes Gregor is wrong, you approaching it will place it in an awkward position."

"I'm willing to chance it, but I won't proceed

without permission. Let me know if you change your mind."

"I will."

Jamal tightened his fingers, still intertwined with hers. "Wise counsel. I'd probably have sicced my wolf on his."

Ilona rolled her eyes. "We need to get along with Gregor, not antagonize him." She flinched as the same malevolence she'd felt before plucked the periphery of her power. "Do you feel that?"

"No. Not directly, anyway." The air around him brightened as he sent power spiraling around them, no doubt seeking what she'd reacted to. Jamal frowned. "I don't feel anything out of the ordinary, but then the barrier has its own hum that obliterates a whole lot."

"Yes, I hear it. Kind of like a low-key buzz that's always there. This is different. Much higher frequency, and I feel it more here." She wrapped an arm around her middle.

"Do you sense it now?"

Ilona closed her eyes. The impression of wrongness had been subtle, barely there but annoying. Now she couldn't feel it at all. "No." She shrugged. "I'm probably imagining things. I'm tired and hungry. It can alter perception."

Jamal wove an arm around her. "Be sure to let

me know if whatever it is returns. Meantime, we're almost to the wagon." His nostrils twitched. "I smell food. Rabbit and greens."

"Guess they had a successful hunt earlier." Ilona's stomach cramped from hunger. That had to be it. She'd imagined the pricking sensation because she'd blown through gobs of magic and her energy levels were failing.

They climbed into the wagon, fragrant with the smells of dinner, and Tairin handed her a bowl and a chunk of flatbread.

"Thanks." Ilona settled with her back against a wall and dug in.

"I can shift and hunt if I need to. Are you sure there's enough?" Jamal asked before taking the bowl Tairin held out to him.

"Yes. Elliott and I have eaten. We finished practice maybe three quarters of an hour ago."

Jamal dug in before he'd even sat down. "Say, did you sense anything strange or out of the ordinary in the past few minutes?" he asked around a mouthful of the rabbit and wild onion stew.

Tairin drew her brows together. "No, but now that you mention it, Elliott thought he did. That's why he's not here. He went to the edge of the barrier to check on things."

"He went, and now he's back," Elliott called softly from outside and let himself into the wagon, pulling the door shut behind him.

"Did you find anything?" Tairin asked.

Elliott shook his head. "Must've been my imagination. All was well where the barrier is thin, and I didn't sense anything amiss betwixt here and there."

"Well, it wasn't just you," Tairin went on. "Father asked if I'd sensed anything weird."

Elliott crawled over to a pallet in the corner and sat with his knees drawn up. "What'd you think it was?" he asked Jamal.

"It was me." Ilona placed her empty bowl on the floor next to her. "I felt an intrusion. It wasn't blatant. More like an unpleasant, prickly sensation that activated my magical center." She rolled her eyes. "After today's practice, I'm surprised I have any magic left to detect anything."

"Know what you mean." Elliott rolled his shoulder blades to the accompaniment of cracking joints. "Is there any of that sweet tea left?"

"Yes. Anyone else want some?" Tairin twisted behind her and pulled a large, metal teapot front and center.

"Me." Jamal grinned.

"I'd love some," Ilona said, "but make sure Elliott has as much as he wants first."

"Eh, we can always make another pot," Elliott said and passed a mug to Tairin. "The thing that sent me outside didn't feel quite like what you described. More like something that didn't belong there waiting outside the barrier. It didn't feel like vampire, though, and it was a long way away."

"Do you still feel it?" Ilona asked and accepted a mug from Tairin. Maybe it was a Romani thing. Elliott might be a shifter now, but his predominant magic was still Rom. Tairin's blood was mixed, but she definitely led with her shifter side.

"No. It was brief and now it's gone. You?"

"Mine went away before we got here, and it hasn't returned." Ilona shrugged. "I've kind of chalked it up to being wiped out and running so much magic through my body."

"Could have been it," Elliott agreed.

They drank their tea in silence after that. Ilona's eyes started to close, and she shook herself back awake. "Thanks again for feeding us. We'll get out of your wagon so you can sleep."

"What are families for?" Tairin smiled.

"I hope I can return the favor someday, daughter." Jamal made his way across the wagon and unlatched the door, waiting for Ilona.

She let herself outside, joining him. "Want to go back to where we left the blankets?" she asked.

"We could, or I could retrieve them and we could lay them out beneath Michael's wagon. Probably a better bet if it rains."

Ilona glanced upward at a dark sky shot with stars. A slip of a moon flirted with the horizon. "No rain tonight. I say we chance it. We can always move if I'm wrong."

"Sure you'll be comfortable so far from everyone?"

"Yeah. I've pretty much decided whatever I sensed wasn't really there. Come on." She extended a hand and he clasped it, warming her chilled fingers. "It was kind of Tairin to share their meal with us. She's an amazing woman. From what she told me, it was her suggestion to approach me—once all of you knew I was hiding in that little cleared area."

"It was her idea, yes. And I'm proud of the person Tairin grew into. Long ago, she and her wolf turned a desperate situation to their advantage. She took a huge gamble, though."

Curiosity sparked. "What was that? I don't

know much about being a shifter."

"Egypt wasn't a kind place for young, unmarried women, so she took to her wolf form. It solved many problems and kept her safe from being robbed, raped, or even murdered."

"But isn't that what shifters do?" Ilona felt confused.

"Yes, but not like that. The human form is always primary. She remained a wolf for a hundred years. That's very dangerous. After so long, she was damned lucky she could even find her human body. A caravan stumbled upon her naked and unable to talk because she couldn't remember how. They took her in, nursed her back to health. I'll be forever grateful to them."

"What aren't you saying?"

"Tairin forgave me for abandoning her. I'm still working out how to forgive myself, but I'm closer than I was when she located me to ask for help with the vampire nest."

"Good. She wouldn't want you to censure yourself. She's not vindictive."

"You don't know her. She was on fire with anger when she showed up outside the shelter where I'd sequestered myself. I didn't blame her."

"Well, she's not angry now."

Ilona slipped between the elm's generous

branches and tucked herself into the blankets. They were damp on the outside from the night's chill, but moisture hadn't penetrated their dense weave.

Jamal joined her, gathering her into a heartfelt embrace. She hugged him back. No matter the reception they received from shifters like Gregor and Rom who hated shifters just as much, she'd made her choice.

"Thanks for being you and opening your heart to me," she murmured.

"Ilona, *liebchen*. The path we've chosen won't be an easy one, but we'll pick our battles. Gregor wasn't one of them. You were wise enough to see that."

"Or maybe I'm a coward at heart and hate confrontations. Doesn't matter." She moved upward and closed her mouth over his.

He kissed her back, and dizzying heat enveloped her. Somewhere in the depths of their lovemaking, she clung to him, crying his name and wishing the night would never, ever end.

THE SAME SILVER clouds from before surrounded her. Her first instinct was to struggle, cut the magic powering her trance, but she forced it aside. The goddess had information, things she needed to know. It was how these involuntary visions worked.

Ach, how the hell would I know that? I've only ever had one of them. Every other vision state resulted from my efforts.

Her breath came faster, and sweat dribbled down her sides. She reached for Jamal, but he wasn't here. Which meant she'd left the plane where they'd fallen asleep, wrapped in each other's arms.

Was her body here—or still back with Jamal? She suspected the latter and vowed to find out more, assuming she returned in one piece.

Same as before, she floated through a cloud forest. The cloud to her right quivered, and a bright red swastika formed, followed by dozens carved into every cloud as far as she could see. In synchrony, they all began to first ooze and then drip blood. Horror clotted her throat until breathing became a struggle. She tried to tell herself the liquid—that had moved from drips to torrents—wasn't blood, but the sharp, metallic stench was unmistakable. The clouds took on a garish, red cast, eerie in the half-light of this place.

It cost her, but she sucked in steadying

breaths. One. Another. Another. When she thought she could do something other than shriek and curl into a helpless ball of terror, she extended her hands, palms upward.

"Goddess. Tell me what you wish me to know."

It was a common enough request when she viewed competing images in a pool or glass. Would it work here?

The medium she floated in exploded, showering her with slivers of something that burned and bit harshly. She wiped blood out of her eyes and off her face as she fell. Just like last time, she touched down easily and looked around. Unlike last time, she was by herself. No Rom. No shifters. Just her.

Another prison camp surrounded her. She must be invisible because guards and prisoners trudged by on either side. Ilona reached for the place her magic dwelt, relieved to find it intact. She started to summon power to move herself back to the world she'd left—or try to—when malignant magic speared her.

Ducking behind a barracks that stank of urine and death, she sheathed her magic fast. The wickedness had vampire stamped all over it. Shit! Were they everywhere? Or did they just lurk in the prison camps where they could feed off misery and blood?

Had the vampire sensed something when she attempted to activate her magic? Worse, did that mean she was stuck here?

Crap! Is there some link between the thing I sensed before dinner and me ending up here? Her head whirled as unknowns piled atop other unknowns into a dizzying mélange that threatened to swamp her.

Come on, she urged, understanding if she didn't pull herself together, she'd be lost.

Think. I have to think. Got to take this one step at a time and solve what I can. Maybe if I can get outside the gates, then I can use magic to break the spell that has me in thrall.

I'm here for a reason, another voice chimed in.

She bit down hard to steady teeth that wanted to chatter. She *was* here for a reason, but what?

Could this possibly be the camp where Aron was?

There weren't that many prison camps in Germany. Not yet, anyway. She looked around. This wasn't Dachau, but she hadn't spent enough time in Sachsenhausen-Oranienburg to get a feel for it.

Running on instincts that had rarely failed

her, she shrouded her telepathy in layers of spells, called her brother's name, and waited.

Minutes ticked past. Lots of them.

About the time she decided she'd read too many war novels with happy endings, a faint scratching tickled her third ear.

"Sissy?" The voice was hollow, faint, almost not there.

"Aron?"

"I told you not to come." This set of words slapped her hard.

The vampire must have noticed too because its foul reek moved closer.

She shut up fast and swathed herself deeper in invisibility. At least she knew why she was here, but she'd have to piece a hell of a lot together on the fly. Could she somehow leverage the same energy that had transported her all the way across Germany to move her brother out of the camp?

She had no idea how dream energy worked, how it had snared her, or how to activate it to move herself back. Last time, the trance had spit her out when it was done with her. Presumably, when she'd seen what she was supposed to.

Ilona concentrated on what she knew. It was easier, and if she lost herself in all the unknowns, she'd sink into despair. As she mentally ticked off plusses, including the unexpected depth of her magical well, she moved toward her brother's energy. Now that she knew he was here, she felt his presence like a beacon.

Maybe I don't have to solve everything right now.

Aron had power of his own. Obviously, not enough to escape, but maybe he was still shackled in iron. How she'd manage to break his fetters remained to be seen, but first she had to find him.

Ilona had never been a praying type, but she prayed now. To Isis. To Arianrhod. To every Celtic and Egyptian deity she remembered. Between prayers, she hoped Jamal wouldn't waken, sound the alarm, and put people at risk trying to find her. Time passed differently where she was, so differently it was possible no time at all had elapsed in the real world since she'd been snared by the trance.

Yeah, maybe if I returned right away, but that's not going to happen. I couldn't leave even if I wanted to.

Dreamer's corridors like the one she was on only showed themselves to Romani seers—at least according to the lore books. She'd always thought the corridors were myth, fabrication.

Until now.

Elliott relied on props to strengthen his ability, which probably meant he'd studied the lore books. Everything she'd read had been on the sly since women weren't allowed access.

Her chances of returning before her disappearance created apprehension were thin. Time might pass differently, but she had to first locate Aron, and then hammer out a way to free him. Presuming Elliott figured things out, which wouldn't be all that hard, he'd plunge headlong into seer magic, hot on her trail. Meara would force her way through too. She was powerful enough, it just might work even though she wasn't Romani…

Stay away, Ilona exhorted, her mind pedaling in tired circles. *Stay away. Remain safe. I'll solve this on my own.*

She'd continued moving toward Aron, and he was close. Just behind the wall to her right. Taking a chance, testing the magic that had her in thrall, Ilona pushed against the concrete cinderblocks and slithered through them as if they weren't a solid barrier. At least it answered one question. Her body was back in the other world. Maybe that meant her absence would escape detection.

And keep everyone she loved and valued safe.

CHAPTER 16

Ilona swallowed a horrified gasp. Aron lay on a dirt floor in a stinking pile of urine and shit stained rags. He was stick thin; sores covered his mostly naked body. She crouched next to him, and his eyes snapped open. The same gray as her own, they burned with fever.

It didn't take healing magic to know her brother hovered at death's gateway.

She wrapped her arms around him, but his body was real. Hers wasn't and her arms moved through him, much as her body had migrated through the cinderblock wall.

"Not really here," he muttered. "Must mean I'm dying. Seeing things."

Ilona started to reply in telepathy, but that was what had drawn the vampire earlier. She didn't have a body here. Did she have a voice?

No time like the present to find out.

"Part of me is here," she said, following it with, "Can you hear me?"

He nodded, his fever-glazed eyes growing rounder. "What manner of magic is this?"

"I don't exactly know." She assessed his ankles and wrists. "They removed your shackles."

A bitter laugh rumbled from his thin chest, followed by a long, racking cough. Aron flapped a hand down his body. "Probably recycled them for someone else. I'm not much of a threat. Hell, I can barely stand anymore."

Ilona remembered her crowded barracks in Dachau. "They put you here all by yourself?"

He drew a labored, noisy breath. "You should leave, and yeah I'm by myself. Made it convenient for the vampire before even he gave up on me."

"I'm not leaving without you."

A flash of her sarcastic little brother flickered across his gaunt features. "Your body isn't here. How do you plan to move me anywhere?" Twisting, he grabbed a bottle filled with murky, gray water and lifted it to his lips.

Ilona rocked back on her heels and glanced around the cell. Maybe six feet square, it didn't contain so much as a pile of straw. A single door was inset in the far wall. No doubt it was bolted from the other side. Two rats squealed in a corner, fighting over something. Another poked a whiskered snout through a hole at floor level, but the others must have convinced it not to join the squabble.

"How long since you've eaten?" Ilona asked.

He shrugged. "Don't know. Every once in a while someone drops food through the hole in the door. I used to be fast enough to get it before the rats did, but I gave up."

She reached hands toward his shoulders wanting to shake him, but dropped them to her sides. "You cannot give up. We can't let them win."

"Oh, Ilona." His eyes sheened with moisture. "I love you, sister, but can't you see? They already have. They know I'm dying. Even the vampire who used to show up to drink from me knows. Haven't seen him for a while. Go back to your life. One of us needs to survive."

He stopped short of saying it wouldn't be him.

She swallowed around a thick place in her

throat. She hadn't come this far to fail. The goddess—or some divine presence—had brought her here. Surely it wasn't only for her to have a deathbed conversation with her brother. A thought slapped her hard.

"You said a vampire drank from you. They do the same with the SS, but it makes them stronger. I know it's alien magic and has a putrid feel, but have you tried to leverage it?"

"Never even occurred to me." Aron shook his head. "I'm too weak to do anything. The time to do that would have been before bad water gave me the bloody flux."

"Look at me."

"Stop sounding like my big sister."

"It's what I am. So far, all you've told me is what won't work. We are going to figure out something that will. I can unlock your door with magic, but it won't do much good if you refuse to help yourself."

Aron pressed to a sitting position and raked his grime-crusted hands through long, greasy hair. "Even if you open the door," he said, "there's no way out of this place."

"Not as a normal human being," she agreed. "Let's take stock of your magic. Hunt for it. Experiment with what nascent power the vampire might have left in you. Try to weave it in with your ability." She softened her tone. "Take as much time as you need. It sounds like no one will bother us."

Hope flared painfully in Aron's eyes, and he straightened his bowed back. "You'd be right about that. I haven't seen anyone for at least a day. They're due to bring me more water, but they might decide even that's too much trouble."

Ilona focused on one of the two bickering rats and directed a beam of power. It shrieked its annoyance just before its body went rigid, quivering in death throes. The other rat ignored it, continuing to feed on nasty-looking strips of something unidentifiable.

Aron stared at the dying rodent, but he didn't need her to spell things out. He rolled to where he could grab the rat. Sinking his teeth into its neck, he drank from it before he stripped flesh from its bones, chewing and swallowing fast.

"God but that was disgusting." He looked up from the grisly pile of bones in his hands out of eyes that might have been to Hell and back.

"I know. I ate plenty of them after I escaped from Dachau. But you're already stronger, I feel it. Do you want the other one before you marshal your magic?"

Aron nodded.

Ilona waited while her brother ate and sorted through his magic. Time might pass differently in the world she'd left, but surely by now someone had discovered her absence. It didn't matter. What did was right here in front of her. Aron was stronger. She hadn't just said that to make him feel better.

For the first time since she'd entered his cell, she let herself believe they might have a chance.

~

JAMAL JOLTED awake with Meara cawing over him. It was still dark, but the horizon had developed a gray, pearlescent glow, so dawn wasn't far off. Ilona was still cradled in his arms. He held her closer and whispered, "Time to get up, darling."

"She's not here!" Meara said into his mind. Light flared, and she morphed into her human form.

"What do you mean she's not here?" Jamal demanded, his brain still fuzzy from being dragged from sleep.

Meara squatted next to him. "Her body is, but

her spirit ranges free. We must figure out where she's gone."

Jamal sent magic auguring into Ilona's boneless form. It wasn't that he didn't believe Meara, but he had to see for himself. Sure enough, the jagged bifurcation where her astral self had separated from the rest of her punched him in the guts. He levered his arm from beneath Ilona's shoulders and tucked blankets tenderly around her.

"How'd you know?" he demanded as he set his clothing to rights and stuffed his feet into socks and shoes.

"I felt her leave. How else?" Meara shrugged. "What worries me is she isn't back yet. If she's separated from her body for too long—" Her words cut off abruptly, as if she decided she'd said far too much.

"What happens then? Will she die?"

Meara nodded. "In a manner of speaking. She'll join the damned who rove the earth forever, unable to leave this plane for what comes next. The Rom use them as spirit guides."

Jamal bolted upright. "Let's go. Let's find her."

"Not that easy. I'm not Romani. I can't track her."

"Who can?" Jamal's guts twisted into a burning mass of snakes.

"Come with me. We'll raise Stewart. He has far more magic than Michael."

"How about Elliott? He's got the same seer magic as Ilona."

"Already thought of him. He'll meet us in Stewart's wagon." Meara took off running, and Jamal paced her.

"We have to find her," Jamal's wolf cried, followed by a long, mournful howl.

"Did you know she was gone?" Jamal demanded, ready to jump down his bondmate's throat.

"Of course not. I'd have alerted you. I was in the other place sharing information about Anubis with the bond animals." The wolf sounded injured.

"Sorry. I'm sorry."

"I understand. I'm frantic about her safety too. We waited long for her."

Stewart, Michael, and Elliott stood outside Stewart's wagon wearing grim expressions. Tairin was there too, looking equally worried. Vreis and Cadr arrived on a run at the same time as Jamal. Their dark hair was sleep-tousled and their blue eyes held an apprehensive cast.

"Do you suppose this is another of those tarnished prophecy things?" Jamal asked.

"I have no idea," Stewart said.

"I don't know what you're talking about," Meara said.

"Was she drawn into the dreamer's corridors involuntarily before?" Elliott demanded.

"Yes," Stewart and Michael said almost in unison.

"You have to say more," Meara made come along motions with one hand.

"There's no time," Jamal protested.

"We all have to understand what we face," Stewart said and focused his next words at Meara. "Romani seers can be drawn into an involuntary trance state using dreams as a vehicle. We call them dreamer's corridors. 'Tis a place your astral self goes, leaving your body behind. Ilona was led there before. 'Tis where she saw that Anubis wasn't what he appeared.

"Last night, she was snagged again. One of the gods or goddesses has likely determined they can use her considerable power to move their agendas forward. Problem is, dreaming time is over and she's not back yet."

"Which means what?" Jamal cut in.

"Either she's wrapped up in a project, or she's trapped and canna return," Cadr replied.

"We must go after her," Elliott said. "If she's

separated from her body for too long, she won't be able to find it again."

"Brother does that ever sound familiar," Tairin muttered.

Jamal eyed his daughter. If she'd managed to shift back to human after a hundred years, maybe things weren't as bleak for Ilona as everyone seemed to fear.

"How do we get there?" He looked around the group.

"I'm not thinking it's *we,*" Elliott said. "I can go. I actually have the feel of her blood, so I'm the logical one to follow her. I can likely raise the same spirit guides I used before."

"Vreis and I will accompany you," Cadr said. "We hold seer ability too."

"None of you are going without me." Jamal stomped in front of Elliott and stared at him.

"Ye're taking me," Stewart announced.

"And me," Meara said. "I've never traveled these paths, and I wish to know more about them."

"I—" Elliott choked and started again. "I'm not sure they're open to anyone but Romani."

"Which would leave you out since you're a shifter now," Jamal said acidly.

"Fine. If everyone is going, I'm not staying here," Tairin said firmly.

"I'm remaining here," Michael said. He narrowed his eyes. "There may be a sorting process along the corridors..."

Elliott turned to Tairin. "Please." His voice vibrated with entreaty. "Remain with Michael. One of the last times I dabbled with strong magic, I raised a demon. I'm not at all certain I won't open a gateway right into Hell."

"Won't happen," Stewart said. "I will guide this casting, but we are too many. Beyond that, odd numbers hold potential. Even numbers may well doom us."

"I'll stay behind," Tairin said. "I want Ilona back safe. Michael and I will lead the other Romani. We'll cast supportive magic to hold the gateway Stewart opens. Make it easy for you to return."

"Thank you." Elliott hugged her.

"I will remain here as well," Vreis said. "That trims your group to five."

"We must be on the far side of the barrier to do this," Stewart said. "Let's go." He took off at a fast clip.

"Get Nivkh to help you with that gateway," Meara instructed before racing after Stewart.

Jamal caught up and followed them past the corral and through the weak place in the barrier. The horses had grazed where they were down to earth and needed to be moved, but he couldn't worry about that now.

The five of them formed a rough circle near the base of a cliff. "Have ye ever done this afore?" Stewart asked Elliott.

"Yes. It wasn't easy, but the spirit guides make it possible."

"That's because ye had to force the magic. Apparently, it swept Ilona along with it."

"Why is that important?" Jamal asked.

"Because it means her magic will be intact. If she didn't call a spell, it wouldn't have drained her ability," Elliott replied.

"Ye must lead since ye said ye have blood markers and guides at the ready," Stewart told Elliott.

"I command both from when we hunted for her brother the other day." Elliott locked gazes with Stewart. "How will you guide if I'm leading?"

"Excellent question, lad. I will open myself. Ye four will latch onto my magic. Once we're all joined, I'll summon the spell to break us away from our physical bodies. It willna be comfortable. Once we're spirit, Elliott will push into the ether with us beside him."

"Will my magic work without my body?" Jamal asked.

"It does for me," Elliott said. "Or it did when I was Romani."

"For me as well," Cadr chimed in.

"We willna discover how any of this will play out until we punt the ball skyward. Ready?" Stewart's gaze darted around the circle.

Jamal blinked. Meara was back in bird form, and she clacked her beak once, sharply.

"Should I be a wolf?" he asked.

"The vulture is my primary form," Meara replied. *"Human is yours. Do not shift."*

"Enough talk. We begin," Stewart said. "Empty your minds. Link to my magic. Once we enter the corridors, this will go quickly. We must not make any mistakes, or we risk being trapped there as well."

Jamal narrowed his focus to Stewart's Celtic chant and latched his power to the Romani's. He knew the language, but this was an archaic form, and he only picked up one word in three. Hot, searing pain began in his feet and raked through him until he felt as if someone had taken a branding iron to his innards.

He forced himself to breathe through the agony that kept him anchored to his body. Once he stopped fighting the sensation, it dropped away abruptly and he floated in a gallery lined with silvery clouds. The others were ranged near him. He felt their distinctive energies. He wondered if he could talk, but everyone else was silent, and he didn't want to risk disturbing Elliott's concentration—or Stewart's casting.

He looked inward, peeling back layers until he found his wolf, grateful for its steadfast presence.

The clouds ruptured as if someone had gutted them. Rather than silver, they ran red. One by one, they dropped away and he fell in an awkward, gut-wrenching arc toward something he couldn't see.

No body, he reasoned. Without a body, falling wouldn't mean he'd end up a pile of broken bones at the bottom of wherever Elliott was leading them. The silver-red around him fragmented into nothingness. For such a violent action, it was absolutely silent, or maybe he needed his body to hear.

Perhaps this place was incompatible with sound waves.

Jamal took stock. He was still falling, but not as fast. Before he could deduce what that meant, he drew to an abrupt halt in the muddy dirt of what had to be a prison camp from the look and smell of it. Shoddily constructed buildings rose on either side of him. The stench of death and rot permeated everything, but it didn't quite mask the reek of vampire.

He reached for magic to make himself invisible, but stopped himself. No one could see any of them. Uniformed guards marched prisoners so close they walked through where he stood.

His vision felt odd, and he blinked to bring things into sharper focus. It worked. Elliott was ahead with Stewart and Cadr behind him, both moving quickly. Jamal rushed after them, surprised a walking motion worked absent his body. He sensed his limbs, but knew they were a long way from him. A sharp peck in the middle of his back told him Meara wanted him to hurry.

"Where are we?" he sent in shielded telepathy.

"Quiet." She pecked him again.

He flinched away from her pointed beak. How could he feel pain absent a body?

Same way I sense myself moving through space. None of that matters. The critical part is finding Ilona.

Could he risk a scan with his magic? It was intact. He'd already checked.

Shadowy figures streamed in front of Elliott. Must be the spirit guides he'd alluded to. The thing Ilona would turn into if they didn't locate her fast. Jamal clenched the hands he didn't have into fists. Why had Ilona been drawn to this place? Was it the same camp she'd been dragged to during her last tarnished vision?

Made sense. Vampires were here. They'd been there too, but maybe they were in every prison camp. Perfect place for them, given their obsession with death. The shadows in front of Elliott flowed into a concrete block building. Elliott disappeared right behind them.

Jamal followed him and Stewart through the wall. Solid cement, yet he walked through it as if it weren't even there. On the other side, Ilona knelt next to a skinny young man who looked like her. Must be her brother, which explained why she was here.

The filthy, stinking man stared at them. "Who are all of you? Never mind that. Get Ilona out of here. Something bad just happened. One minute she was talking with me, exhorting me to draw enough magic so we could both escape, and then she just checked out."

"How long ago did that happen?" Stewart demanded.

"A minute. Maybe two."

"Och aye. 'Twas the spirit guides. They recognized she'd overstayed her magic and claimed her."

Jamal moved to where Ilona knelt and tried to pull her against him, but his arms went right through her. Because neither of them was really here. "We can talk in here?"

"So long as no magic is expended, it's probably safe enough," Elliott muttered. "Damn it. This is my fault. I'm the one who brought the guides."

"Doesn't matter. We have to hurry. How can we move her out of here?"

"Blood calls to blood," Stewart said. "Lad."

"Yes. My name is Aron."

"Aron. Wrap your arms around your sister and do exactly what I tell you."

"Yes, sir. I'm not very strong, sir."

"We'll take care of that part," Elliott said, his voice harsh.

Cadr moved behind Aron and propped him up. "Let me help you, laddie."

"We'll have to be quick," Stewart warned. "Once I summon power, if any vampire is close—and I do sense them—they'll come running. Magic draws them like nothing else but blood."

"Looks like I'm the only one here with blood,"

Aron mumbled and knelt in front of Ilona, surrounding her with his arms. Cadr supported him from behind.

Her eyes were closed and her form slumped. Jamal wanted to wrap magic around her, spirit her to somewhere safe where the rift between body and spirit could heal, but Stewart was running this show. Competing priorities—never mind magic—could trap all of them.

Celtic flowed from Stewart, the purity of his words a counterpart to the death, rot, and wickedness pounding against them from every quadrant. Elliott moved in front of Ilona and Aron, arms extended, and joined Stewart's incantation. Cadr added his voice to their chant.

Sour, discordant energy sped toward them.

Vampires.

The tableau with Aron and Ilona at its center wavered becoming insubstantial.

"Get them out of here," Jamal cried. "I'll deal with the vampire. Do whatever you have to, but make sure Ilona gets to safety."

"Oh you will, will you, puny shifter?" The cell door clanged open and two vampires charged inside.

"My puny shifter will have help," the vulture cried. The words were garbled rolling from the bird's vocal chords, but Jamal didn't have time to think about that. Meara grew until she was twice her normal size. Surging forward, she buried her beak in one of the vampire's necks and wrapped long, sharp talons around the thing's neck and shoulders. It tried to bat her off, to sink elongated fangs pulsing with hunger into her, but she evaded its efforts. Magic boiled from her. Enough to make Jamal squint against the glare.

He dragged the silver stake out of his pocket with magic when his fingers refused to close over the weapon. How he could have it—and his clothes—absent his body made no sense, but he'd sort this whole, bizarre nightmare out later. He let the other vampire charge him, timing his strike to maximize the vampire's forward motion. When it leapt on him, he was ready and utilized magic to drive the stake into its chest. Ichor that reeked of the charnel pits of the damned rolled over him, but he kept magic focused on the stake, twisting it to make certain the thing would die. He might not have functioning fingers or hands, but magic was a fair substitute.

The vampire writhed, bellowing in death throes that Jamal hoped wouldn't bring ten more like it running. In the face of Meara's magic, no one would even notice his, so he threaded strands around the struggling vampire to muffle its cries.

"Dead enough," Meara said into his mind.

He glanced at her in time to see her extract an eyeball and crunch it down. She'd done that before. Must be a special vulture treat.

"Your body is here?"

"More than yours, but less than usual," she replied in her usual enigmatic fashion.

"I'm hoping you'll explain that later. Do you know how to get back?" He could figure it out, but no reason to if Meara had it nailed.

The vulture cawed raucously. *"Of course I do. Open your magic to me. And let go of that abomination. I don't plan to transport its sorry carcass anywhere."*

Jamal extracted his stake and directed a jot of magic to drop it back into his pocket. As handy has it had become, he'd never let it out of his sight again. Meara's power pounded against him, and he opened a channel for her to link to his magic. Before he could ask her anything else, the cinderblock walls fell away and he rolled onto the dirt in front of Stewart's wagon.

Jamal lurched upright. People—shifters and Romani—were packed into the small space all talking excitedly. Where was Ilona? Had Elliott and Stewart and Cadr gotten her back safely? How about her brother? He'd looked terribly ill. Jamal pushed power outward, seeking the woman he loved, but he couldn't find her. He wanted to ask the people gathered around, but wasn't certain how much of their journey he could disclose without invoking Stewart's or Meara's ire.

The air around Meara shimmered, flaring blue-white as she shifted. "Nice piece of work we did." She slapped him on the back.

"Never mind that. Where's Ilona?"

Meara narrowed her eyes and multi-hued light flowed around her. "Follow me."

Maybe it was her undeniable power, but the crowd parted before her and she led him to a protected spot between Michael and Stewart's wagons. Two Romani women worked over Aron, cleaning his wounds and pouring tea down him alternating with what smelled like boiled grains.

Ilona lay wrapped in the same blankets he'd tucked her into. Stewart, Elliott, Cadr, Vreis, and Tairin worked over her, their magic thick.

Jamal dropped to Ilona's side, and pulled her into his arms. "What's wrong?" he cried. "She's here, but I can't sense her."

"Lay her down," Meara said. "They carried her

body here from where you left her and pieced what they could back together, but much of her still walks the dreamer's corridors."

"Let him hold onto her," Stewart said. "It may well make the difference and draw her back to this world."

Jamal clutched her, stroking hair back from her forehead and crooning in Coptic mixed with German. He looked at the others over her head and wished he hadn't. None of them looked hopeful.

"How long before we know?" he asked.

"I doona have an answer for ye, lad, but I've never known one like this to return to the living." The lines marking Stewart's forehead deepened.

"This one will." Aron staggered into the clearing wrapped in a clean blanket. "I will not let my sister sacrifice herself for me."

"You're too ill." Tairin ran to him. "Go back to the women."

"They can cure me once we have Ilona back." He swayed on his feet, but his eyes burned with determination.

Jamal beckoned him forward. "I'd be honored to share magic with you. Help me find the woman we both love."

Aron's eyes widened as he staggered toward Jamal. "B-but you're a shifter."

"And you're Romani. Still willing to help me?"

The corners of Aron's mouth lifted in a grim smile. "You betcha. This isn't any odder than anything else today."

CHAPTER 17

Ilona drifted in black nothingness. She'd been kneeling next to Aron. He was much stronger after consuming the two rats she'd killed for him. And he was making progress sorting through the magic at his disposal. The vampires hadn't left much of their essence when they fed from him. Just enough to keep him alive, but their magic smoothed the way for his own ability to shine through. She'd never realized he inherited some of their mother's seer magic, but he'd explained he didn't want Valentin to exploit him.

She gritted her teeth against each other. Never mind she didn't have a body anymore. Aron had told her how relentlessly Valentin pursued him, his attentions escalating after their mother died. It had grown so bad, Aron took to sleeping in unexpected locations. Places Valentin couldn't find him. Because the caravan leader was basically lazy, he'd never expended the energy to locate Aron's various hiding places.

She rolled from side to side, restless in the ever-present dark. Powerful magic had dragged her from Aron's side, and that was the last she remembered. When she came to herself, she was floating in this void.

A tremor ran through her. She had to get back. Aron needed her. Jamal would be worried. So would Stewart and Elliott and Tairin and all the rest of them. Maybe they'd take some horrible risk to locate her. She could never allow that to happen.

No. She had to do something.

Ilona curved her body into a ball, wrapping her arms around her knees. At least her arms didn't cut through her knees, but what did that mean? If she was back in her body, nothing felt right.

Her mind bounced from topic to topic. Where was Aron? What happened to him? Was he able to escape the prison camp on his own?

Ha. Not very fucking likely.

What had pulled her from his side? It hadn't been vampires. She recognized their peculiar brand of power.

Ilona tried calling. Her voice bounced back at her, echoing crazily, but at least she could still talk.

My magic. How could I forget about it?

Feeling stupid and remiss, she reached for the place her power dwelt, relieved beyond words to find it intact.

"All right." She spoke out loud to steady her racing pulse. "Getting out of here should be simple enough."

Ilona tapped the rich vein of power, giving the command that should reunite her with her sleeping form, wrapped in Jamal's blankets.

Nothing happened.

She tried again, upping the ante on her magic. Maybe she was trapped behind some powerful blockade, not unlike the one back at the gypsy and shifter encampment.

Still nothing.

She stretched out her limbs, trying to grab hold of something, anything. Maybe the physical feel of something beyond her body would help anchor her.

I have to try harder. Maybe I got the wrong spell...

Time blitzed past. She should have been exhausted, breathing hard, but she couldn't seem to push herself out of the inertia dragging at her. Strands of something wet and sticky kept trying to trap her, but she tore away each filament that wrapped around her.

Those scared her worse than anything else did. Who was trying to wind her into a giant spider's web?

"Relax." A voice called from the blackness.

Panic twisted her guts into a knot. "Who are you?" she shouted.

"Doesn't matter," another deeper voice replied. "Let yourself go. Float. Still your mind."

"Soon you won't remember a thing." The first voice was back.

"Won't remember what? Where am I?" She felt anxious. Chest tight, throat constricted, and her voice sounded as if she were sleepwalking.

"Why the life you left," voice number two said. "Let it happen. It will anyway, and it's much more pleasant if you don't fight it."

"I don't want to forget my life." She tried to shout, but her voice came out a squeak.

"You will eventually. We're trying to help.

We'll come back later. Maybe by then, you'll have come to accept things."

"Never." She stuffed a hand into her mouth and bit on a knuckle, enjoying the pain. At least it meant she could still feel something.

Amid clucking, cooing, and other soothing noises, the voices retreated.

Ilona pulled herself through the blackness with a swimmer's stroke, hunting for the people who'd spoken to her. She'd find them and drum the truth out of them no matter what it took. She had plenty of magic to threaten them, maybe even kill them if she didn't like their answers.

After a while, she quit swimming. She wasn't tired, but she'd given up. She'd never find them; they were gone. Besides, it didn't matter. Nothing did. Where she was wasn't so bad...

"No!" she screamed, and this time her voice shattered around her.

"I can't grow complacent. Once I give up, I'm done for."

Determination kindled, and she reached for her magic again. It was still there. She visualized the encampment and willed herself to go there. And then she did it again. And again. And again.

Different spells.

Different magical mixes.

Nothing created so much as a flicker in the endless, undulating darkness.

Tears gathered, dampening her cheeks before they dropped into the void that surrounded her. Jamal. She'd finally found a man to love. Aron. She'd almost freed him.

Finally and almost. Not good enough.

I cannot give up. I will not give up.

Fire, heat, pain bloomed around one shoulder. She shrieked, twisted, batted at whatever had hurt her, but the pain dug deep, holding her in its clutches. Why was she under attack? Had the voices grown tired of tolerating her resistance?

She shrieked, followed by another. The pain moved. This time, her other shoulder caught fire. Why couldn't she feel her attacker with her hands? She reached in every direction, but her efforts cut through empty air.

Shit, aw shit. I'm losing my mind.

~

DESPERATION ROCKED JAMAL. He'd done everything he could think of, employed every magic both with Aron and on his own. Ilona's brother was weak, but to his credit, he'd kindled every last iota of magic at his disposal, working to draw his sister back from the dreamer's corridors.

Jamal locked gazes with Meara. "Please. I have to. No more choices."

Rabid determination blazed from the vulture shifter. "You have my permission. Even if it locks one of my bond animals in hell with her."

That was the risk. Jamal understood full well. He'd bite Ilona, infuse shifter essence into her, but then it was up to her. She'd have to shift. Something that was excruciatingly difficult here on earth might be impossible in some border world at the edges of infinity. If she failed to shift, the wolf who volunteered to bond with her would be lost as well.

He'd asked his wolf to troll for possibilities and hadn't bothered it since. The request was almost beyond the edge of reason, and he wouldn't blame any bond animal for refusing what might end up a death sentence.

"I found someone," the wolf said.

"Does it fully understand all the—"

"Yes. Why do you think I was gone so long? Do it now before there's no chance of success at all."

Jamal winced. The wolf had lobbied—and lobbied hard—to do this first, not at the tail end of many failed attempts to draw Ilona back. He let the shift magic take him, heedless of his clothes ripping.

Bending his head, Jamal bit one of Ilona's shoulders, letting the bond animal's essence flow through him. *"Thank you."*

"I shall do my best," the wolf assured him.

"I'm sure you will." Jamal transferred his powerful jaws to Ilona's other shoulder and completed the transformation ritual.

Elliott knelt next to Ilona, chanting over her. He'd barely managed to shift to escape vampire poison, and he'd been here. On Earth. Not imprisoned goddess only knew where.

"Come on, Ilona," Elliott urged in Coptic. "You can do this. Try. Reach for your wolf. Let it out."

Jamal let go of his hold on Ilona's shoulder. Her body hadn't flinched beneath his assault. What were the odds she could even hear Elliott?

I have to believe she'll find her way.

"Yes, you do," Meara said from behind him. "Find your primary form, and we shall help her from here with magic as best we can."

Jamal morphed back into his human body and

knelt over Ilona, holding her close. "Shift, darling. Let the wolf in you loose. It will find its way back to me and free you from purgatory."

Word of Ilona's plight had spread through the camp like wildfire. Shifters and Rom alike raised their voices in prayers and spells all aimed at drawing Ilona back to them. Magic eddied and pulsed around Jamal.

If times hadn't been so desperate, everyone working toward a common goal, heedless of who was Rom and who was a shifter, would have warmed him. It would have pleased Ilona too.

Jamal tried again, clutching Ilona's boneless form close. "Let the wolf out. Shift. Trust the magic. It will not fail you."

ILONA GRAPPLED with the thing she couldn't see. Her shoulders were on fire and she hurt so much, she felt nauseous. The fiery sensation had moved beyond her shoulders, and her body felt like it wanted to rip itself in half and spill her insides all over the inky black void.

"Let me out," a voice cried.

At first she thought it was the voices from

before. The ones that had suggested she'd be trapped here forever.

"Shift!" Command rang heavy in the word. *"I can save you, but you must believe in me."*

"But I'm not a shifter," she protested, wondering what kind of bizarre parallel universe she'd fallen into.

"You are now—if you let it happen. I told Jamal I'd do my damnedest to save you. Do not let him and his wolf down."

"Jamal? I— I don't understand. He's not here." Pain hazed her brain, making it hard to breathe, let alone think.

"Jamal isn't here," the voice agreed, *"but I am. I'm your bond animal. We don't know one another, and if you don't pull your head out of your ass and shift, we never will. If you don't have it in you to do this for you, do it for me. I'll be stuck here right along with you if you don't shift. I took a chance on you, Ilona Lovas. I did it because a good man loves you and thinks you're worth my sacrifice. Don't prove him wrong."*

Her heart thudded hard against her chest. Was that what the pain in her shoulders had been? A wolf biting her? Even if it were, that didn't explain the ripping, tearing agony pummeling her now. She closed her teeth over her lower lip until she tasted blood.

Jamal's words crashed over her.

"I'm sorry I can't offer you an opportunity to become a shifter—not without breaking one of our cardinal laws."

"Unless your life is in danger," the voice in her head added. *"This qualifies. Damn it, at least try to do this while the energy is hot. The first shift is always hard. The longer you wait, the less possible it will become."*

"You can hear my thoughts?" she ground out from between her gritted teeth.

"Of course. Reach for me. Let me out."

She'd curled into a tight ball to combat the excruciating sensations rolling through her. Maybe it wasn't possible to shift like that.

What am I thinking? Maybe this is some kind of trap. If I relax, the voices will swoop in and seal me away forever.

"Jamal's wolf told me you wanted to be a shifter. Did you lie to it and Jamal? If you did, and we're locked in this world between the worlds for all eternity, I will make what's left of your life a living hell. Do not test me, human. Shift. Do it now!"

She ground her fists into her eyes, trying to force form out of the blackness. It didn't work.

Was Jamal's wolf nasty to him? How about Meara's vulture? She snorted back a grim laugh. Meara was plenty unpleasant on her own.

No, she calls it like she sees it. Doesn't waste time sugarcoating anything.

The thing inside her was waiting. She felt its impatience and its growing desperation. The black void wasn't going anywhere. Apparently, neither was she. She'd tried every magical combination and permutation in her arsenal, but nothing had created the slightest flicker in the endless black.

"Tell me what to do."

A long, undulating howl ripped through her. *"Finally. Open your magical center as wide as you can and reach for me. I'll use it as a conduit. Once it's open, keep it that way. This will hurt. A lot. The first time is always the worst. It will take all your magic to hold a gateway for me to use—and all mine to make it through. If you get cold feet, sabotage our efforts, we won't have enough strength for another go."*

"Got it." Ilona unclenched her fists and spread her hands in front of her to maximize her casting. "Get ready. I'm opening myself now."

She dug deep, pouring magic through the reservoir that held her power. She didn't stop until she ran wide open. At first, she thought the wolf had exaggerated. If there were really a wolf inside her at all. Maybe she was hallucinating. Imagining someone had dropped out of nowhere to save her from the void. She was desperate to escape before her mind crumbled to nothing. Welcoming an imaginary savior wasn't beyond the pale.

"You have to believe." The wolf's voice was strained.

Of course. She knew that. Magic depended on believing in it, ceding control, and suspending a natural disbelief in what you couldn't see and smell and touch.

Ilona pictured a wolf in her mind's eye. The one that formed was dark gray with lighter gray markings. It was beautiful. She wanted it to be free.

"Perfect. I can do this. Hold steady."

Ilona sucked in a breath, holding it. Even though she girded herself, she wasn't ready for the excruciating pain that attacked her from all sides. Her head exploded. Spots danced before her eyes. Bones cracked, skin stretched and contracted at the same time. Shrieks rang around her, tortured cries that hurt her ears, but she couldn't shut down the agony emerging from her mouth.

She wanted to ask the wolf how much more, but didn't have the energy to do anything but hang on by her toenails. Or maybe she had claws by now. In a deep, secret part of herself, she wanted the wolf to be real. She truly wanted to be a shifter. Wanted their enhanced magic and her very own bond animal. It would make loving Jamal easier too, but he wanted her no matter what kind of magic she held.

His unconditional acceptance burned a path through her, and the pain began to ease.

"Is it done?" She tried to form words, couldn't, and repeated the question in telepathy. *"Is it done?"*

"Yes. You can't speak because you no longer have human vocal chords."

She moved her limbs to test the reality of a different body, arched a shorter spine. Elation raced through her like high voltage, and a series of triumphant howls filled the void.

"Easy," the wolf cautioned. *"That was only the first part. We still have to get out of here."*

"How do we do that?" She was so excited, she ran in circles, extended claws digging into the fabric of the void.

"Cede our shared consciousness to me. Meara wasn't certain of this, but according to our legends,

this place is only for Romani whose spirits have lost connection with their bodies."

"Go on." Her tongue lolled. She felt it drag out one side of her jaws.

"I will keep this simple. I'm going to envision the place I left everyone and use our shared magic to open a path. Once it's there, we will walk out of here."

"It can't be that easy."

"We won't know until we try. Picture Jamal. That will help."

Ilona sorted what belonged to her and what belonged to the wolf. It took a while because she wasn't used to sharing her mind. Once she'd shunted control to the wolf, she let Jamal's face rise before her. His beautiful tawny hair and haunting liquid eyes with their amber centers.

"Believe in us," the wolf reminded her.

A shiny path lined with pointed rocks unfolded before them. They hurt her pads, but she didn't whimper when the wolf loped along the glittering footpath. It appeared before them as they needed it, and she suspected it vanished behind them, but she didn't look back. Somehow, she deduced it wasn't permitted by this particular brand of magic.

Voices blasted out of nowhere, buffeting her from all sides.

"You cannot leave."

"Cannot leave."

"It's not permitted."

"You broke the rules. You're still Romani."

"No. She's not."

"She tricked us. Tricked us. Tricked us." The final word turned to a howling sibilance, and something grabbed her from one side.

Ilona couldn't see, but she closed her jaws around where she thought the attack came from. A bitter cry told her she'd hit gold even though it felt like she'd bitten through air.

"Never mind that," the wolf urged. *"Faster. We're almost there."*

They ran and ran. Her breath came fast as she panted, still not used to the wolf's body. The voices came and went. So did hands that slid through her fur. Finally, just when she'd decided the wolf's *almost there* estimate was so much hype, the black ceded to gray.

She blinked against the unexpected light, narrowing her eyes to slits. To her surprise, an eyelid she didn't possess as a human shielded her from some of the brightness. She was still running hard when the gray shattered and she dropped onto sandy earth in front of a gypsy wagon.

Thinking with her dual consciousness didn't come easy, and it took her a moment to recognize the wagon as Stewart's.

Jamal scooped her into a hug, digging his hands into her fur. "Ilona. Christ! I am so glad to see you. You're beautiful."

She wriggled in his embrace, licking his hands and face, but she didn't want to lose sight of the reason she was here.

"Thank you," she told her wolf. *"I probably don't fully understand the risks you took, but thanks for the boot in the ass."*

"You're welcome." The wolf sounded pleased with itself.

Stewart pushed in front of her, joined by Meara, Elliott, and Tairin all talking at once. Cadr and Vreis crowded close too.

"Silence." Stewart held up both hands and knelt next to her. "'Tis grateful I am that this worked. 'Twas far closer than I would have liked."

"You'll have to tell me more when I'm human again." She licked his hands and his chin.

"You have to let me through," a familiar voice shrilled. "She's my sister."

Aron.

With Jamal still hanging onto her, Ilona twisted in time to see her brother force his way through a crowd of gypsies and shifters. He stopped dead, staring at her, and then sent a jot of uncertain magic zinging toward her.

Jamal let go of her. "Go to him," he urged.

"It's me," Ilona said and padded to Aron. Her pads were sore from the magical path that had led out of the hellish void, but it was a small price, given she and her wolf were free.

"That's what my magic says." Aron rocked from foot to foot, looking ever so much better than when she'd been dragged from his side in the prison camp.

"Trust it. Magic never lies." She dropped onto her haunches, waiting.

Aron's features worked with emotion and he launched himself to where she sat, wrapping his arms around her. "Sissy. Aw, Jesus, Sissy. I was so worried about you. The women, they kept telling me not to fret, but you were gone a long time."

"How long?"

"Two days since I showed up here."

Shock boiled through her. She'd only thought a few hours had passed. She leaned into Aron, reassuring him with her touch and licking his face.

Jamal walked over to them and placed a hand on Aron's shoulder. "Thanks for all your help working with me to draw Ilona back from where she was lost. Looks like the women took good care of you."

Aron glanced up and grinned. "You're welcome, and they did. It was like having half a dozen mothers."

Ilona looked down her snout at her brother. *"My recollection was you weren't overly fond of having even one."*

"True enough, but that was only when she was telling me what to do." Aron rolled to his feet. "We'll talk more when you're back in your Sissy form."

"Indeed we will."

"What would you like to do?" Jamal asked her.

"What do you mean?"

"I could shift and we could hunt for a bit, or you could shift back to human."

"What do you want to do?" she asked her wolf.

"Why ask me?"

"You're the true hero here. You took a huge chance on me and then made sure I didn't blow it by not believing in the gift you offered."

"If it's truly my choice, let's hunt with Jamal's wolf."

"I heard that." Jamal grinned. "Give me a minute and I'll take off my clothes. I already ruined one set while we tried to rescue you. The folks here will get tired of offering me shirts and pants if all I do is shred them."

She tilted her chin. *"Can I watch?"*

"Sure, but you have to follow me to where you're the only one who can." He quirked a brow. "Got to give a fellow some privacy."

Meara dropped a hand onto her shoulder and Ilona twisted to meet her gaze. "Welcome to the pack, sister. You have half an hour to indulge your wolf, who was indeed a hero. Then I expect you back here. Nothing's changed, and we still have battle plans to craft."

"We hear and obey," Ilona's wolf spoke up.

Its formal tone surprised her. She had a whole lot to learn about who she was now. Maybe Elliott would help since he was in the same situation…

"Coming?" Jamal asked.

"Yes. Meet you on the far side of the barrier." She turned to Aron. *"I'm so happy you're safe."*

"No one's truly safe," he murmured, "but at least I'm still alive to do battle with those Nazi bastards."

"That's true for me too. Not much I could've done from where I was trapped."

"I want to hear more about that." He stroked her fur.

"And I want to hear what happened after you left Dachau."

"It's a deal." He smiled gamely.

With a final nuzzle to Aron's hands, she trotted after Jamal. Everything else could wait.

CHAPTER 18

A Few Minutes Before

Jamal watched the ball of gray light explode. Shifters and Rom had been holding it together with their combined magic, but it eluded their control. His heart shattered right along with it. Where was Ilona? Had the wolf even found her?

He thought he'd felt them moving closer, but their magic had imploded. Maybe he'd been wrong about sensing them at all. He raced into the center of the most powerful casting he'd ever been part of. The air still pounded, pulsing with magic that pricked his skin and made his bones feel like mush. Surrounded by crashing, pounding power, he felt her still and reached with everything in him. His magical well was low, but it didn't matter. The only thing that did was the woman he loved. Stewart and Meara flanked him, adding their magic to his and chanting furiously.

In a blaze of blinding light, Ilona burst from the center of the shimmery magic. Breath whooshed from him, and heat filled his chest with relief so profound it almost brought him to his knees. Her wolf was stunning. Dark gray with lighter gray markings, and her same turbulent gray eyes.

He threw himself to the ground and wrapped her in a tight embrace, still not believing their gamble had worked when every other approach failed. She was a shifter now. Just like him. She'd said she wanted it, but would she resent being forced into changing her magical identity?

Only time would tell.

Right now, his heart spilled over and cracked open from unbridled happiness. She was here, and she was still his, judging from her effusive tongue.

"All is well between Ilona and her wolf," his wolf reassured him.

Jamal didn't press for details. It didn't work that way. Conversation between the bond animals was private. It would be wrong for him to probe.

After the first rush of greetings, he'd suggested a hunt. She needed to get used to her bond animal's form, and that was one of the easiest ways. Surely her first shift had been excruciating, particularly at her age. He'd ask about it, but not right now. Now was a time to glory in their animals' sleekly muscled forms.

"Ha! Made it in time to see you strip," she said as she ran lightly to him.

"How do you know I didn't wait for you?" He smiled. Joy was very near the surface. It ran counter to his usually taciturn nature, but he didn't push it away. They'd earned these moments. He'd be a fool to throw them away in favor of caution.

"Even better." Her tail swished from side to side, and she locked her gray gaze on him. *"Hurry. Meara only gave us half an hour."*

Jamal unlaced stout boots and tossed his borrowed pants and shirt atop them. The shift magic took him, fluid and righter than it had ever felt because his mate stood by his side. She took off running and he gave chase, catching her tail in his teeth and giving it a swish.

"Do you know the best thing about this, other than having you back?" he asked.

She turned, flanks heaving, eyes shining. *"No. Tell me."*

"Everyone laid their differences aside. Rom worked next to shifter. Everyone gave getting you back everything they had."

"I didn't plan to have this conversation as wolves, but where exactly was I?"

"In the place between worlds where the Rom spirit guides live. They're Rom who got separated from their bodies for too long and couldn't find their way back."

"Aha. Those must have been the voices that told me I'd never leave."

"At least according to Stewart, if you'd been there much longer, you never would have. It's why Meara gave permission for me to bite you."

Breath plumed from Ilona's open mouth. *"It will take time for me to figure out how all this works, but how'd you come up with a bondmate for me on short notice?"*

"You could have asked me," her wolf joined the conversation.

"Okay, if I asked you the same question, what would you say?"

"That I'm a sucker for challenges."

"It was my wolf," Jamal said. *"It found a wolf*

willing to risk going after you."

Ilona bowed her head formally. *"Thank you."*

"You're most welcome," Jamal's wolf replied. *"We're wasting valuable time. Can we hunt now?"*

Whuffling laughter rose from Ilona. *"I've eaten plenty of mice and rats raw as a human."*

"They're far better when you're a wolf," her wolf informed her.

Jamal raised his snout, scenting the air. When he caught a whiff of nearby prey, he crept toward it. Ilona followed, staying downwind so the creatures wouldn't scatter.

When he got close, he executed a practiced leap and brought his front paws down on three mice who'd made the mistake of remaining right next to each other. Ilona sashayed close and snapped up two of them, crunching through small bones.

"Amazing," she said. *"Who'd have thought they'd taste so good? They're scrumptious, succulent."*

"Another wolf," Jamal made short work of his own mouse and deployed both nose and ears locating more game. Ilona had to be half-starved. She'd gone for days with nothing to eat.

HIS TIME SENSE as a wolf wasn't particularly

sharp, but he herded them back to where he'd left his clothes when he was certain they'd used up their allotted half hour.

"Look!" Ilona trotted to his pile of clothes. Someone had laid a skirt and tunic atop the heap along with a cream-colored wool sweater, stockings, and her shoes.

Jamal summoned shift magic and started to dress. "Guess someone didn't want you to have to walk back into the camp stark naked."

She milled around the clothing heap, nosing it, and whining.

"What's wrong?" Jamal knelt next to her to slip his stockings and boots back on.

The gray wolf hung its head. *"My wolf says shifting back won't be as bad, but it hurt when I shifted. A lot. Not saying I'm not going to find my body. I'm gearing up for it, but it's like sticking my hand into a flame."*

He wrapped his arms around her wolf form, stroking her rough outercoat. "It gets better. One of the problems was you were so old."

"Thanks."

He held her tighter. "Not what I meant, and you know it. Everyone's first shift is excruciating, but the pain doesn't last as long when you're twelve or thirteen. After a few transformations, you'll be able to walk through the change with no more discomfort than a mild, cramping sensation."

"My wolf says to turn things over to it."

He scratched behind her ears. "Do you believe it?"

"I do. I didn't when it first showed up in my mind. Figured it was one more manifestation of the voices that had been tormenting me."

"What made the difference?"

"I thought about you. And I had nothing to lose. I'd tried to get out of where I was with every spell at my disposal. None of them worked."

"Shift," he urged. "Don't think about it, just do it."

She paced away from him, panting from nervousness. The air developed a familiar shimmer, and Ilona stepped through. Her body was striking with full, high breasts, a flat stomach, and hips that flared to long, shapely legs. Jamal could have gazed at her forever, and his blood heated with desire.

Smiling, she threw herself into his arms and wound her arms around his back. "You were right. It wasn't all that bad this time. Much faster and not nearly as intense."

"I was right too," her wolf said, sounding

pleased as only a bond animal could.

"Thank you as well," Ilona told it.

She tilted her head back, eyes glittering with adoration. Her full lips were parted, and he wanted to kiss her, but they'd had their playtime. It wasn't fair to the rest of the group for them to take more time for themselves. Besides, if he kissed her, he wasn't at all sure he'd have the discipline to stop there.

"I know." She kissed him once. Fast. Sweet. Before he could crush his mouth down over hers for a more satisfactory connection, she squirmed out of his embrace and squatted next to the clothing pile, dressing hurriedly.

"Guess we're lucky it wasn't raining. Clothes do dry, but they're unpleasant to put on when they're wet." She straightened. "Catch me up. Aron looks like he'll make a full recovery."

"He will. Once the Rom women got hold of him, they dosed him with a decoction of herbs that cleared whatever infection was causing his fever. He's been eating like a horse, which isn't surprising. And he was determined to help me when I cast spell after spell, trying to lure you back. Those Romani spirit guides sure held on tight."

Ilona frowned. "That they did. It was like once

they had me, they owned me. They were furious when I found a way out of there. Or maybe they felt cheated because I wasn't Rom anymore, and it meant they had to let me leave. Back to Aron, though. A vampire was feeding off him. Will it have some kind of retroactive effect?"

"Stewart didn't think so. In a backhanded way, that might be the only reason Aron was still alive when you got there. Most of the vampire essence has faded, though. If you asked Aron, he might tell you he misses the added boost to his magic."

"Whew! Thank the goddess he'll be all right. When I got swept into the dream world again, I had no idea why—until I found him."

"If we hadn't followed you with those spirit guides in tow tracking your blood, you probably would have been fine."

She shook her head. "No. I couldn't figure out how to bring Aron back with me. I didn't have enough magic. We'd just gotten to the point of me deciding I needed to unlock the cell and shroud us with invisibility so we could get out of the prison camp when you showed up."

He gripped her hand, lacing his fingers with hers. The small action reinforced that she was really and truly back here with him. "As they say, all's well that ends well."

"Ah, but we're far from the endgame with all this." She chewed her lower lip. "Will I still have seer ability?"

"Probably. In truth I don't know, but Meara is a seer, and I've known other shifters with that particular magic. Elliott's prophetic magic remained after he became one of us."

"Good to know. Even if I lost that gift, Aron has psychic ability. He's untrained, but the potential is there. I suppose he inherited it from Mother, same as me."

They made their way to the central gathering area. Someone had kindled a fire in the pit and greetings flowed. Everyone wanted to hug Ilona or grasp her hand. He felt the suppressed emotion in her, saw it in the sheen of tears across her eyes.

Meara motioned them toward her, and Ilona said, "May I thank everyone?"

"Be quick about it," Meara replied, her manner abrupt but not unkind in vintage Meara style.

Ilona made her way around the circle, positioning herself so everyone could see her. "I want to thank all of you. Jamal told me how you laid aside your differences and gave unstintingly of your magic to bring me back among you. My wolf and I appreciate everything you did."

She took a breath before going on. "I was Romani for twenty-seven years. Now I'm a shifter. This will take time to sort out and get used to, but I will fight just as hard for you as you did for me. My wolf promises it will as well."

Cheers followed her as she made her way back to Jamal's side.

Even Meara offered an approving nod. She raised her hands, and the crowd fell silent. "These past days were excellent practice working together. Building on that teamwork, we'll storm Sachsenhausen-Oranienburg as originally planned."

Nivkh joined her. "We will spend what remains of today making certain our group assignments are sound. Assuming nothing untoward occurs, we will leave tonight. I connected with several bear shifters who own transport vehicles with covered flatbeds. They'll be waiting for us later today a few miles down the mountainside where there're decent roads."

"Questions?" Meara glanced around the crowd. When no one spoke up, she flapped both hands. "Get moving. Find your groups."

Jamal headed for where they'd practiced before. Ilona kept pace next to him. "Just so you're not surprised, Aron added himself to our group," Jamal said. "Not that we've had any time to prepare for staking vampires, but he found out about the raid on Sachsenhausen-Oranienburg, announced he was going, and made it most clear he'd either take your place or fight alongside you."

Ilona rolled her expressive eyes. "That would be Aron. He's always been strong-willed."

"Must run in the family." Jamal sent a pointed glance zinging her way and she laughed.

Gregor was waiting for them. He strode straight toward Ilona with purpose burning behind his eyes. Jamal inserted himself between them. "Watch yourself, man."

"Really?" Gregor skewered him with annoyed hazel eyes and pushed around him, holding out a hand. "Welcome to the pack, sister."

Ilona stared at his outstretched hand, but didn't make a move to grasp it. "That's the same thing Meara said to me."

Gregor nodded. "It's a standard greeting for new shifters." He dropped his arm to his side. "Look, Ilona, I'm sorry. I'd have offered my hand even if you were still Romani. I learned a lot about myself over the time you were gone. I was wrong. Many of the ways shifters—and Romani—have treated each other needs correcting. I can't do anything about anyone else, but I do have control over what I do. How about it?" He stuck out his hand again.

Ilona grasped it. "I'm sorry too."

"For what?" Gregor released her hand.

"I reacted, got angry. Didn't even try to understand."

"I'm here." Aron ran to them, breathing hard. "I want to practice. You guys have had a chance to blend your magic, but—"

"Whoa, youngster." Jamal ruffled his hair. "You're a pretty important cog in this wheel. We need your Rom magic to strengthen what we have."

Aron's gaunt face split into a brilliant smile, and he mock bowed. "At your service, sir shifter."

It was a great note to begin on, so Jamal mapped out their first drill.

NIGHT HAD FALLEN HOURS EARLIER. Jamal, Ilona, Gregor, and Aron were bunched into the back of one of the transport trucks along with two other groups of three. Cadr and Vreis were there, but Jamal didn't know the others. They had three amulets among them—only one for each group—but plenty of silver stakes. Although bumpy, the ride wasn't too uncomfortable since the rough, wooden truck bed was cushioned with stacks of blankets.

So far, no one had stopped them, and they'd passed through several gated checkpoints. Jamal suspected the driver, who was a bear shifter, had employed magic to confuse the guards. Either that, or he'd levied suggestion, which would have had the same effect.

The truck had pulled off the road a few minutes before. Trees grew thickly, providing at least some cover. According to the driver, they were about fifty miles north of Munich, which was better than he'd hoped they'd do. Jamal grabbed a stack of blankets and jumped down from the truck's high bed. Ilona followed him with Aron by her side.

Gregor shifted and melted into the woods, presumably to hunt. Everyone else bedded down in the truck.

Jamal had hoped for a few hours of privacy with Ilona, but he would never tell her brother to go away. He idolized his sister, and his delight at being reunited with her was apparent. Locating a tight grove of evergreens that shielded them from all sides, Jamal spread out the blankets. Aron snatched up one of them and started back the way they'd come.

"Hey!" Jamal called after him, keeping his voice soft. "Where are you going?"

Aron turned back long enough to flash a smile at Jamal. "I'm not that young. I understand plenty. If I'm too close, I'll put a crimp in things between you and Sissy."

"Don't be silly," Ilona began.

"I'm not. I won't be far. Don't worry, if the bogeyman comes for me, I'll squeal like a scalded cat." He waved jauntily before disappearing into the darkness.

"Do you think he'll be all right?" Jamal asked, not wanting to court danger for the young Rom, whose spirit was cheerful and infectious. No one remained gloomy for long when Aron was nearby.

Ilona nodded. "Yeah. He's resourceful. Besides, the driver said we'd be on the move in just a few hours. Four in the morning, wasn't it?"

She laid down on a blanket and held out her arms. Moonlight played over her dark hair and striking features, casting them in bas-relief. Ilona opened her arms. "Neither of us knows what the next few days will bring."

He lay next to her and enveloped her in a heartfelt embrace. She wove her outstretched arms around him. The feel of her pressed the length of his body was heady, intoxicating. Her wildflower scent rose, surrounding them with its alluring fragrance.

"Ilona, *liebchen*." He stroked hair back from her face and cradled her head in his hand. "I love you. You'll live a long time now that you're a shifter. Many human lifetimes for us to be together."

"I hope so." Her gray eyes softened with tenderness. "I— I love you too." A soft smile gathered at the corners of her mouth. "That makes twice I've told you, and so far I haven't choked on the words. I've never cared deeply for a man before."

"I'm honored."

Her full lips parted in clear invitation, and he settled his mouth over them. He wanted to be gentle, take things slow, but he'd almost lost her and the specter of how close a call they'd had made every moment with her precious. Made him want to devour her with kisses. Made him want to run away with her, take her where no one could ever harm her again.

For once, she wasn't in his head. Running might preserve their lives, but it would never happen. They'd fight alongside their people.

Her lips moved against his, rich with promise, and she opened her mouth, welcoming him. Jamal stopped thinking about anything beyond the magic and wonder of the woman next to him. He trailed kisses down her face and neck, licking the hollow in her throat. He'd seen her naked body today after she shifted, and an image of her high, full breasts with their brown, puckery nipples drove him to pull her tunic up so he could take them into his mouth.

She pressed into his kisses, capturing the back of his head in both hands as he moved from breast to breast. Her nipples grew long and hard as he laved them with his tongue, and his cock shot to attention. It was uncomfortable, bent at an odd angle inside his trousers, so he reached a hand to free himself. The slight touch of his fingers sent sensation cascading through him.

Ilona wrenched away from his mouth long enough to turn in a half circle so she could push his hand away from his ridged flesh, replacing it with her own. Heat circled his glans as she took him into her mouth, kissing and sucking.

He thrust against her touch, hips moving of their own accord, and pressed a hand beneath her skirts and between her legs. Slick heat met his questing fingers and he pushed them into the dark, magical place deep inside her. She tightened around his fingers and sucked harder on his cock.

His heart leapt into triple rhythm, thudding against his chest. A familiar tightening in his balls told him it was time to up the ante. If he didn't get inside her, he'd come in her mouth.

"Let go and turn over." His voice held a raspy edge, thick with wanting her.

She lifted her head, but didn't let go of him. "Turn over how?" she asked breathlessly.

"Up to you, but hurry. I have to be inside you."

She twisted out of his grasp and smiled much as he imagined one of the Sirens might just before flipping over and getting on her knees. Her rucked up skirts displayed the perfect globes of her ass. Between them, her sex gleamed in the moonlight, surrounded by dark spiky curls.

Jamal groaned and heaved forward, unable to resist. Wrapping a hand around himself, he guided his cock into the scorching heat of her body, shuddering as she closed around him. Fully encased, he reached forward and rubbed her distended nub.

Ilona arched her back and rocked against him. He withdrew and plumbed her, walking a fine edge. Too much more stimulation, and he'd be lost. Her nub swelled under his touch, stiffening still more. Ilona muffled a cry just before her body dissolved around him in a flood of heat and quivering muscles.

He rode it out and kept touching her, determined to bring her to a second peak before he gave in to his own need. She closed a hand over the one he stroked her with, altering his rhythm and cadence. So lost in lust, the world could have ended and he wouldn't have noticed, Jamal drove into her, and she met him stroke for stroke. Just when he didn't see how he could stave off his climax for even ten more seconds, she convulsed around his shaft, and he let himself go.

Semen pulsed from him in a climax so intense he wanted it to last forever, sure if it did he'd be transported to another world.

Breathing as if he'd just run a race, he let himself down atop her and rolled them onto their sides. "That was amazing, incredible. We could do this all night, but we should sleep."

She tightened her body around his cock still buried within her. "Thanks for being you."

"You and Elliott prove something," he said.

"What's that?" she asked, her voice sleepy.

"It hit me front and center when you said *thanks for being you.*"

"Sorry, I'm dead on my feet. You need to say more."

"It's pretty simple, really. You're the same person, whether you're a shifter or a Romani. Elliott too. Who we are transcends our magic. Makes the animosity between our people seem ridiculous."

Ilona snuggled closer. "I fell in love with a philosopher."

"And I fell in love with the most incredible woman ever. I'll shut up now, so we can both catch a few hours' rest."

"Make sure we're up in time."

"Promise."

Jamal tightened his hold on her. The next days would be hard, but he'd make certain nothing happened to Ilona or her brother. No matter what the cost.

"We'll make sure," his wolf spoke up. *"You never asked me formally, but I approve of her as your mate."*

"I already knew that."

"How?"

"You'd never have found her a bond animal of her own if you didn't already believe she was part of our pack."

The wolf whuffled softly, and its contentment lulled Jamal to sleep.

CHAPTER 19

Three Days Later
Half a Mile from Sachsenhausen-Oranienburg

Ilona was invisible, but she still felt exposed in the late morning light. Their groups were approaching the prison camp from different angles on foot, having left the trucks a mile or so back. They'd done the best they could to conceal the five large vehicles, and Ilona hoped to hell that they'd still be there when they were done. It would be a long walk home, otherwise.

A thought struck her. She didn't really have a home. Not anymore. The plan was to regroup behind the magical barrier with the gypsies and shifters who'd remained behind, but she had no idea if she'd ever see that place again.

My home is with Jamal now. And Aron.

They hadn't discussed it, not in so many words, but if things blew up on them, they'd remain together and find safety as best they could. Gregor would be more than welcome to throw his lot in with them—if he were so inclined.

Early this morning, the bird shifters had flown an aerial reconnaissance, which identified three gates. The birds hadn't seen any vampires when they overflew the facility, but that didn't meant they weren't there. They could have been masking their energy in one of the many buildings or regrouping in a nest somewhere nearby. Regardless, each group had at least one amulet and many silver stakes.

The rest of the journey from southern Germany had been nerve-wracking. Their luck from the first day hadn't held, and they'd been stopped multiple times. One stop turned into a bloody skirmish, and they'd killed all five guards. The confrontation provided opportunity, though. Their driver stole a uniform from a burly dead German. Things had grown easier after that since he'd taken the man's papers too and told the next checkpoint stops he was transporting prisoners to Sachsenhausen-Oranienburg.

A few guards had peeked into the back of the truck, but no one gave them any more grief after that. Everyone was on edge, though. Every single time the truck had rolled to a halt and they heard their driver barking answers, Ilona's stomach clenched into a hard, painful knot. When they'd finally met up with the other trucks in the middle of last night, everyone had similar stories to tell.

Their driver wasn't the only one sporting a purloined German uniform.

She wrenched her attention back to the present. This was more than a quick raid. If they were successful, every German solder inside the camp wouldn't live to see the moon rise, and the prisoners would walk free.

It was a bold plan, outlined by Meara, Nivkh, and Stewart in the wee small hours before dawn. Their logic made sense. It had been far harder to get here than anyone anticipated. So long as they were here, dealing out maximum damage was the only reasonable approach. They wouldn't be returning.

They'd move inside, strike fast and hard, and make a run for the trucks before anyone could raise an alarm. Stewart's first stop would be the communications building, and by now he'd probably already cut the phone and power lines.

Not that the German officers couldn't drive to secure reinforcements, but by the time they returned, it would be too late. The damage would be done, and the shifters and Romani long gone.

She hoped.

Jamal walked on one side of her, Aron the other. Gregor was in front, his gaze darting from side to side as he assessed danger. She felt his wolf hovering close to the surface.

As if thinking about Gregor's wolf drew her own, it said, *"Shift. I'm a better fighter than you."*

"It may come to that," she told it.

"If it does, don't wait too long. Remember, it takes time to fully shift, and we're vulnerable during the transition. Particularly to vampires. They can trap us between forms and kill us that way."

"Got it." Her mouth was dry and her hands clammy. She flexed her fingers to encourage the rest of her muscles to loosen.

"Look at that!" Gregor pointed at a small, side door that had just opened in the prison camp's outer wall. He darted forward, and the rest of them followed.

It wasn't one of the three main entrances Meara had sketched in the dirt for them, but it would do. Uniformed officers hustled an oblong box that looked heavy out the door and left it standing open. Who knew? Maybe there were other boxes inside, and they were returning to move them as well.

Gregor didn't hesitate. He bounded through the open door, gesturing for them to follow. Sure enough, the same SS were headed right toward the open door with another of the coffin-sized boxes suspended between them.

What the hell were they? In Dachau, the SS hadn't bothered with caskets for dead prisoners. And then it hit her. These must be for vampires. Maybe the prison included a woodworking shop.

How convenient.

Her inner voice was droll, but it took effort to mask her horror at how closely vampires were entwined with the Reich.

Ilona forced her attention away from the caskets and took in the prison camp. It didn't look much different from Dachau or Esterwegen, the place Aron had been. A quick intake of breath from her brother told her he remembered his imprisonment all too well. All the camps stank of urine and shit with a sickly-sweet overlay of death and rot.

Ilona swallowed a snort. Vampire heaven.

Kind of like turning pigs loose in a garbage dump. Were the rest of the groups inside? She scanned the sky. Meara overflying the camp was their sign to begin once everyone was in position. So far, the vulture wasn't there.

Prisoners plodded past on one side of them, herded by guards wielding bullwhips with rifles slung over their shoulders. No one cast a second glance their way, and Ilona breathed a little easier. The worrisome element that could sense them would be vampires, and at least so far Ilona hadn't picked up their rotten emanations.

More prisoners streamed by. One woman snapped her head up and stared right at Ilona. The black-haired woman had to be Rom. Ilona shook her head and risked telepathy. *"Say nothing. We're not here."*

The woman ignored Ilona's warning, broke out of line, and started toward them. A guard dragged her back, landing a blow across the backs of her legs with his whip. The woman shrieked and fell to her knees in the dirt crying. "The devils are here." She pointed. "Shifter devils. I tell you true. Shoot them before they drag us into Hell with them."

Gregor herded them forward, but the

woman's cries followed. "The shifters are moving. Don't let them get—"

The harsh reverberation from a pistol fired at short range battered Ilona. Outrage flooded her. They'd shot the poor woman to shut her up. She spun, wanting to flatten the guard with magic, but Jamal grabbed her arm and made a chopping motion with one hand.

"One less to feed," a guard muttered and walked away from the woman, who was bleeding in the dirt of the prison yard. "What the hell is a shifter? Do you know?"

"Eh, they go crazy in here," another guard said. "She was talking shit. We should just kill all of them and be done with it. Cheaper. Easier." He dusted his hands together.

The other guard punched him in the upper arm. "We don't get to make those kinds of decisions. We just work here."

"*Ja.* I remember." He grinned, displaying teeth discolored from chewing tobacco and prodded the small group of prisoners. They moved forward, keeping their eyes trained on the ground. No one made a move toward the woman whose shrieks had faded to dying gurgles.

Aron sidled up to her. *"I saw far worse in Esterwegen. Hell, Valentin wasn't any saint when it came to doing away with people who figured out what he was."*

"I know. I remember," she replied.

"There!" Gregor pointed above them where Meara's distinctive form winged a circular flight path to ensure all the groups saw her.

"We will remain together," Jamal cautioned. *"No one takes any side trips. We can't afford to dilute our energy hunting for anyone."*

Ilona nodded. So did Gregor and Jamal. Each group had an assigned sector of the prison camp. They were close to theirs, but not quite there yet. She hurried down a side alley with the others until the map she'd committed to memory jived with what spread before her.

"This will go fast," Gregor cautioned.

"It has to." Jamal nodded sharply. *"If we tarry, reinforcements will show up about the time our magic is fading."*

Vampires could slow them down a whole big bunch, but Ilona didn't bother to mention it. They all knew. According to information Stewart had obtained from goddess only knew where, the camp had roughly sixty resident guards, headed up by half a dozen SS. Those were their first priority. Many of the other workers were prisoners, who should welcome freedom.

"Well, lookie there." Gregor jerked his chin at three SS sauntering toward them. Two had cigars clamped between their teeth. *"I'll take the one on the right."*

"I've got the middle one," Ilona said. *"Aron and I."*

Jamal didn't bother calling his target.

Power boiled around them as they sent killing blows designed to stop the men's hearts. It came off splendidly. The three Nazis crumpled into the dirt without so much as a whimper. Surprised looks bloomed on their faces as they clutched their chests before they fell. If Stewart were correct, they'd just wiped out half the SS contingent assigned to this camp.

She felt the backwash from power being expended all around them, and her elation over killing the SS faded. All that magic was like waving a red flag in front of a bull if any vampires were within a five-mile radius.

Can't worry about that now.

Aron grabbed her arm and spun her around. Guards herded more prisoners. She focused on two of them. Aron's power was a great boost to her own. Maybe it always had been, but they'd never tested it before. Guards crumpled around them. After a brief volley of confused shouts, the prisoners rushed toward the nearest gate, jostling each other until some fell. Others hauled them upright, and the crowd moved on.

"Keep moving," Jamal urged. *"Things are going well."*

It was solid advice. The other fourteen shifter-Romani groups were dealing out similar damage, and pandemonium was quickly spreading through the camp. Shouts rang out, and the harsh *rat-a-tat* of weapon fire filled the air. The stench of gunpowder thickened. Two groups had been in charge of opening the gates in hopes some of the prisoners who weren't too downtrodden would take the opportunity and flee. It was working. They passed close to the front gate and saw a mass exodus.

Ilona silently wished them well. Many would be recaptured, but not all of them. This had gone far more smoothly than she'd dared hope. At least so far, no one had even challenged them—beyond the Romani woman who'd died.

Of course, they remained invisible, but still…

"Time to leave." Jamal wasn't bothering with telepathy anymore. No reason to amid the shouts, screams, and howls. If that weren't enough, gunfire still pounded all around them.

Ilona stopped worrying about vampires. If they were going to show up, they'd have been here by now. She turned in a full circle, raking the camp with her gaze. More than anything, she wanted to make certain the guard who'd shot the Romani woman was dead. The woman's only sin was she'd been indoctrinated to hate shifters, scarcely a mistake worth dying for.

"I vote for the door we came in," Gregor said. "It's out of the way, and we'll have a clear shot to make a run for the trucks."

"Good plan," Jamal agreed. "I don't see any guards still on their feet. Our work here is done."

Ilona and Aron joined them as they ran back the way they'd come, retracing their steps. She kept her eyes peeled for the guard, but didn't find him lying in any of the numerous pools of blood. Lots of other guards, and at least ten SS beyond the ones they'd killed, lay scattered like forgotten tin soldiers.

Thirteen plus SS was a good haul. She was savagely glad there'd been more of them than Stewart's intelligence indicated. Vindictiveness heartened her. She wanted every single Nazi bastard deader than dead. If she had her way, they'd have suffered a hell of a lot more.

"Ilona!" Aron's cry drew her up short. She'd been certain he was by her side, but his voice came from several feet away.

She spun. Her first instinct was to freeze, but a vampire had come out of nowhere and it was bearing down on Aron, a feral grin stamped on its perfect face.

Jamal and Gregor ran up on either side of her. "Looks like we get to do what we practiced for." Gregor sounded positively delighted.

A shiver tracked down Ilona's spine. Why had the vampire singled out Aron? It had to be because of the one who'd fed on him. Maybe the fuckers had some way of figuring out who'd be a good candidate for their next easy meal.

Jamal flashed the stake. "Let's do this. Before his buddies show up."

Ilona ground her teeth together. How true. There was never just one vampire. They traveled in packs. The vampire was closing on Aron, who stood rooted in place. After his first, frantic summons, his face had relaxed into an almost dreamy expression.

"Goddammit! That thing has him in thrall," she screamed.

"We need to take it down," Jamal shouted. "Once that's done, its spell will dissipate."

Fine. But it never should have nabbed Aron in the first place.

A rush of protectiveness almost blinded her with outrage and fury.

She and Gregor pelted toward the vampire, discarding their invisibility spells. The thing had to see them to react. If all it felt were magic, it'd likely ignore them in favor of the waiting meal. Aron twisted his head to one side, baring his neck, and she kicked herself for not recognizing how his time in Esterwegen had marked him.

"I don't think so," she screeched closing the distance between them and the vampire fast. Aron barely blinked as she raced past him arm in arm with Gregor. Jamal remained invisible, magic muted down to nothing, as he circled to get into position. He was behind the vampire now and running full out, stake extended.

Ilona willed him to strike fast and hard, killing the twisted creature who lived off rot and death.

The vampire focused eyes the color of fine emeralds on her, and his perfect lips parted in a seductive smile. "I like you. You have spirit. You also share the blood of my sacrifice. Should make things…interesting."

"Interesting how?" she countered. Jamal was almost there. Just in case, she pulled her dirk free, brandishing it in the vampire's face.

The thing laughed at her. "Really? Little

shifter bitch. That pathetic blade wouldn't harm a rabbit."

"True enough. It might not be terribly effective against someone as powerful as yourself." Gregor smiled as if he were having the most prosaic conversation with an acquaintance.

Obviously pleased by the flattery, the vampire's smile broadened. "You're clearly part of the group that's turned this whole place into the most delightful smorgasbord. Those Nazis are a bunch of stupid bastards. We appreciate them dead more than al—"

Jamal launched himself at the vampire, burying the stake in its heart with a force that drove it into the dirt. Ilona and Gregor raced forward, pulling magic like mad things to hold the vampire in place while the silver stake killed it.

Something closed on Ilona from the side, but she couldn't take her energy off the vampire. They'd almost won. Then they could grab Aron and leave.

"Stop!" Aron shrieked. "You're killing it." He threw himself on her back and began clawing her.

"I've got this," Gregor said. "Get your brother under control."

"We've got this," Jamal corrected. "He's almost

dead. Not a very powerful one. No bugs crawling out of him."

Ilona wrenched away from Aron, who was dragging his hands down her back and shoulders. She refocused her magic and saw the vampire's black-tinged spell throb around her brother. It was weakening since the vampire was in its death throes.

"Aron!" She made her voice stern. "Stop. This isn't you."

"He was kind," Aron protested, whining. His eyes held a dull, dead aspect. "Said he wouldn't drain me."

That did it. Ilona dug deep and doused her brother in a flood of purifying white light.

His gray eyes snapped open and came into focus fast. A horrified expression crossed his face. "Shit! Aw crap! It had me, didn't it?" Twisting, he ran to the downed vampire and kicked its face.

Jamal yanked the silver stake out and bolted to his feet. "We're done here. Let's go before any more of them show up."

Aron was still kicking the vampire. Tears and snot streaked his face as he cursed it.

Ilona stuffed her dirk back into its sheath and grabbed one of Aron's arms. Gregor took hold of the other. "Pull yourself together right now,"

Ilona hissed. "Time to go. We can sort this out later—and make sure it never happens again."

With Jamal behind them, they ran for the gateway. "Make yourselves invisible," Jamal called. "Lots of ground to cover outside the camp."

It was a good reminder. Ilona summoned power and draped it over herself and her brother.

"I can do my own," he muttered. "I'm enough of a failure today."

Her heart went out to him. "Wasn't your fault," she said. "Just something about vampires we didn't understand—until now."

She'd wondered why they hadn't bothered to show up. Surely, they'd sensed the camp was under attack. The vampire's words came back to her. *Those Nazis are a bunch of stupid bastards. We appreciate them dead more than alive.* Even though the vampire hadn't gotten the last word out, it didn't matter. And it explained a whole lot. Maybe the vampires would end up unlikely allies after all and help drive the Reich into Hell.

Yeah, right. Talk about wishful thinking...

They passed through the same doorway they'd used to enter the camp and ran. The streets were clotted with prisoners who'd escaped. She mentally urged them to get farther away while they had a chance. They stuck out like sore thumbs in their striped prison garb. What she didn't see were other shifters or Romani from their groups. Or sense any of their magic. Had the others left the camp that much ahead of them?

Guess we'll find out soon enough.

The town's roads gave way to forested track. They rounded a familiar corner only to find all the trucks gone.

"Aw double shit! This is my fault," Aron groaned.

"No one's fault. We did what we had to. We'll figure something out." Jamal dropped an arm across Aron's shoulders.

No reason to waste magic on invisibility or telepathy, so she released her spell. Much like the escaped prisoners, they needed to put distance between themselves and the camp they'd liberated. She was about to suggest moving on quickly when the hunting cry of a vulture raked across her ears.

"Follow me," Meara called and flew slowly away from them.

"Where do you suppose we're going?" Ilona asked Jamal.

"Probably a shifter den," he replied. "They're

all over, so maybe there's one close by. I was getting ready to search once we discovered the trucks left without us."

"Naw," Gregor spoke up. "I bet she's leading us back to the trucks."

"What's a shifter den?" Aron asked, not sounding quite so downtrodden.

Keeping an arm firmly around him, Jamal launched into an explanation, and Ilona could have hugged him for being so kind to her brother.

CHAPTER 20

Jamal kept an eye on Meara's winged form. She flew slowly enough for them to plot a trajectory and follow her through the trail-less forest. Aron trotted next to him, not looking quite as devastated as he'd been earlier. "You doing okay?" Jamal asked.

"Yeah. I had no idea I was so vulnerable to vampire coercion." He shook his head, and dark hair tumbled into his eyes. "One minute I noticed it, and the next I was baring my neck for its fangs. Christ! I hate them. How could I just lay myself out like a trussed goose?"

"They must have marked you somehow," Ilona said from where she loped on Aron's other side.

"Can you unmark me?" Aron turned his head toward his sister.

"Probably. I need to confer with Stewart. If there's some way to eradicate vampire tracings, it might be in the lore books."

"Meara and Nivkh might know as well," Gregor said. "This forest makes me feel safe, but I'm sure we're not. Anyone have any idea where we are?"

Jamal used magic to take some bearings. Meara was leading them northwest rather than south. Where were they going?

"This isn't the right way," Gregor muttered, as if he'd read Jamal's thoughts. Maybe he had.

"It's not the way we came," Jamal agreed. "I'm sure Meara has something in mind. She's not one to move forward without good reason."

"Probably so. I'm still reeling from Anubis being a sham." Breath hissed from between Gregor's teeth, steamy in the chill air. "That man was like a god to me."

"He was to all of us," Jamal broke in. "I haven't let myself think about his loss."

"Probably a good strategy. It's not as if we don't have other problems that are far more pressing."

"Look!" Aron jutted his chin skyward. "She's circling. Probably means she's going to land."

Jamal aimed for a point in the center of Meara's aerial circles. It turned out to be a cleared area at the end of a rutted road. Meara shifted midair in a blaze of light and was human when she touched down.

"Glad I located you," she said. "You were the last ones out. What kept you?"

"Vampire," Jamal said, skimping on the details for now. "Where are we headed?"

She eyed him with asperity. "Figured you'd know we weren't moving south. One of the trucks will be here soon enough. They can't travel as fast by road as we could overland."

"What happens once it gets here?" Gregor asked.

"We're making a run for the Netherlands. There are places we should be able to cross the border. Once we're there, Stewart plans to get us aboard a ship for the British Isles."

Ilona drew her brows together. "It's closer than going back to Munich—at least the Netherlands are—but how safe is it?"

"We have a window, but it's a thin one," Meara replied. "Right now, the Netherlands are neutral. Hitler will invade, but not until the middle of this year. Maybe May. Maybe June. My visions can't tack it down any closer than that."

"So all we have to do is cross the border," Ilona muttered. "That's a pretty big hurdle."

"It's not any riskier than transiting Germany north to south again," Jamal countered. "Particularly since vampires have certainly discovered the one we killed by now. Our scents are all over it. They'll be furious, hell-bent on revenge. In truth, I'm surprised they haven't caught up."

Aron skinned his lips back from his teeth. "You heard the vampire. He called the prison camp a smorgasbord. They'll come after us, but not until they can't drink any more blood." The corners of his mouth twisted into a disgusted moue. "They don't like it nearly as well once it's congealed."

"So we might have bought ourselves a few hours." Ilona fisted a hand and pounded it into a tree.

"What?" Meara raised her silver-gray brows. "There's more to this vampire story. Tell me."

"Jamal didn't say anything when you first got here, but the vampire caught Aron up in thrall. We have to shield him—or teach him how to shield himself so it doesn't happen again."

"Not liking the sound of that." Meara stalked in front of Aron. "I'm going to lay my hands on you. You will remain absolutely still."

"I understand." Aron's tone was solemn, and he straightened his spine.

Jamal knew the feel of Meara's power, daunting and reassuring all at the same time. It built and eddied around Aron, creating a pulsating vortex. Unlike the solid red whirlwind she'd created around Elliott while battling to save his life, this one was translucent and shaded from green to pale blue.

Ilona edged next to Jamal and gripped his hand. "What's she doing?" Rather than telepathy, her voice was a faint whisper next to his ear.

"Not sure," he whispered back. "Judging from the colors, cleansing any remaining vampire taint."

As he watched, fang marks rose on Aron's neck, outlined against his tanned skin. Meara blew on them, and they disappeared, only to be replaced by another set. Horrified fascination filled Jamal as the twin puncture marks appeared again and again.

"Oh my God! How many times did they feed from him?" Gregor said from behind them, clearly watching too.

Jamal grasped Ilona's hand harder. This must be hell for her, seeing hard evidence of her brother's abuse. That he'd survived was little shy of a miracle. Gradually, Meara's power receded. She moved her hands from the crown of Aron's head to his feet before straightening and folding her arms beneath her breasts atop her curtain of hair.

Aron bowed his head. "Thank you. I feel the difference. I wasn't aware of how deep they'd gotten their slimy talons into me."

The corners of Meara's mouth twitched. "Watch that talon talk, you'll provoke my vulture."

"Sorry. Poor choice of words." He raised his clear, gray eyes and looked at her. "How about a simple thank you?"

"Accepted." She leveled her discerning gaze on him. "Young man. You will not be immune to vampire mind control. No Romani is. The part I altered is this. They'll no longer be able to immobilize you from fifty paces and lure you with honeyed words about what an honor it is to be their next meal."

Aron looked from Jamal to Ilona to Gregor. "The vampires didn't stop you in your tracks. Why?"

"Shifters have built in safeguards. Vampires

can't control us with their minds. Likely it's why they've pretty much left us alone," Gregor replied.

"So it would be better to be like you."

Meara shook a finger at him. "No. That's flawed thinking. We need every type of magic wielder. We strengthen each other. If every Rom became a shifter, the dynamic balance of magic in the world would be altered—with disastrous consequences. The goddess created all of us, which means we each have a role to play."

The deep rumble of a truck moving slowly toward them caught at the edge of Jamal's sensitive hearing. Soon there'd be a few more of them, and there was safety in numbers.

"Did we sustain any losses today?" he asked Meara.

"Yes. A bear shifter and a raven. They'd entered one of the guards' barracks. Thought they'd killed everyone, and they were on their way out when the room exploded, trapping them." The corners of Meara's eyes pinched with sorrow. "I saw it through the raven's mind. It was a grenade. The guard who detonated it died along with them, but that's not any comfort. My shifters are worth a thousand of any Nazi."

Gregor murmured the shifter incantation for the dead. Brief and to the point, it asked the goddess to speed them to their afterlife. Jamal and Meara joined in.

"Come on." Meara motioned. "Let's go meet that truck. The last half mile of road in here is just as bad as what's beneath our feet."

"You'll have to teach me your prayers. Like the one you just invoked for your dead," Ilona said as she walked up the deeply rutted dirt road next to Jamal. Puddles overflowed some of the ruts. "Do you have lore books like the Rom?"

He shook his head. "Not so much. Most of our tradition is passed on orally. For now, it's more important for you to learn how to control your new mix of magics. Things like invocations can come later."

She sent a crooked half grin skittering his way. "Yeah, probably right." She angled her head to one side. "My wolf just informed me it will help."

"Of course it will."

"I want one," Aron said. "It'd be like the best imaginary playmate of all time. One that made your magic strong and could turn you into—"

"Weren't you listening to Meara?" Ilona looked askance at Aron.

He shrugged. "Yeah, but it's still..." He started

over. "I'll focus on making my magic as strong as I can."

"Good plan." Jamal ruffled his long hair.

The boy's mother had been dead for a year. And his father had been gone for six. Jamal wouldn't be intrusive about things since Aron didn't need an overbearing parent, but he made a silent vow to help the young Rom when and where he could.

Ilona squeezed the hand he still held. *"Thank you,"* she said into his mind, and he knew she'd been eavesdropping on his thoughts.

Footsteps pelted down the track toward them. Jamal extended magic and recognized Nivkh and Stewart. Meara, who was ahead, had probably already met up with them.

"Hurry," she called.

Jamal broke into a run. Ilona and Aron kept pace. Gregor pulled around them, sprinting ahead. The truck idled just beyond, and Jamal followed everyone into its high bed. By the time he made certain Ilona and Aron were safely inside, the truck was already rolling. He leapt into it, letting its canvas sides down to hide them from casual observers. Not that anyone would be in this forest, but the road had to lead to a more populated area.

Michael was in the truck, along with Elliott, Tairin, Cadr, Vreis, and several shifters and Rom Jamal didn't know. Tairin smiled warmly at him. Elliott did too. Jamal settled atop a stack of folded blankets and asked, "When will we meet up with the others?"

"We won't. Each truck is on its own getting across the border," Stewart answered and made a sour face. "We dinna plan this over well. One of us—" he pointed at Meara, Nivkh, Elliott, and Stewart "—should have been in each truck. That way each of our vehicles would have contained a strong magic-wielder."

"Nothing to be done about it now," Nivkh said.

Jamal buried his thoughts. It would take more than magical strength to see all of them safely out of Germany. Luck would play a part. So would cunning and outthinking their many adversaries.

Vampires. Nazis. And the odd German citizen anxious to collect a bounty for helping the Reich.

Meara looked up from where she sat cross-legged, her back leaning against a hay bale that somehow hadn't gotten transferred to feed the horses. It seemed as if they'd left the protective barrier several lifetimes ago, but it had been less than a week.

"You are correct that we have many adversaries," Meara said. "But we also have a few tricks up our sleeves. If we manage to cross the border, our biggest problem will be vampires. They know no borders."

"Let me outline what I have in mind," Stewart said. "The only ones here who've heard my full plan are Cadr, Vreis, Meara, Michael, and Nivkh."

Jamal leaned closer, not wanting to miss so much as a single detail.

"Do ye all speak Gaelic?"

A mixture of yesses and noes rose from the group.

"Och aye, 'twould be a wee bit safer, but 'tis more important that ye all understand fully." He blew out a long breath and placed his hands on his folded knees. "The British Isles are friendlier to magical workings than Europe. 'Tis easier to cast spells there, and our magical roots are more available. I doona believe the Germans will occupy England, Scotland, or Ireland.

"This decision to leave wasna lightly come by. I'm worried about my caravan, and Michael holds concerns about his as well. If they remain hidden beyond the barrier, they may well be able to wait out the war without incident."

"I sent one of my birds to deliver that message," Meara spoke up.

"Aye, and I am verra grateful." Stewart turned his dark gaze her way.

"As am I," Michael concurred.

"I trust I can do more good on the far side of the North Sea than sitting watch over my caravan. I hope 'tisn't a decision I come to regret." Stewart raked one hand through hair that had come half-unbraided. "Moving forward, 'tis my belief—but I may well be wrong—that we can link to the power inherent in the British Isles. Mayhap even scare up some of the little folk to aid us in our efforts, or the Fae, if they're not still embroiled feuding with their dark cousins."

"My brother and I can help with that," Cadr said, his tone solemn.

"Aye, I used to know a cadre of Fae. I'm certain they'll still be where I remember in their barrows beneath the Scottish Highlands," Vreis murmured.

"Thank you," Stewart replied. "Reinforcements for our efforts are more available there than here. Yet 'tis a gamble. Any who doona wish to leave Europe are free to return to the encampment behind the barrier or any other place of your choosing. I had this same conversation, albeit an abbreviated version, with everyone afore their trucks left."

"Do you have any idea how many opted to remain in Germany?" Elliott asked.

"A handful. They sorted themselves into one truck. More will leave us in the Netherlands. A place free from Nazi occupation was appealing enough to many that they were willing to risk the border."

He straightened his spine. "Questions?"

Stewart waited for several minutes before he said, "We're in uncharted waters. I'll depend on all of you to help craft sound decisions as we move forward."

The vote of confidence from the Scotsman warmed Jamal.

The truck wasn't swaying as much, which meant they'd returned to better road. It also meant their chances of being stopped went up. "How long will it take to get to the border?" he asked.

"Depends how many times we're waylaid," Meara replied. "If all goes well, we should be there by tomorrow night. We have to cross at night," she went on. "I've played it both ways. Vampires are strongest then, but if we draw enough magic to render all of us invisible for a daytime crossing, we'll draw their attention too."

"Damned if you do, and damned if you don't," Tairin muttered.

"Indeed," Elliott chimed in.

The truck rolled to a stop, and Jamal girded himself. Had something gone wrong already? Was a pack of vampires bearing down on them? He sent magic spiraling outward, but didn't sense anything amiss.

The driver, another bear shifter wearing a stolen German uniform rolled back a corner of the canvas. "This is a good place to stop," he announced. "Another few miles, and we'll be on the main road through the mountains. Nowhere to pull off then for a very long time. We can rest up and get moving once it's dark."

Meara clapped her hands together. "Shifters! Hunt your food. It will save stealing provisions. Get enough for the Rom here too."

Jamal followed Ilona and Aron outside. The afternoon was chilly, but it wasn't raining. "Wish I could hunt with you guys," Aron said.

"You can, and in a way you're really good at." Ilona smiled at her brother. "I hear a creek. It can't be more than a few yards away. "How about catching us some fish? We can cook them along with whatever Jamal and I hunt down."

"Thanks, Sissy. Will do." His face wreathed in smiles, Aron loped toward the sound of rushing water.

"Ready to hunt?" Jamal asked.

"Soon. Maybe we could walk a little first?"

He wrapped an arm around her. "Sure. Anything you'd like, *liebchen*."

When they were a little way from the others, she turned to him. "Thank you for accepting Aron. It means a lot to me. He never really spent much time with his father, and Valentin was a shitty human being, a lousy caravan leader, and scarcely someone for a young boy to look up to. It wasn't just because he liked men. He could've had an eye for the ladies. It wouldn't have mattered. He was still a small-minded bigot."

"You don't have to thank me." Jamal held her against him. "We're a family. I never got to see Tairin through to adulthood. It's like the goddess has given me a second chance." He leaned close, inhaling her scent. "Are we going to Britain with Meara and Stewart and the rest of them?"

"Yes. It feels right to me. When I get a chance, I'll see if I can't use my seer gift and gather more information." She caught her lower lip between her teeth. "Is that what you want? I should have asked you first."

"It feels like the right path to me too. Nothing is certain, Ilona, but I'm happier than I've ever been. I love you, and no matter what the next months and years bring, they'll be brighter because we're together."

Her eyes sheened with tears, and she clung to him. "I couldn't have said it better myself. I went from having nothing to having everything."

"You never had nothing." He tilted her chin up and lost himself in the wonder of her changing eyes.

"What do you mean?"

"You've always had yourself. You're one strong woman, darling. It's why I was drawn to you. Why I fell in love with you."

"I hate to break up the love fest," his wolf inserted dryly, *"but are we ever going to hunt? I'm hungry."*

"I am too," Ilona's wolf said, punctuating its words with a howl.

Jamal chuckled. "You heard them. Better get those clothes off fast. Before they chew us to bits from the inside out."

"You just want to see me naked."

"Yeah that too."

In a flurry of light and magic, they left their

clothing draped over a dry tree branch, summoned magic, and let their wolves loose.

YOU'VE REACHED the end of *Tarnished Prophecy*. The next book, *Tarnished Journey, Soul Dance Book Four,* begins where this one left off. Everyone still has to escape Germany, and it's possible Stewart might find a love of his very own. Read on for a sample.

ABOUT THE AUTHOR

Ann Gimpel is a USA Today bestselling author. A lifelong aficionado of the unusual, she began writing speculative fiction a few years ago. Since then her short fiction has appeared in webzines, magazines, and anthologies. Her longer books run the gamut from urban fantasy to paranormal romance to science fiction. Once upon a time, she nurtured clients. Now she nurtures dark, gritty fantasy stories that push hard against reality. When she's not writing, she's in the backcountry getting down and dirty with her camera. She's published more than 50 books to date, with several more planned for 2017 and beyond. A husband, grown children, grandchildren, and wolf hybrids round out her family.

Keep up with her at www.anngimpel.com or http://anngimpel.blogspot.com

If you enjoyed what you read, get in line for special offers and pre-release special reads. Newsletter Signup!

TARNISHED JOURNEY, CHAPTER ONE

Stewart Macleod paced in a rough circle, skirting the collection of shifters and Romani gathered in small groups. He'd declared a rest break, but everyone was too keyed up to sleep. A few of the shifters were combing the forest for food for the rest of them. The shriek of a vulture on the hunt told him Meara wasn't far away. It had been drizzling all day, and now fog was moving in. He encouraged it with a bit of magic. Anything that would shield their presence might help.

They'd avoided Hannover and Osnabrück as they transited the northern portion of Germany, selecting backroads that had stressed their truck's ability. There'd been a few places where they'd all had to get out, but luck had been with them. They hadn't broken an axel or even had so much as a flat tire.

The Netherlands border wasn't far. Crossing it would push one problem—Nazis—to a backseat. Vampires would still plague them, but he hadn't sensed any since they'd passed Hannover. Was it because the Reich was using every single one of the fell creatures they could get their hands on?

The more he thought about it, the likelier it seemed. Vampires reveled in blood and death. Sex ran a hot second. The Nazi prison camps provided lush opportunities for both feeding and fucking, a resource far too rich to be ignored. Vampires might disparage the Reich, but they weren't above using them to meet their needs.

A corner of Stewart's mouth twisted downward into a grimace. Hitler and his henchmen might believe they had vampires under their thumb, but they'd be in for a rude awakening someday.

Och aye, and we can only hope 'twill come sooner rather than later.

For once no one was bothering him. No questions. No "Hey, Stewart, come here for a moment," requests.

It gave him a much-needed opportunity to lay out his plan for getting the group across the border and examine it for holes. Critical elements he might have missed. They'd be abandoning the truck soon—not much choice, even though not having it created other problems. Every road had border crossing guards, and they prowled the terrain near their stations. The Nazis knew good and well that once someone moved into the Netherlands, they were home free.

The safest way across was on foot for the Rom and in shifted form for everyone else. He ticked off names of the principal players. Nivkh, Tairin, Elliott, Jamal, Ilona, Meara, and Gregor were shifters. All wolves except for Meara, Nivkh, and two other bear shifters, one of whom was their driver. That left himself, Michael, Cadr, Vreis, and Aron in their human bodies, along with three other Rom from Michael's caravan.

He thought about his own caravan hidden behind a magical barrier a few miles outside Munich. It was hundreds of miles away, and he hoped to hell they'd be safe. He hadn't always been a caravan leader. In truth, he'd only adopted the Romani mantle a mere century before. Or perhaps it had been two. Regardless, he'd pulled off the deception swimmingly—until a few days ago. Jamal was sharp. He'd asked pointblank what Stewart was, having intuited his magic didn't match Romani energy patterns.

Fortunately, Jamal had the good sense not to keep picking at the topic once Stewart told him it was off-limits. He swallowed a snort. Romani magic had dwindled until only a very few had much left. But Jamal was a shifter, and an old, canny one at that. Leave it to a shifter to call him out on his long-running deception.

Before the Nazi problem had heated up, he'd toyed with the idea of translocating his entire caravan to Scotland, but he'd waited too long. He hadn't understood how the Reich solidified its powerbase so quickly—until he realized their mass hypnotism was fueled by vampire coercion.

A squawk from Meara's vulture was followed by a flash of light as she shifted midair and somersaulted to his side, landing lightly. Silver-gray hair fell to the ground, providing both cover and warmth. Her shrewd amber eyes still held an avian cast, and she looked more raptor than human as she regarded him.

"Mind if I join you?"

He met her gaze, not fooled by her words. She was one of the first shifters and always had a motive. "Ye're not asking a question. Not really," he countered. "State what's on your mind."

The prickly jab of magic pierced him as she surrounded them with warding. Along with it came the odor of clay baked under a sun far hotter than it ever got in Germany—or the British Isles. It was the scent of many of her castings. Whatever she had to say, she apparently wasn't interested in being overheard.

"Everyone's too worried to pay us much heed," he said, keeping his tone neutral. The vulture shifter could be touchy and had a short fuse.

She shot a pointed look his way. "So you want them to listen in when I inquire whether now is the time to reveal what you are?" Without waiting for him to respond, she went on, "The shifters will take their animal forms. Crossing the border unnoticed should go smoothly for them—"

"Unless a vampire notices," he cut in.

"Unless a vampire notices and chooses to act on the knowledge," she corrected him. "Shifters are immune to vampire mind control. They've pretty much left us alone because of that, preferring to focus on more tractable prey."

Stewart waited. Meara clearly had a plan of her own for spiriting them across the border into the Netherlands. One which she was about to promulgate. Perhaps it was less risky than his.

"You're quiet," she observed.

"Ye're far from done. If I interrupt every few seconds, ye'll never finish."

The corners of her mouth twitched, but didn't quite form a smile. "True enough. All right then. By my count, there are eight of you who are stuck in human bodies. Seven if we take you out of the equation, but bear with me."

He made come along motions with one hand, not wanting to respond to her gambit about taking himself out of the equation. She sensed he was different, much as Jamal had, but he'd been evasive in the face of her earlier probing. Was she hunting for information?

"What is your true name?"

Stewart started, not expecting the question. He shook his head. "'Tisn't important. I havena used it for centuries, and no one remembers who I was."

Meara frowned, drawing her gray eyebrows into a single line. "Surely your gods would. Shifters don't have such things, but the Celts had them in droves."

"Aye, true enough. If any recall who I was,

none have chosen to speak with me for a verra long time."

He cut the flow of his words. Part of his plan hinged on those same gods, who'd discounted him for hundreds of years, still being tethered to Earth and capable of responding to a summons for aid. It was one of the biggest unknowns in his strategy, and one he hadn't spent much time worrying about. He had to get to Scotland first, and that was far from a given.

Even if the Celtic gods had left for other worlds, the British Isles would still concentrate his power, and everyone else's as well. But it might not be enough to subvert the Nazis and their war machine.

Meara narrowed her eyes. The gesture made her look even more like a vulture. "Skipping your name, you were a Druid high priest, correct?"

"Good guess. I was the highest-ranking Druid in Britain. 'Tis why I'm close to immortal."

She narrowed her eyes further. "What does *close to immortal* mean?"

He shrugged. "I'm not exactly certain. Danu, Gwydion, Arianrhod, and a few of the others got into an argument over activities at one of the Druid temples. We had an overabundance of corrupt priests, and I had to sanction them. Not one of the proudest moments in our priesthood, but—"

"Sanction as in kill?"

"Yes." An image of bodies smoldering atop a pyre flashed through his mind. He pushed it aside.

"Interesting. I had no idea Druids were so bloodthirsty."

"We're not." Defensiveness raced through him like a hot tide. "Times might have been different then, but some transgressions deserve death no matter what the era."

"Now it's me who's doing the interrupting. You brought this up to answer my question about immortality. Go on. I'll bite my tongue."

Stewart had a hard time imagining her sitting on her opinions, but kept that thought to himself. "Not so much more to tell. Druid priests provided a buffer between the Celtic gods and everyone else. The gods didn't want to have to deal with anyone but me after the problem I described earlier, so they told me I'd live a long time."

"That's it?" Meara's nostrils flared. "No rough estimates?"

Stewart shook his head. "After the first five hundred years or so, I stopped expecting to drop dead and just went with the flow. Modern times have made it harder to slip out of sight and reappear elsewhere. 'Twas one of the reasons I opted to masquerade as a Rom. They're wanderers and more likely to escape notice. I've had to change caravans a few times, but luck—or something—has been with me. I've run into freshly leaderless caravans at just the right time. A dollop of coercion mixed with a dash of compulsion were enough to put me in charge."

He stopped to consider his next words. "Other than bullying my way in, I've never taken advantage of the Rom in my caravans. I needed a position where people would accept my magic, and the Rom never questioned me. I couldn't very well be a shifter. Druidry has seen a bit of a resurgence, but nothing where I could lose myself and be invisible. Not much in the way of other magic wielders left in the world."

"You forgot vampires." A feral expression etched into her ageless face.

"As if I could. You asked me all these things for a reason. What do you have in mind?"

"I've been playing with a few options. It would be safer for the Rom to be invisible, but that level of expended magic fanned out over a large area is sure to attract vampires, if any are in the region."

"What does any of that have to do with exposing myself as a Druid?"

"I was hoping you'd have some special magical tricks at your disposal."

"Tricks that would reveal I couldna be Romani if I employed them, eh?" Stewart cleared his throat. "Nay. Sorry. I havena any magic bullet that will transport the eight of us who aren't shifters across the border. We'll have to pray our good fortune holds. I dinna expect we'd get this far without notice, yet we have."

"You're planning to leave the truck on this side, right?"

"Aye. Too difficult to find a route past the border that won't entail searches and requests for papers. None of us have them except the driver, and those are stolen. The communications network turns slowly, but by now the name on his identification might be on a list that would alert a border guard."

"I've cut that deck a few ways. We'll need transport on the other side. It's either that or a very long walk to the docks in Amsterdam where we can find a ship. Over sixty miles through settled country, places where a pack of wolves and a few bears would stick out like mismatched shoes or stockings."

"Better if we angle north and try for a ship around Eernshaven."

"So more than sixty miles and even more reason to hang onto the truck. Shifters can still take to their animal forms to cross the border, which would leave Rom in the truck. Not so big a challenge to make it appear no one is there when the border guard checks the back, and I can magic up the driver's papers to make certain they're not flagged as stolen."

"I don't like it. What if the guard is one of the SS who've parleyed with vampires and holds some of their magic? Worse, what if the guard *is* a vampire?"

Meara looked askance at him. "Have you seen even one vampire actually working for the Reich? Never mind in a menial, boring position where they'd be standing beside a little booth for hours checking an endless procession of vehicles?"

Stewart winced. "No. Maybe I'm overreacting, but this border idea was mine, and I'm the one who'll have to live with it if we lose anyone during the crossing."

Her harsh expression softened, and she stopped walking and laid a hand on his arm. "The odds of all of us making it across aren't good. You have to know that."

"I do, but I doona wish to add to the risks."

"How were you thinking we'd cross the Netherlands once we put the border behind us?" Her question was soft, but her penetrating gaze never left him.

"Stealing a vehicle." When he said it out loud, the words pinged sourly. Talk about danger. And an immediate one at that. Even if they removed the plates, most cars were easy enough to recognize.

"Stealing, eh?" She snorted. "You've traveled with the Rom so long, you think like one. We'd need at least two vehicles. Maybe even three to accommodate everyone, which means we'd have to split up. Nothing like three stolen cars caravanning across the country."

Breath whistled through his clenched teeth. "You made your point. We'll chance it with the truck. You were just overflying the area. I bet you have a suggestion about which border crossing station we should approach."

She rolled her eyes. "I like to think I'm not quite that transparent."

"Why go through a quarter hour of conversation? Why not just tell me what you wanted to do?"

"It's always better if we come to agreement.

No one likes being force-fed another's ideas. Turns out we can remain on the road we left before this break. It's as good as any other, and I didn't sense vampires. Which isn't to say some couldn't show up between now and nightfall—"

She snapped her fingers, but before she could say anything, he spoke up. "No reason to wait for nightfall if we don't need darkness to shroud ourselves. Vampires are strongest at night, so we're better off rounding everyone up and going right now."

"You read my thoughts. I'm off to work on the driver's papers. See you on the other side." Light flashed around the vulture shifter just before she vanished.

Stewart hustled back to the group and rattled off names. "Change of plans. Into the truck with you."

Cadr jumped to his feet. Loose black trousers were tucked into a battered pair of leather boots, and a heavy navy blue sweater was tossed over a lighter woolen top. Curly dark hair fell to his shoulders, and his blue eyes crinkled with concern at their corners. "Och aye, and I thought we were waiting for the dark to better hide ourselves."

"'Twas my original plan as well, but Meara

talked me out of it. I was going to leave the truck and chance it on foot, but she helped me realize how badly we'll need transport big enough to hold all of us once we cross the border."

Cadr cocked his head to one side. "Are the shifters still crossing as animals?"

"Aye, 'twill be just us Rom in the truck. Ready your magic. We'll weave a ward to render ourselves invisible." Stewart loped toward the truck, still calling names. By the time he got to there, everyone was loaded into its cavernous bed, and he joined them.

Meara lifted the canvas and stuck her head inside. "Drape the blankets over yourselves. Rather than invisible, try a spell that makes the lot of you appear dead."

Michael shifted his swarthy, thickset body and nodded in her direction. "Brilliant. Most people are uncomfortable enough with death, they won't wish to examine corpses too closely."

She cracked a rare smile. "Not just corpses. Dutch citizens returning to their native soil for burial." She dropped the canvas side, and the truck's beefy engine roared to life.

"Thank you." Stewart directed his telepathic comment to the driver.

"Why thank me? It's my truck. None of you could figure out how to drive it on short notice."

"Because if it weren't for us, ye could join the other shifters and cross in your bear form."

Laughter rolled through Stewart's head. When the shifter stopped chortling, he said, *"Yeah, like a bear in the middle of winter isn't something that would make folk sit up and take notice. We're supposed to be asleep."*

Stewart almost thanked him again for interrupting his hibernation cycle, but didn't. The less magic expended right now, the better.

"Do you believe we'll be all right?" Aron asked, his gray eyes pinched with worry. At sixteen, he was the youngest of them. Ilona was his sister, but she'd very recently become a shifter because there were no other options to call her back from a borderworld inhabited by Romani spirits.

"Come here." Stewart beckoned. "Ye can join me beneath my blanket."

Aron scooted across the truck's rough bed. "Thank you. I'm scared."

"Rightfully, so, lad," Michael said. "It's not as if you haven't had a rough go of it between the Nazi prison camp and vampires feeding off you."

Aron straightened his thin shoulders and pushed long, dark hair out of his face. "Meara fixed the bad places in me. Vampires can't find me anymore."

Stewart heard a tremor in the lad's voice. "Ye said the words," he exhorted. "Now ye have to believe them."

"Yes, sir."

Stewart arranged a blanket, lay on it, and motioned for Aron to lie next to him before he draped another blanket over them. The truck pitched and rolled on the dirt road before getting back on asphalt. It wouldn't be long now.

"Open your minds to me," Stewart instructed and wove a spell with all their various magics. Death was easier than invisibility. He even added the stench of decaying flesh to make it more realistic.

The truck rumbled to a stop, and he heard a guard demanding papers. Aron edged closer, and Stewart's heart went out to the boy. In many ways, crossing on foot would have been easier. At least movement provided an outlet for the adrenaline that had to be pouring through everyone scattered across the truck's bed.

Heavy footsteps moved around the truck, and Stewart tightened the web he'd woven around them all. Next to him, Aron flinched and started to shake.

"They can't see me anymore, can they?" Even his telepathy was breathless.

"Ssht. Remain still." Stewart sent a thread of power outward. He'd been so focused on protecting everyone inside the truck, he hadn't bothered to check who was headed their way.

Vampires.

Goddammit! He followed up the English curse with a string of Gaelic ones, but kept them locked in his head.

Meara's intervention might have moved Aron beyond vampire gunsights, but the lad was still sensitive to their presence.

Thank the goddess for small favors.

Vampires would enjoy dead cargo, but maybe not long dead. Stewart upped the ante on the rotten carcass smell until he wanted to gag.

Someone pulled back a corner of the canvas and dropped it in a hurry. "Whew! That's terrible."

"Are you certain?" a second voice demanded. "I'm hungry."

"Not for those you aren't," the first voice responded.

The canvas was pulled back a second time, followed by the truck's springs complaining as someone jumped into the bed. "Pick me up on the other side of the border," the vampire who'd just entered their truck called cheerily to his companion. "Easier to find something back here than to grab any more humans. They're touchy as scalded cats. Superstitious too."

"Meet you in the Netherlands, but not until well past nightfall. Just jump down when you're done. I'll find you later," echoed from next to the truck. Its engine whined, and the gears ground as they engaged. Tires thumped as they rolled through the gateway and into a country free from Nazi domination.

One problem at a time, Stewart told himself. Getting the crossing behind them was huge.

He'd just begun to reshape their shared magic to snare the vampire when Aron bolted upright and launched himself at the creature. His lips were drawn back from his teeth, but no sound emerged. Even terrified, he understood the necessity of not drawing undue attention to their truck.

The vampire's eyes widened and it crooned, "Our Nosferatu goddess is smiling indeed. Look at that luscious morsel." Red hair cascaded down broad shoulders, and eyes the shade of raw emeralds glimmered with hypnotic charm.

"I'm no one's morsel," Aaron snapped and

wrapped his limbs around the vampire, grappling with it.

"Love it, just love it when there's a bit of a challenge." The vampire's mouth opened to display its fangs.

Aron twisted away from the deadly incisors, but the vampire was fast.

Before it could sink its teeth into Aron, Stewart wrapped power around the vampire, coil after coil of shiny cord, but it didn't slow the creature down.

"I've got this," Cadr grunted and lurched past Stewart with a silver blade drawn and ready.

Sensing the deadly metal, the vampire twisted away from Aron. "Now you're just making me angry. You don't want to do that. I can make short work of the lot of you."

"Really?" Michael pulled a silver blade of his own and shot forward. "Try it, vampire."

CPSIA information can be obtained
at www.ICGtesting.com
Printed in the USA
BVHW060008250223
659171BV00010B/1307

9 781959 551065